A BOOK OF THE 13TH SPECIAL FORCES GROUP

ALIEN ABDUCTION WAR

STEPHEN STOLLER

NEWMAN SPRINGS PUBLISHING
320 Broad Street
Red Bank, NJ 07701

First originally published by Newman Springs Publishing 2021

This book is a work of fiction. Any similarities to any living or deceased individuals or actual events are purely coincidental.

ISBN 978-1-63692-959-0 (Paperback)
ISBN 978-1-63692-966-8 (Hardcover)
ISBN 978-1-63692-967-5 (Digital)

Printed in the United States of America

To Teresa.
Without you, I would not have pushed forward.

CONTENTS

CHAPTER 1

GREETINGS

The pickup truck bumped down the country road in the usual fashion, semicomfortable but not luxurious. The paint was in surprisingly good shape, considering the harsh winters up here in the Adirondack. On the other hand, the engine was in beyond good shape. Robin Lincoln had a guy who he had paid to make it awesome. The guy also worked on the frame and suspension, making the old workhorse into a stallion under the original design.

Robin was a man who liked to be prepared. What for, he always said, was up to somebody else. Although the "what for" was up to someone else, he felt you were ultimately in charge if you were prepared.

He was headed home after being down in town doing what he called his chores, such as shopping at the general store, getting a few essentials at the hardware store and some ammo at the local hunting tour guide shop, and—last but not least—hanging out with a few of the citizens and chewing the fat.

He had not meant to stay out so late, but Buck Lawrence who owned and ran the local gas station was on a roll tonight. He was telling one funny story about the events of the last year after another and having been away for a year Robin had laughed so much his stomach was still sore.

Robin tuned the radio to the nearest station, which was forty-five miles away in a larger city. It was late, around ten thirty in the evening, so he knew it would be local news and local talk shows for the next few hours. He did not mind the talk radio instead of music. It reminded him he was home, and it felt downright good. That is what having to be away from home did for you. It made you appreciate being back a whole lot more.

Robin was about five miles from home when the radio stopped talking and started scanning on its own through the channels. Robin's brow furrowed as he looked from the road to the radio back and forth. With a humph, he slapped the dash over the radio for no other reason but to take some action, any at all. He tried to imagine what kind of disturbance would cause such a reaction to an AM/FM receiver. The pickup then jerked as the power left and returned, as if the engine had been completely interrupted from its one single purpose.

"What the…" Robin said out loud, startling himself with the sound of his own voice.

The truck did not jerk again. It plainly started coasting as the engine did a complete turn off by itself. Without the power running, the steering was a bit stiff, but being in top form, Robin was able to steer the truck to the shoulder, next to an open field.

He sat there confused and angry, staring at the dash, like somehow he would see a light and slap his forehead and go, "Oh, that thing, that's what happened," but it was not working.

He grabbed the key in the ignition and turned it. It was dead—no click, no noise, whatsoever. Even knowing how the results would turn out, he tried three more times, issuing a growl as he accepted it was not going to work.

Robin was not a mechanic nor really a car enthusiast, far beyond just loving to drive them and appreciating the function and form of the conveyance. Although he had a base knowledge of the parts and their function, so minor repairs or fixes were in his roundhouse.

He sighed as he opened his door and started for the front of the truck. When he got to the front, he realized he had forgotten he had to pull the lever under the dash to pop the hood so he could open it. "Mother of pearl!" he swore as he stomped back to the cab to hit the lever. Robin did not go in for foul language, though he did believe there was a time and place for it, and god, did he ever have those times; but as a rule, he knew the fouler and dirtier he got, the angrier he became. So to keep calm and lighten his mood, he found creative ways to say curse phrases.

He leaned in the cab and reached down and pulled the lever, releasing the hood catch. Standing up and stretching, hearing his spine crack and align as he did, he resumed walking back to the front of the truck.

He slipped his fingers under the hood and found the last impediment to the engine, the latch that released the hood catch. Raising the hood, he noticed a small light bulb attached to the underside of the hood came on as expected. It was a feature on all vehicles around the world and must have been declared essential, so it was installed on all makes and models. Though in truth, they were not created equal. This one had obviously been where the manufacturer had skimped and saved.

"Crap, if I had a little more light, I could at least see what the hell I'm looking at," he said to himself as much to the trees or the local animals that may be watching.

From behind Robin, light enveloped him, and he could see the engine as if he were in bright daylight with the sun right behind him. So much so he even felt a warmth emanating from it behind him.

"Thanks," Robin said over his shoulder as he peered in at the engine.

He slowly turned his body, squinting his eyes, knowing that the light source would strip away any night vision he had if it caught him full in his eyes.

"What the fuck!" Cursing was definitively correct at this juncture.

Facing toward the light, it seemed to dim a few lumens. He could make out a structure behind the light and the light emanating out of an opening. Much like the bay of a C-130 aircraft or a Chinook transport helicopter, or even an Osprey heliplane thing.

As these thoughts ran through his mind, he saw three smallish figures disembarking from the entrance and coming down a ramp. He could not focus on these beings; but he could tell they sure as hell were not humans. As they proceeded forward toward him, he saw no clothing or weapons on any of them. He stood completely still as they approached, as if he were frozen. They seemed to have no fear or regard for Robin as an attacker.

One of the things stayed about fifteen feet away as two of the remaining continued forward, one to each side of him. The slightly heavier and taller one to his right and the slimmer and shorter one to his left. He immediately thought of them as Fat Man and Little Boy. He knew where the names came from in his head and was very amused at himself.

Fat Man on his right came even to his side first. Robin did not move, even as the chubby cherub of a creature reached out with its long gray fingers and grasped his hand lightly. The touch was repulsive and felt like a cool clammy octopus grasping his hand.

Little Boy came even with his left side and grasped his hand, as if he were a small child needing the comfort of adults to be led to dinner, bed, or a new classroom.

He felt the tug of both arms as they stepped forward, compelling him to move.

Stepping forward, he came even with the aliens he knew were called the grays, at least that is what most of the Earth's population saw in stories, pop culture, and myths of the present. He suddenly realized he was being abducted. He knew the concept, but it just completely dawned on him he was watching this unfold as a spectator, but now his brain kicked in.

These little fucks were trying to abduct him! Fat Man and Little Boy were going to walk him up to their leader, and they would all skip happily into the big flying saucer and fly away.

The two ushering grays on each arm were half his stride, so he took a stride twice as long as normal to the front of them. This seemed to confuse them. He heard slight chirps to which he assigned as "surprise" in his mind as they froze in their steps. Which was exactly what he counted on. Now as his arms were behind him like two wings about to flap, he gripped the little clammy hands tight as he made a fist with each hand.

Another little chirp from the grays brought a slight smirk to Robin's face, and he noticed the leader turning his head like a cat or dog, trying to understand what he was seeing.

Robin tightened his arm muscles to increase his power as he swung the two grays up off the ground as if he were flapping his powerful wings. He brought the two gray bodies together in front of him, colliding their small frames and heads together with a satisfying crunch. He did not know if the sound was the result of bones, cartilage, or some other damn thing. He just knew it sounded unbelievably bad if you were a small gray thing.

Bending slightly forward, he looked down to see the damage. Fat Man had a huge slit in his head, and blue goo was flowing from it. Robin could see inside, and solid material was spilling out. It could not be a good thing for Fat Man. As for Little Boy, he was hanging limply, rolling his head around in what looked like an unnatural manner, though Robin was not sure if that was usual or unusual.

Fat Man seemed like deadweight, and Little Boy seemed to be in life-threatening condition, if not dead also.

The leader, who was now about eleven feet away, had both his flailing arms and long ass fingers in the air, screaming, like E. T. in the movie. Robin smiled as the thought came into his mind, *Waving his hands in the air like he cares a hell of a lot.*

Behind the leader, Robin saw movement in the entryway. It appeared that a fourth member of the crew was responding. The fourth alien, Robin noticed, had an object in his arms and was pointing it toward him.

Robin's training kicked in, and he pulled the limp body of Fat Man he was still holding in his right hand up in front of him as a shield and leaned toward the left. A bright light erupted from the end of the object and caught Fat Man's body as Robin took three steps to the left. Fat Man's body first blew blue goo onto Robin. Then it heated and disintegrated, leaving Robin with just the hands in his grasp. Dropping Fat Man's hands, he reached to his side and pulled a Springfield Armory .45-caliber handgun, drawing and firing as he put the body of Little Boy up as his second shield. The light flashed again, and the same result occurred, more blue goo on Robin. And he saw the fourth alien fly back up the ramp into the ship after catching two of the three rounds Robin had released. The third round had hit the leader just at the right shoulder, taking that right arm completely off.

The leader, spouting blue goo, ran up the ramp, and the light started to compress. Robin realized the ramp was closing. Just for good measure, Robin pointed the .45 handgun at the ship and fired two more rounds. He heard the satisfying pings of the bullets striking metal. He was under no false belief that it did any damage. It was just a "f—you" to the little bastards.

Robin noticed red and blue alternating lights as the ship powered up and lifted off the ground. He heard a bang as a door closed and heard boots running on the pavement. Out of the corner of his eye, he saw a Smith and Wesson .40-caliber gun in a two-handed grip next to him. "Hey, Mackey. Out on patrol, I take it," Robin said as matter of fact.

"Yep," Deputy Sheriff Mackey said as he holstered his weapon, "just out on patrol. And you?"

"Ah, just heading home, shooting some aliens. You know, just a Thursday night," Robin said in as casual a conversation manner as these two always had.

"Yep," the deputy said, straightening up and looking over at Robin, "just a Thursday night. Hey, what have you got there?"

Robin looked down and noticed he was holding the two arms of Little Boy in his hand still. "Oh, just Little Boy's hands," he said, holding them up.

"Little Boy?" Mackey asked.

A smirk and light chuckle came from Robin as he explained the naming of the two fallen grays. Mackey laughed a little louder than Robin had. Both men looked down at the hands Robin was holding. Then they looked to the two in front of them and the full arm the leader had left behind. Robin looked down first at his shirt. Blue goo, which he surmised was their blood, was all over him.

"Want to head on down to the station? Clean up in the locker room?" Mackey looked away and down the road. "Should give Sheriff Donovan a call and a heads-up."

"Yep. Got a change of clothes in the back of the cab. Hey, do you have any bags we can put these in?" Robin said as he waved the hands around like a schoolkid would excitedly do, spritzing Mackey with a few drops of blue goo.

"Yep," replied Mackey as he wiped goo off his face. He went to his trunk and took a box of bags out and handed a couple to Robin and took a few himself.

Once the pair had picked up and bagged up all the severed limbs, they threw them into the bed of the pickup and headed back to the sheriff's station.

Robin Lincoln, senior master sergeant of the US Army Special Forces, was not surprised that his truck started up in the first try this time. He also knew he was going to have to call his commander and report the event. He would either be laughed out of the service or questioned by higher-ups for the next ten years.

CHAPTER 2

THE LEADER

The leader stumbled through the ship, grabbing the sleek walls with his remaining arm. A subordinate crew member rushed to him and placed its hand over the wound in the shoulder, hoping to slow the loss of life fluid.

They made it to the medical room, and the crew doctor administered to the leader. He expertly healed the wound, but there would be no growing the arm back or putting it back on, especially considering they had left it back planet side.

The leader pushed his way out of the medical room and back into the passageway and headed to the lab area. The doctor and the crew member followed, trying to keep pace with the enraged leader.

A team of scientists was working on a human they had picked up a couple of hours earlier. Looking up, they saw the leader enter the room enraged and chirping out things they had never heard from the leader before. When he stormed up next to the exam table and stared at the placid human lying on it, they backed up out of his way.

"Give me the scalpel device," he said to the nearest scientist who held it nervously. "Now!" he yelled in their chirping language not usually used in this manner, for they did not anger easily.

The scientist did not like the tone this visit was taking, but he hoped the scalpel device was not to be used on him. "Yes, yes, Leader, here it is," he chirped in fear, carefully handing the device to the leader as he kept his body as far back as he could.

Taking the device, the leader held it tight in his hand, the left, the only one he had now. He stared into the face of the human who could not react to the angry alien because he was suspended in a field that kept him from movement, speech, or any other action other than just thought and watching what was happening.

A strange chirping came from the leader, not something his crew was used to from him. It was their way of laughing or the equivalent thereof.

He showed the device to the human and turned it on in front of the human's face. The laser scalpel lit up, and the leader began to start peeling skin off the human layer after layer.

Although in great pain and distress, the human, Jerry Owens—farmer, single man, aged thirty-two—was screaming inside his brain, for the restraint system kept him docile and quiet.

The leader knew this and chuckled as he took great pleasure taking apart this human. It was not exactly the revenge he craved for the loss of his limb—oh, and his two crew members also—but it was a start.

The crew quietly left the leader to his task and went to find other assignments. It would not do to be around if the leader was not satisfied with just taking apart the human.

CHAPTER 3

THE WAR ROOM

The third floor below the White House was known as the war room by all the military men that met with the president on a weekly basis, if not a daily one.

Only the president and the Secret Service and, of course, the past presidents and others whom the presidents had allowed knew how many floors were under the White House.

General Hansen realized no one could tell. By way of the elevator, you slid in your ID, and wherever you were scheduled to be that day, it announced your destination and took you to it. Rumor was that the computer that ran it was an artificial intelligence (AI), one of the best made, and it controlled the floors under the White House and all safety and security.

He slid his White House ID, and a green "accepted" flashed on it. A voice on par with Siri, Alexa, or Google Assistant said, "Good morning, General Hansen. Today you will not be going to floor 3 as usual. We will be going to floor 6 as per request of the president."

General Hansen scrunched his face and made a humph sound as he pondered what floor 6 could be. As a lifelong military man, he was never surprised or thrown off with changes. It saved his life many times and made him the most successful leader of the Army Special Forces. He preached his philosophy on adaptability to his men, telling them they must be flexible in order to be able to rise to any threat or misfortune.

Hansen was successful because he treated his men with respect and showed appreciation for their intelligence. It had not hurt that he came from their ranks and rose in rank due to heroic feats. Overall, the general was down-to-earth and humble but held great confidence in his intelligence and abilities, and he was right to do so.

General Hansen had been due at the usual White House military briefing on Thursday. So when he received a call to report today, Tuesday, he was a bit thrown off as he wasn't aware of any significant incidents within the last twenty-four hours since the usual meeting was confirmed yesterday.

Riding down in the elevator, which was only used to access the lower subterranean floors, he wondered even more so what this could be for. Take the moving up of the date of his White House visit, then add a pinch of going to a new unknown floor, and you've got a mystery; and one that might even challenge his skills. He loved and lived for a challenge to his skills.

The elevator stopped and informed him that he was on the sixth floor and a uniformed Secret Service agent would escort him to the proper room. A slight smile crossed his face. The voices and the way the new computers were now talking always amused him. He was not a Luddite by any means. He had a Google Mini at home; and the family, including him, used it all the time. What he really wanted was a building and a system like this at Bragg. Now that would be cool, except he would make it play music for people waiting.

There was no bing, just the voice saying, "Door opening," as it slid open to reveal a young man in dark urban gray digital camo and carrying a M4 Carbine and a sidearm.

"Sir, welcome. President Parker is in the briefing room, and if you would follow me, I will escort you and show you the way," the young man stated. And it sounded as if he said this fifty times a day, and he may have.

"Lead the way, young man. I'll try to keep up. You know us, old generals," Hansen said in an amused tone.

"Yes, sir, I know those old generals," he said as he turned to the general with a smirk and a wink. "On the other hand, I know this general. Keeping up isn't going to be a problem. It's slowing you down."

Hansen laughed out loud. He liked this young man; he seemed to be quite a capable man.

After making a few turns and down through several active open areas, they came to a door which had two similarly dressed and equipped guards on either side of the entry.

"General Hansen, arriving for the meeting."

Hansen thought the young man was talking to either guard on the door, but neither reacted at all.

"Identity scanned and confirmed. Slide authorization card and retinal scan," the elevator voice stated.

"I don't have a card," General Hansen said to the disembodied voice.

The two flanking guards smiled as Hansen's escort produced a card and placed it into a slot the general had not noticed before, and a beam shot out and scanned the young man's eye.

"Ah, not me," Hansen said, making light of his error.

"No, General, not you. Senior Agent Masters," the voice said, producing chuckles from all four men.

"You're a sassy computer, aren't you?" Hansen asked, not really expecting an answer.

"Well, actually, I am not a computer but an AI program. And yes, I was made sassy. You may call me Annie."

"Well now, Annie, glad to meet you, I think."

All four men chuckled again as the door slid open, revealing a futuristic conference room.

The newly elected president James Parker was up at a table, getting a cup of coffee, and looked over at the arriving people. "Well, it sounds like Annie is as entertaining as ever. Come on in." Parker had a slight Southern tint to his speech. It was what put him into the charming and down-home category. Parker had won the previous fall election, not in a landslide but in a clear margin of victory, quite obviously the country's choice, no question.

Hansen entered and walked over to the president, smiling, as the president put out his hand. Hansen took it, and they shook hands. Hansen respected and liked Parker. Parker had been a helicopter pilot for the Army and flew Apaches till he retired and went into politics. Their paths probably crossed on numerous occasions on one mission or other in the Middle East.

"You met Senior Agent Masters there. He's one of the good guys," Parker said as he pointed toward the young man. "I don't go anywhere without him."

Masters nodded in affirmation, and Hansen could tell he was just a little embarrassed by the attention.

"Fine young man, Mr. President," Hansen said as he nodded back to Masters with a slight smile.

The president grabbed a muffin and strolled over to the conference table in the middle of the room and took his seat at the head of the table. "Please grab a coffee and a muffin or two and come sit next to me," Parker said as he signaled to the chair on his immediate right.

"Sir, I'm going to call for Sergeant Andrews and her team to set up now if that's all right?" Masters asked as he pulled a radio from his belt, got the nod from the president, and completed the task.

After taking a couple of bites from a great-tasting pistachio muffin and a few sips of one of the best cups of coffee ever, General Hansen looked over to the president who was finishing off what appeared to be a double chocolate muffin. "So, Mr. President, is this meeting just you and I, and are you going to say, 'I'm sorry but'?" Hansen said in a joking and in a serious way.

"General, may I call you Reginald, by the way?" Parker asked in a genial way and waited for a reply.

"Mr. President, the way I see it, you may call me whatever you want. I have to answer," the general put it as plain as he could, not sure what this game was.

The president eyed the general steady, not giving anything away, and the general kept eye contact. Masters shifted a bit as the quiet in the room became thick. It was obvious the two men were sizing each other up. Both had seen their share of combat in and out of Washington, DC.

The president made the first move. "See, therefore, I invited you here first an hour ahead of anyone else." He took a sip of coffee and continued, "You are exactly what you seem to be."

"I don't follow," the general said, not sure what exactly was happening.

"You see, I have been made aware of some information recently, as in when I was briefed taking over as president. Information that is not officially known or even acknowledged behind closed doors." Parker took a sip of coffee, seeing if he had gotten the general's attention, and he had. He could see the gears moving in the general's eyes. "I felt I had to act now, fast, as there was an incident last night, one that could not be ignored." He paused to let General Hansen catch up.

"Okay. And my role in this, whatever it is?" Hansen asked.

The president pulled up closer to the table and the general. "I'm sorry I don't mean to be so… How should I say it? So covert about this. It's just not a subject people tend to find serious, but it very much is."

Hansen's brow furrowed at the last statement. "Well, Mr. President, whatever it is, I will certainly not make light if you judge it to be so serious," he said, gesturing to the surroundings.

"Yes, your reputation and record speak for itself," the president said in a more sedate tone than he had used before.

Technical Sergeant Louise Andrews and her team entered, wearing their Air Force urban digital camo fatigues, and began manning rows of equipment set off to the side on a raised platform like an orchestra. In a way, they were like an orchestra. They sifted and disseminated info into the meeting like a harmonious unit, so the participants did not have to pause in their planning.

"Well, the incident that occurred last night involves one of your men and, might I say, fits exactly what my planning was going to involve." He looked at General Hansen and saw he had not had a chance to hear of the incident. *Good*, he thought.

The president began speaking and pointed at Sergeant Andrews. "The incident involved Master Sergeant Robin Lincoln, currently assigned to the Fifth Special Operations Group, out of Fort Campbell,

Kentucky." Parker paused as on the large screen on the wall ten feet from the end of the table a picture and information on Sergeant Lincoln appeared. "Now Sergeant Lincoln is currently on leave, after a tour in the Middle East. He resides in the Adirondack Mountains near Lake George region." A small photocopy of the leave orders and a picture of his address and a history of the home appeared to the right of the screen while the picture of Lincoln stayed to the left.

Parker looked over to the general, seeing he was impressed with the setup and quite enthralled with the presentation, no doubt wondering what could have happened with his man. To his credit, he did not interrupt the president. "Okay, Reginald, stay with me here. On his way home last night, he had an encounter with what can only be classified as alien life-forms." Parker paused and waited for Hansen to react.

"Humph" was all he got as the general kept his head turned to the screen. A copy of an Air Force incident report replaced the previous view of information on the right of the screen.

"Let me summarize the event. You will be able to go over all the information when we're done," Parker stated.

"Of course," the general said, trying to digest everything he was seeing and hearing.

"Your man was stopped and assaulted by these aliens, as they tried to abduct him."

General Hansen laughed. "That was a mistake. They wouldn't stand a chance against Lincoln."

"Funny you say that. They didn't." Parker paused and looked over at the general as the next photos were placed on the right side of the screen.

On what appeared to be a table in an interview room of a police station, five bluish gray thin arms with extralong fingers lay, apparently cut off at whatever passed for elbows, all except one which appeared to have a piece of shoulder intact.

"The Air Force responded and picked up your man and the limbs. Apparently, one alien got away without his arm, and all that is left of two others was their arms."

The two men sat back in their seats, the general rubbing his stubble, contemplating the incident.

"Okay, Mr. President, lay out what you have in mind. I know you didn't call me in here just to let me know one of my men was involved." Hansen had an idea where this was going, but he needed it to be mapped out by the president because, if he was correct, this would be a tough assignment.

"I take it you figured out where I'm going with this?" the president asked, knowing that he had picked the right man.

"Yes, I do, and I'm trying to decide whether to ask for retirement, a raise, or to be committed."

The president laughed and slapped Hansen on the back. "Well, if this goes south, two of those options will be for both of us."

The president, with the help of Sergeant Andrews, mapped out the plan and structure the president worked out.

CHAPTER 4

BLUE BOOK

Master Sergeant Lincoln sat in the rear of the unmarked twenty-passenger jet with a cooler next to him containing the parts of aliens. He was accompanied by two Air Force captains from intelligence and three armed air police sergeants. All but Lincoln just stared at the cooler. Apparently, when faced with actual tangible evidence, these men were in shock. Although they belonged to a unit formally known as Project Blue Book, none of them expected this level of confirmation, one that could not be refuted.

"Master Sergeant, did you get a good look at their ship?" the captain on the right asked. He was the shorter of the two Air Force captains, and he had a mustache. Both captains looked to be about twenty-eight or twenty-nine. His name tag read Anderson.

"No, unfortunately, there was a bright light emanating from the interior, and it looked like a ramp had been lowered," Robin said, keeping his hands holding up his head as he leaned forward in his seat, looking at the floor of the plane. "Haven't you ever seen one of these or faced these little gray guys?" Robin asked, sounding a bit skeptical that they had not had any contact, yet this was their job.

The other captain whose name tag read Roberts answered Lincoln, "No. We have tried and thought we would have by now, but there really isn't any physical evidence like what you have. My god, all we have had is evidence that wasn't enough to stand up to any and all testing." He swallowed and continued, "I mean this." He motioned with his hand to the three sergeants and he and Anderson. "We are all the Air Force is putting on the subject anymore. There are so many civilians out there doing it they figure we would be last to find out."

Robin looked up and gave him a perplexed look. "So why even assign anyone to it if it's so impossible for you to succeed?"

The five Air Force men laughed.

"Because," Anderson answered, "this is a real subject people complain about, and the higher-ups don't want to look unconcerned or stupid. But they also don't want to look concerned or stupid."

This time, they all laughed, including Robin.

The air police technical sergeant kind of smiled and asked Robin, "So are you the sergeant at arms of your unit?"

He was going to mindlessly reply when it hit him; the others all chuckled. And Robin kept an even face and said, "Haha."

Then Roberts could not help it. "So it was arm-to-arm combat?"

Robin tried to stay stoic, but he did snicker at that one.

"You know you may be in trouble, considering they were unarmed," the youngest air police sergeant said. His name tag read Kowalski.

Robin rolled his eyes, and they all laughed, as Robin said, "Oh my god, that was awful, but very funny."

The tension had been released, and the six men fell into pleasant, if not silly, conversation to the end of the flight to the infamous Area 51.

Master Sergeant Robin Lincoln always wanted to see "behind the curtain" of the site, and now he was going to see it and be center stage in it at the same time.

CHAPTER 5

COMMAND

The leader reviewed the recording of the attempted abduction, where the human murdered his two men and violated him, removing his arm with an archaic projectile. The usual rage he controlled inside bubbled up from his center, causing a low growl issuing forth from him, so uncharacteristic. Cutting the captive human had not abated his need to punish the one who took his arm.

He noted the location in his mapping controls of where the incident occurred so he could go back to it when he wanted. Looking over the footage, he noted and scanned prominent markings of the human and his conveyance. Placing the information in the analyzing system and having it on constant watch to catch the offending human, he envisioned the torture he would unleash on the beast. If only he had a chance to tag the beast, he would exact his revenge now; but given a second chance, no, when the next meeting came, the human would pay. This pleased him, and a noise like a grating chuckle came from him.

The crew was weary of the leader after watching him gleam with pleasure as he dismantled the human they had subdued. While the leader had been harsh with them before, watching the gruesome pleasure he took, even if it was just a human, as he cut, cut, and cut at the thing's flesh made them even more weary.

The navigator did not like the humans much anyway; their skin was too squishy, but even he had to admit the leader did some disturbing things to the one they had. Command would not like it, and if they pursued the one who had attacked, he was sure that Command would be terribly upset. Which would move Navigator to Leader, and that would be fine. So Navigator decided he would let Leader go on the course he had set, to find the human.

Navigator and Leader were pulled from their separate paths of thinking as an alarm went off, notifying Signal to answer the communiqué from Command. Signal hit a button and pushed a few levers, and Command appeared on a three-dimensional display to the front of the control cabin.

Command consisted of five gray beings of an elder status and marked by red stripes on their left facial area known to humans as a cheek. One Stripe being the center figure while Two Stripes and Three Stripes sat on either side, finally flanked by Four Stripes and Five Stripes on the outer area. Each stripe commanded a dozen ships in this territory of space.

The crew sat quiet, the leader eyeing the five with a squint of annoyance. He was not in control of his self being.

The five, studying the crew and Leader, passed comments to one another, the sound on their side obviously muted.

"Your appendage is gone" was not a question but a statement given by One Stripe. "Your crew do not look at full strength. Why have you not advised us, Leader Three?" One Stripe leaned forward with a scowl upon his light gray countenance, challenging Leader Three to misstep and make the mistake of speaking sharply in return to Stripe One, which would be a fatal mistake.

Navigator held his breath. With the mental mode of Leader, he hoped he was about to see Command give the ship over to him.

A small moment of anger crossed the leader's face like a cloud on a stormy day. As angered as he was, he did not make it to leader by being a fool; no, he reigned back his anger. Leader Three, being the commander of the third ship in Stripe One's forces, bowed his head and got off his seat to kneel on one knee like an appendage to show submission to One Stripe.

One Stripe leaned back, and a hint of a smirk crossed his features. "Well, I await this information, Three," One Stripe stated in a much less threatening tone. He had been appeased by Leader Three's actions and response.

"A human resisted the immobilization, and because of the lack of capabilities by two of my lower crew, it was able to fire a projectile. The projectile was unexpected by them, and it struck and removed my upper appendage. The two lower crew were, due to their mistakes, ended." The leader rubbed the space where his arm was attached to remind the command that he was stricken by the lower crew's mistakes.

One Stripe did an exaggerated nod and huffed, a sign of acceptance of the details of the report.

The tension the leader was feeling released as he found he was waiting for Command to demand his execution. He had not realized that he was, in fact, thinking that was a possible result.

"What of the human who inflicted the harm to you?" One Stripe stated, expecting to hear of his capture or death.

The leader paused. "He produced his projectile and took another lower crew. At the same time, he removed my appendage. There was more to the human than a usual one. Another human transport had arrived with unknown amount inside. The action to leave was the only action to take." He had made his case. He sat and stared and waited for his fate.

The command shut off their audio feed and were animated in a discussion.

Leader Three sat there, watching the discussion. He did not fear his death. He wanted vengeance first. The grays, or Aldions (Al-d-ons) as they called themselves, had always been a very vengeful race. As he watched, he saw all of command nod in agreement, and audio was returned.

"Leader Three, we are not pleased at the loss or the lack of punishment to the human." One Stripe took a long-projected breath. "Keep a watch for this human. Should you come across it, use discretion, but take care of the problem only if you come across it. Do not make this a priority, I warn you, and only once for the next will be your end." With that statement and a forceful thrust of a finger, the command was gone.

Leader Three let out a breath he did not know he was holding, as his shoulders and head sagged momentarily with relief. He looked over pointedly at Navigator who would take over if he were to be executed. Navigator had the good thinking to busy himself and not show any reaction at all. Leader Three knew what he was thinking just the same. A fire of anger still raged in his heart. He would have to quell it somehow. At the least he would have to plan to have Navigator have an accident, which would be no loss. Besides, Engineer was his supporter and would do anything he asked. Yes, the more he thought, the more he focused on how to get what he wanted. First would have to be the human—yes, the human.

CHAPTER 6

SPECIAL MEETING

Sitting in a bunker room in the infamous Area 51 was exciting for Master Sergeant Lincoln, but the fact that he brought alien arms to the party was a career highlight. As a Special Forces 18Z (operations sergeant for his team), he had been through quite a few things that most people never see. Anyone would agree that, first, an alien attack, then a call by the major general in charge of the United States Army Special Forces was either a good thing or a major bad, bad thing.

Major General Reginald "Reg" Hansen, commander of the Special Forces Division, also Robin's old boss, walked into the conference room that Robin was sitting in. Robin put down his coffee and donut and stood at attention as the general walked in. The other military in the room did the same including the Project Blue Book Five, as Robin thought of them.

Of course, as the general entered—which was impressive enough—the president walking in behind him was just icing on the impressive cake.

General Hansen scanned the room, recognized Master Sergeant Lincoln, smiled, and walked over with his hand out to shake Lincoln's. "Master Sergeant, it's been a while since I last saw you. I believe it was just Sergeant then," he said, chuckling and shaking the hand.

"You are right, sir, and I believe it was just Major then, not General," Lincoln said as he smiled.

"Quite right. Back in the Tenth Special Forces Group, in Stuttgart, as I recall," said Hansen, looking a bit wistful.

"Yes, sir. Just don't bring up that woman and the two British SAS guys." They both laughed.

"As long as you leave out any story of the Polizei and the Second Cavalry." Hansen gave a wink to Lincoln.

"Oh, definitely. I almost forgot that one," Lincoln said, coughing into his hand.

"Hmm, best that one be forgotten." Hansen looked around, noticing the other people in the room again.

The president motioned for everyone to take their seats. The president and the general withdrew from their respective briefcases several file folders apiece. The size of which made Master Sergeant Lincoln think that they had more in mind than just a briefing of his encounter. He squirmed a little in his seat and sat up straighter. From experience, he knew things were about to get complicated.

The president cleared his throat and began speaking as he opened a file. "At the security meeting, I spoke with the joint chiefs of staff. General Mathews of the Air Force, General Stein of Space Force, and General Worth of the Army." He paused as he flipped a paper or two. "I have informed them all that Major General Hansen will be in charge of a new unit that will be under Special Forces Army but detached to Space Force and using Air Force assets. Now all of you present will be involved, and I need your input as well as that of General Hansen. We discussed this, and we feel that we can start to organize the unit with your initial help." He finished the last statement and gestured to Major General Hansen to begin.

"Master Sergeant Lincoln, we are going to build a new Special Forces Group. Its intention will be to combat the aliens however we can. That is why the group will be detached to Space Force with assets of the Air Force in concert together." He looked at Master Sergeant Lincoln who looked as if he had an idea or two. "Any ideas, Master Sergeant?"

Robin Lincoln smiled. "Yes, sir, I do. First, I would like the group to be the Thirteenth Detachment Alien Hunters. And if I'm guessing, I get to be on Operational Detachment Alpha One,

ODA. I would like to have Captain Steve Ryan and Chief Warrant Officer Lee Tanaka as my commanding officer, CO, and assistant commander."

"The Thirteenth, huh? Why that? Not worried about being unlucky?" the general asked with a ponderous look on his face.

"Unlucky for whatever we run across, sir, but certainly not for us. Plus, it's always been my lucky number," Lincoln said, leaning back, crossing his arms over his chest.

The general smiled. "Well, knowing you and that you're still in one piece even after the other night, I can't dispute your choice. If the president is good with it, I'll start there. And my thoughts exactly on the captain and warrant officer. Now put together a list of the rest of your team and for one more." The general wrote on a pad next to him.

"Will do, sir," Robin replied and jotted a couple of names he thought of. Off the top of his head, he would give it thought. The people he suggested needed to not only be top operators but have the flexible minds to deal with the otherworldly.

The president opened another file. "Okay, the general and Master Sergeant Lincoln have things on the Army end in good hands. Next, Space Force has Space Force Base Canaveral and Patrick Space Force Base, both in Florida, about half hour of each other. That is where you will be based." He paused, evaluating to see if the group was following him and to give any one a chance for him to clarify anything.

"Technical Sergeant Andrews—although I hate to lose her, she is the best—I'm going to assign you to the unit as the Annie computer AI handler and my go-between." He smiled at her and nodded.

"Captains, I believe the general has assigned you to be with headquarters where you will liaison with the Air Force and also do the interviews and intelligence gathering and your three sergeants will accompany you." The president smiled. "I think you will be happy with your accommodations on Canaveral. I was briefed that a cold war section was built under and to the east of the launch area and, per my request, has been allocated to you."

"One thing," the general interjected to the group, "this is more secret than what Delta Force does, so understand it is of utmost importance that it remain clandestine."

They all sat and contemplated the gravity of that last remark, imagining how the country, the world for that matter, would react to what they were unsure of and, if confirmed, how they would freak out.

Lincoln had doodled out an outline of an alien head and a circle with a line through it, "no aliens" symbol, putting 13 up top and an A and an H to either side.

After the meeting ended, General Hansen called over Lincoln. "It's like you thought this out a while. Why is that?"

Robin nodded his head and said, "Well, after my incident, it's all I could think of. How were we going to deal with this threat?" He looked at the general who just nodded in agreement but was quiet, waiting for Robin to continue. "Sir, I knew this was the only solution that realistically had any chance at working and still maintain innocence on this planet. I know also that you and I know and have observed one way or another the operators of all teams in Special Forces."

"Yes, that's for sure, kind of my job as commander of Special Forces," the general joked, giving them both a chuckle at the situation.

"Yes, sir," Robin said, smirking, "and I have taught and tested quite a few. One way or the other, we can pick the teams that will stay focused and flexible. We can't have people who will be unable to handle the truth."

"That right there is the truth, Sergeant Major, so don't screw it up." The general smiled.

"Hmm, I see how this is—half the work, all the blame," Robin said as he patted the general on the back.

"You know it, just like always," said the general, standing up.

"I know all right. Still got a scar from that blonde you left me to fend off," Robin said, laughing.

"Oh, right, almost forgot that one," the general said, rubbing his chin in remembrance.

They both laughed and headed out of the conference room to catch a flight to Patrick Space Force Base.

As they came up out of the facility and headed for the airfield, Robin shook his head and looked over at the general. "So I get to fly with a two-star, and my luck, he has a C-130 for a plane. Tell me, do we get to land or are we jumping?"

The general chuckled and replied, "Tell me, Master Sergeant, how many more jumps till you move up wings?"

"Oh no, sir, senior, it is a bit off. And I don't want to get it this trip." Robin was a jumpmaster but had a few more jumps and a course to get senior jumpmaster.

CHAPTER 7

MISIDENTIFIED

Leader Three was looking over the scans. It was the fourth time in the last day he had ordered the ship back over the region where the human escaped.

The crew was showing signs of uneasiness. They had not picked up any other humans yet. Their quota was in danger, and Command would be very ready to punish all the crew. Not to mention Leader himself obsessing over the violent human.

"Aha!" Leader shouted. Half the crew jumped and let out minor noises of fear. Leader had been scanning and found a trace of the conveyance the human used and was able to trace it back to where it was sheltered. Quickly, he routed the course on his command controls and gave orders for the crew to comply.

Leader looked over at Navigator, who was studying him. Navigator was startled to be caught staring so blatantly, and he hurried to turn and assume some tasks.

Leader furrowed his brow at the bitterness he was having toward Navigator. He scanned the rest of the crew. Weapon and Engineer were both working at their station. When they looked up and saw Leader watching, they both nodded in support with him. Operation was watching things play out. He had always played his allegiance close, not pledging any way till it was necessary to. Leader admired that in him.

They had locked on to the location where the human should be, and when Leader gave the order to seek and destroy the human, the ship sped away.

*****

Deputy Warren Mackey pulled Lincoln's pickup back under the shelter twenty feet from the house and shut it off. He loved the silence of the mountains, the voice of nature, and just the pinging of a warm engine cooling. Opening the door, he breathed in that fresh cool mountain air and sighed. He sure did appreciate Master Sergeant Lincoln letting him use his truck. All he had to do was watch his place when Lincoln was out on deployment, which was often.

Mackey got a broom from the foyer of the house and jumped up in the bed of the truck, popped the tailgate down, and started sweeping. He had borrowed the pickup to transport two cords of wood he had purchased and needed to store at his house before the season got too late or snow fell. He swept the usual debris left by the cut wood out onto the grass. After finishing, he stood up in the back of the truck and stretched.

Having his arms at eye level, he studied the hair on his forearms start to stand on end, all of them at one time. His brain processed the information, and he noticed a subtle whine he missed at first. Instinct took over, and he said, "Shit," as he threw himself backward out of the bed of the truck and over the side, turning as he fell to land on his front, not his back.

Searing heat hit him a second later and a cold rush of air against his left foot edge. He looked down and saw smoke trailing off the side of his boot, well where the side should be. It was not bleeding, but it appeared as if from the pinky toe to his heel was missing but cauterized perfectly. Mouth hanging open, not feeling anything on his foot for the moment, he looked up at the truck, seeing a huge scoop from tail to front in the center just gone from the truck, about a foot from it being split in half.

"What the…" he trailed off as he looked over to the whining noise and saw an unidentified flying object (UFO), well clear as day a spaceship not of this Earth. For the second time in as many seconds, he realized he needed to move.

Jumping up, forgetting about the foot, he took off toward the house and the open door. He had planted his good foot to push off, but as his missing-toe foot hit the ground, he just did not correct for it. He fell face-first and slid off to the left. Falling usually was bad luck, but this time, it saved his life. The next shot flew through the space where he would have been if he had stayed up. Quickly looking over to the house and the spot where the shot did hit, he saw smoke and little flames dancing on the edges of a circular hole in the first two layers of wood construction.

Mackey rolled over on his back and saw the ship maneuvering, he was sure, to line up another shot. He rolled to his right as hard and fast as he could to get clear, just as a heat flash went by his face and a geyser of dirt erupted next to him.

Stopping just as fast as he was rolling, pain erupted in his ribs. He looked and saw that he had rolled hard into a tree trunk and was covered in scorched earth.

Leader Three shouted as he missed three times. He hit the land button, and the ship hit the ground without the usual stabilization. He pointed at Navigator and Security and got out of his command seat and grabbed a weapon, tossing one to each of the former. He pushed Navigator in the lead spot as he hit the controls to lower the ramp access.

Mackey pulled himself up, using the tree for stability, and he pulled his off-duty weapon from a holster in the small of his back. He could not use his left foot for stability. It was awkward without the missing section. He tried to pull in a lungful of air to get himself limping toward cover. He figured out he must have done some sort of damage to his ribs or lungs or both because only half a lungful worked on the side that had full-on pain.

Limping over to a set of logs stacked for cutting, he made it just as the ship plopped down on the ground. A ramp opened, and three smallish aliens came filing out. Warren looked them over and at first thought how cute they were. Then he realized they just tried to fry him. Looking them over a second time, he noticed what could not be mistaken for anything else but weapons, in their cute elongated fingered hands.

Warren Mackey shook his head and looked over the pack again as he lay behind the logs and rested the gun barrel over the top, sighting and using the logs for stability. He took aim and watched as the second in line pushed the first one out of the ship.

Navigator screeched a mad remark at Leader, the coward putting him out front. Pushing at that, it was plain rude. Now Navigator would focus on undermining Leader. It would become his mission.

Warren blinked the sweat from his eyes out of the way as it stung him. What the hell was he sweating for, he thought, as he lined up a shot. The aliens were grouping up, trying to figure where he had gone.

Leader poked Security in the chest, asking why he did not follow where the human went. Security explained he was behind him and blocked by the other two. He had no view of the human. Leader stomped his foot and shouted at the two to find the human.

Mackey lined up a shot and pulled the trigger three times, just as the group started to move.

Navigator, having a sense of direction honed by years doing his job, turned and stepped one step toward where the human had to be. After his first step, he found himself staring up at the sky and treetops. He blinked his wide eyes, confused by the turn of events. Leader, he saw, was running in circles, screaming.

Security was sitting on his butt, looking as confused as Navigator felt. He felt warm and wet on the side of his head. Security ran through in his mind what just happened. He heard three ancient projectiles being launched. One struck Navigator on the side of his head, taking out a large chunk. The second projectile hit the weapon he held in his hand, the projectile knocking him down with force and heading in a new trajectory toward Leader's foot. Security looked down and saw two pieces of his weapon where one should be, and Leader was running in circles in pain from the projectile hitting him dead center of his foot.

Navigator tried to say something, but it appeared he had liquid in his mouth. His body urged him to spit it out. He tried, but it hurt, and more just took its place. He also could not answer why it was getting darker. He saw the burning star overhead.

Security tossed aside his broken weapon and picked up Navigator's. He sighted it and hit the tracking button to get a precision shot on the human behind the downed forest sticks. He aimed carefully and shot.

Warren was getting ready to shoot again when he saw a flash and his wrist felt so cold. He looked at it to see why and was shocked to find his hands and gun gone and smoke rising from where they had been just a moment ago. The desire to scream was overwhelming him. Of course, it was fighting with the need to run away.

Security stalked over to the logs where the human was lying in obvious shock. Keeping his weapon in his offhand, he grabbed the human by the collar and started dragging him to the ship and the ramp. The human did not squirm or attempt to move. He just held his appendages together and was making pathetic noises. Security could not wait to put the holding field on him. As he dragged the human past the still-screeching Leader and the dead Navigator, he looked at both in turn and gave a humph and continued toward the ship.

Mackey could not formulate thoughts, let alone make his body respond to the thoughts. He was vaguely aware that he was being dragged across the ground. And he noticed the ship getting closer, some horrible screeching, and a terrible smell. In his head, he started screaming. The smell was from his burning flesh—wait, no, that was wrong, burned flesh at the stubs where his hands had been. His head struck something, a lip of something to be exact, then the tug of gravity, and some sort of metal material sliding down his back. No, not sliding down his back, he was being pulled up the ramp into the spaceship. Deputy Sheriff Warren Mackey could think of only one thing to do—pass out, which he did.

CHAPTER 8

HOME SECRET HOME

The ramp of the C-130 Hercules dropped to the tarmac. Major General Hansen and Master Sergeant Lincoln walked down it, oblivious to their surroundings as they were deep into conversation on the unit, the men, and even the equipment required.

A young airman first class saluted the general and informed him he was escorting them to the headquarters of their new unit. Holding his salute, he resigned that the two were not going to stop or pay attention when the general brushed his hand toward him to carry on and that they would follow.

They climbed aboard an Air Force blue six-person golf cart, and the airman peeled away into an older-looking hangar. It looked capable of easily holding three of the C-130s. That's how big it appeared. That seemed to be the only impressive thing about it.

Entering through the slight opening in the main hangar doors, the golf cart passed several small assault copters known as Little Birds, several Apache helicopters, a Chinook helicopter, and three of the new helicopters that were about to replace the Hueys from Vietnam fame. Four of the new helicopters replacing the Blackhawk were also there. Crews were working on them, making them ready for duty. All were marked with the Space Force markings and were dark gray to set them apart from the other branches.

Both the general and the master sergeant stopped talking as they took a visual inventory of what they had to work with. A satisfied grunt came from the general, and they went back to their discussion.

The golf cart stopped at what appeared to be a large freight elevator just slightly past the middle of the hangar opposite of the helicopters and the workforce with them.

The airman got out and went over to the elevator and swiped a card and used his whole hand in a slot for a biometric scan and then spoke to allow a voice recognition capture while doing a retinal scan.

Hansen and Lincoln watched as the elevator doors parted and a freight elevator, beat up and unkept, awaited. They exited the cart and got to the airman and stopped before entering.

Hansen asked, "You said we were going to our HQ. Please tell me this is a joke."

The airman, obviously nervous, replied very seriously, "No joke, sir, we are going to your HQ. We enter the lift."

"Then we get out and we're in the HQ?" Lincoln asked.

"Oh no, Master Sergeant, we take a tram," the airman said.

"A tram? Son, are you pulling a two-star general's leg," Hansen said in a command voice.

"No, no, sir. Please just enter and you will see," the airman pleaded.

Both men were trained killers and exceptionally good at what they did, so they entered the elevator full of curiosity.

"Welcome, General Hansen and Master Sergeant Lincoln. We will be proceeding to level U4. That is the tram level." The distinctive female voice was the same as from the White House.

"Annie, is that you?" Hansen asked as Lincoln stared at him like he was crazy. The general looked at him and said, "I know it's a computer, but it's an AI." Lincoln nodded like it made sense, not sure if it really did.

"No, sir, I am Charlene, the third-generation AI, and assigned to assist the Thirteenth Special Forces Group in their new home. You met Annie in Washington. We are not the same."

"Okay then," Lincoln said. "Will you be throughout our facility, Charlie, or just in here?" Lincoln asked. He decided Charlie was a better fit for a name for the AI, and it—she—didn't seem to mind, as she answered to it.

"I will be running most of the system from here to Canaveral Space Force Base where your training, housing, and HQ will be. The base has an underground and underwater base that runs the distance of about five miles. It is extremely covert and uses a tram to go between Canaveral and Patrick bases. Since the system is completely underground and underwater, it makes your teams and you the most clandestine unit there is." Charlene seemed a bit excited and proud of the fact that she was running it.

Lincoln caught himself. "She." He already started thinking of "it" in human terms.

The elevator stopped, and the doors opened.

Charlene spoke, "Gentleman, if you would follow the airman to the tram, he will direct you to your new home." The AI paused, then said, "I hope you enjoy interacting with me as much as I will with you."

"I look forward to it, Charlie, and thanks for the welcome," Lincoln responded as they stepped out. He was not sure, but it sounded like the ding of the doors as they closed was just a bit more harmonic. Lincoln wondered if that was an AI way of blushing or giggling. He shook his head. What the hell was he thinking.

A Space Force three-star general awaited them as they were led down a hallway which opened out to what appeared to be a subway platform. "Welcome, gentlemen. The tram will be here in a minute. I am the base commander and not in your chain of command, but I hope to work together since your needs will flow through my office."

Even though it was worded as a veiled threat, none of the men took it as one, and it really was not meant as one.

Hansen smiled and said, "General, been there before, so I can promise the sergeant major here will do as much as he can, and he has my ear. Any men I assign here will know the rules."

"Good to hear. I figured as much. You and I are pretty much the same in that we have a job to do and you put us here. Let me do it and stay out of my way."

The three veterans laughed, and inside, they knew any friction in the future would come from outside and not here with these men.

General Patterson, the base commander, gave them a brief history of how the facility was even thought up. During World War II, aviators for the US were trained in Florida, but fear of the Germans attacking left the Army Air Corps a bit afraid that it would be an enticing target to hit if all the facilities were visible. So training structures and aircraft storage bunkers were built underground. Then came the start of developing the atomic bomb and rockets. Since a facility had been started and was still unknown, the government added more to the facility. Once the space race and ballistic missiles were coming into play, a civilian agency was put on top of the government facility. More was added for secret projects and projects most still do not know ever were conceived. Through the years, it had been expanded and grown to be quite modern. The president, knowing he wanted to form a unit and a clear course, began updating and filling out the facilities. No name had been given it, and it was going to be up to group 13 to make it their own.

General Patterson, General Hansen, and Master Sergeant Lincoln toured the structure and picked out their offices and quarters.

"Master Sergeant, I'm going back to Bragg to start the transfers. You are in charge here till I send the new team members here." Hansen stopped for a second and thought. Then he continued, "I have to go about it slow as not to draw attention by having too many people moving about at one time."

"Well, sir, just start with my team. We chose almost all the men and just some HQ staff. That way, we can get up and running and feel our way into this," Lincoln said, having thought about this already. No one was going to question the Special Forces about the number of men on one team moving about. Just business as usual.

"Yes, just what I was thinking." Hansen rubbed his jaw as he thought about his next words. "Master Sergeant, I think, in the orders, it will just say to report to Space Force Base Patrick and see you for orientation. I don't know if you're going to catch flak at first till they know what they are being assigned to, but be prepared." He then looked over to the other general and said, "No problem with you if I use Patrick as our reporting destination?"

General Patterson patted Hansen on the shoulder and said, "Nope, no problem on my end. If you want, I have a couple of buildings sitting empty. You can use them as decoy offices."

General Hansen smiled. "That would be outstanding. We could rotate men through there one team at a time, just to be seen."

"That is the perfect idea, and as far as fielding the complaints, well, as soon as they understand our mission, all that will be forgotten," Robin Lincoln said as the men strolled through the facilities that could have been mistaken for a complete underground city.

Major General Hansen headed out for the Pentagon, then to Fort Bragg to begin the transfers and creation of the Thirteenth group while Master Sergeant Lincoln and General Patterson began coordinating the setup of the facility.

Patterson detailed a platoon of his security police, all who held top clearance, to assist in the furnishing and installing of most of the facility.

Master Sergeant Lincoln greeted Technical Sergeant Andrews and a group of "computer geeks," newly reassigned from the Air Force to the Space Force, who took pride in explaining their "geek" to the master sergeant. The geeks swelled with even more pride as Lincoln welcomed them to the Special Forces and handed them a group pin, which they were to wear above their name tags. The symbol was the traditional sword and banner "*De oppresso liber*," with a green 13 set with the sword between the 1 and the 3.

Lincoln watched as the computer crew stared at the pin and could not stop smiling. He shook his head and headed to the underground hangar, chuckling as he went.

Walking into the hangar area was surreal. It was twice the size of the hangar on Patrick Base that they entered to catch the tram over. There were four lifts to take aircraft up and out to the "abandoned" runway and large NASA (National Aeronautics and Space Administration) hangars.

Aircraft, whether it be helicopters or planes, would be towed onto the lift and raised up into one of the abandoned hangars unseen and then proceed out to take off and reverse the process on return, effectively hidden from notice.

Robin Lincoln saw some activity at lift 1. Apparently, some of the air support unit was arriving and setting up camp.

Master Sergeant Logan was directing a Blackhawk off the lift, the first arrival of the aircraft to be housed here.

"Logan, don't scratch the bird before she even gets into action, you old dog!" Lincoln yelled across the large bay.

A barreling laugh emitted from the stocky, tough-looking man. "Speaking of dog, is that Robin Lincoln messing up my pretty floors with his dirty ass boots?"

Lincoln let out a howl of laughter. The two had known each other since they both were assigned to Special Forces. Master Sergeant Logan ran a tight ship, and every bird he was entrusted never failed. He looked like a biker in size and attitude, and he was a perfectionist when it came to his birds.

Logan directed three of his crew in parking the Blackhawk in its new home and spot. He turned and stuck out his hand to Lincoln, and Lincoln grasped it and pulled the man in for a pat-on-the-back greeting.

"Looking good, my friend. Welcome aboard to the Thirteenth," Lincoln said.

"Shit, you named it. Didn't you, Robin? The Thirteenth, really?" He shook his head, unzipped his sleeve pocket, and pulled out a chewed and half-smoked cigar, his signature prop. "Should have known you'd be involved. So what's the deal? Why the new team? And this is way out there for a base," Logan said as he waved the cigar around the open space, taking in the one of six hangar bays on the facility.

It seemed like a lot, but when it came down to it, a new group and the current groups of Special Forces contained four battalions of four companies each. Now most groups split up locations to different bases, but that wasn't the plan for the Thirteenth yet.

"Don, you are just going to have to wait for my speech when my whole team arrives and more of the HQ staff get here. Plus, the computer squad isn't set yet." Lincoln winked and watched as the lift rose again up to the roof as it slid open above inside the hangar. Lincoln pointed at the lift and nodded to Logan. "Looks like you got some unpacking to do. See if you can't find the mess hall when you're done. I'm buying."

They laughed. And Logan said, "If there is food, I will find it."

"Really, Don, it's good to see you and have you on the team." Robin patted him on the shoulder and turned to head to check on the rest of the activity going on.

The master sergeant found three of the detailed security force men pushing crates on dollies down a wide hallway.

"Master Sergeant, these are the new armor packages. We were taking them to the armory. Is that okay?" one of the men asked.

"Just fine, Sergeant. Keep on."

The men rolled by Lincoln to the armory, which was more like a locker room armory hybrid. All the gear and weapons would be ready for each member of the teams and the barracks rooms and office section set aside for each team and each company. So far, only one battalion was scheduled to go online at this time, so each company got a section of the facility, but quarters and offices were available for two more battalions. For the hundredth time, Robin realized how large this facility was. He shook his head as he continued down the hall. At least the teams were not going to be sitting on top of each other. If they even bumped into each other, it would be a miracle.

"Master Sergeant, there is a tram coming in with members of your team."

Robin froze in the hallway, and it took a second for him to realize it was the AI talking through the comms. He sighed and said, "I'm going to have to get used to that. Thanks, Charlie. If I can find my way to the platform, I will meet them." As Robin finished speaking, he saw a path of lights in blue come on along the wall, hopefully showing the way to the platform. "Charlie, you're an angel, my girl. What would I ever do without you?"

"You say that to all the AIs, Robin."

Robin smiled and winked at the ceiling. He thought he heard a hint of a purr in the AI's voice. Once again, he had to remind himself it was a computer. "Yeah, Charlie, but I only mean it when I say it to you." He could swear he heard Charlene giggle, but that was impossible, right?

Thanks to Charlene's direction markings, Robin made it to the platform with ten minutes to spare.

Robin Lincoln had no idea who was coming in on this tram. The team was being assembled as quietly and as low-key as could be done. General Hansen had not a chance to tell Lincoln who he was able to reassign yet. Hansen was picking individuals that he and Lincoln had discussed, but he would not be able to confirm any sort of order.

"Charlie, how many are coming in on this tram?" Lincoln asked just out of curiosity.

"There are six, Robin, three from the Space Force and three members of your team."

"Thank you, my dear." This time, Lincoln was sure he heard a giggle.

The tram pulled into the platform, and Lincoln smiled as big as he could. His new commanding officer and old friend, Captain Steve Ryan, came out first. The man was as big as a mountain and just as impossible to knock down. He was all muscle in a six-foot-five broad frame of an Irish temper and also the smartest commander he had ever known.

Right behind him, an inch shorter and built the same as Ryan, was Sergeant First Class William Junius—Wild Bill to anyone who ever knew him as a friend. The two operators were among the best, and both had gotten their dream of becoming Delta Force members—well, until Robin asked for them for his team. He would probably hold that little fact till further down the road.

"I should have known, Robin Frigging Lincoln, you could mess up a wet dream, and you did, didn't you?" The captain had a scowl, and both his hands dropped his bags and went to his hips in a stance that made Lincoln swallow hard.

"Son of a bitch, Lincoln!" Wild Bill repeated the same action as Steve Ryan. It was why people called them "twins," on occasion.

"Oh, you had better have a good story for this. Do you know how long and how hard I worked to get into Delta, do you?"

"I guess I will by the end of the day, sir." Lincoln smiled, but it did not seem to have the effect he wanted. Wild Bill growled and took a step toward Lincoln.

Captain Ryan put out an arm and stopped Bill. "Talk and it better be good, or I'm going to let Bill rip your arm off and beat you with it."

Lincoln put both hands out and gestured for them to wait a second for him to explain. He really did not think they were this angry, but he knew the mission and they did not. All they knew was they were pulled from their dream assignment.

Sergeant Gabriel Herndon was a weapons sergeant from the Tenth Special Forces Group, the unit stationed in Germany. He came out and was taking a bite out of an apple. Calm and relaxed, he said, "I'm not as, um, angry as these two. But I am curious what this is about and why I got picked, Master Sergeant, since I don't recall working with any of you." He continued to eat his apple.

Wild Bill and Captain Ryan turned and looked at the six-foot sergeant and lost a little of their anger. Lincoln could see it in their faces.

"Well, can we head to the team room, or do I need to stand here and dish it out? You guys know me, well, except for Herndon."

The twins relaxed and agreed to listen to Lincoln and to go to the team room.

Captain Ryan said, "So you said 'team.' I guess this isn't just an op then, is it?"

"No, sir, we will be the first team of the first company of a new group." Lincoln let that settle in.

"Did you say 'new group'?" Wild Bill asked.

"Yes, and you are slated to be the 18F of the team, the first time you have been an assistant operations and intel sergeant of a team," Lincoln said, knowing the answer already and knowing Bill had wanted that position for a while.

"Shut up! No way!" Bill lost all his anger and smiled.

Sergeant Major Lincoln motioned for the three operators to follow him to the team room.

"Is it safe to come out yet?" came a voice from inside the tram. Lincoln recognized the voice of one of the Project Blue Book Air

Force—no, wait, now Space Force officers. The two captains and one of the air police technical sergeants came out with big smiles on their faces. Obviously, they knew how this was going to go. They must have gotten the feel of that from the attitude of Ryan and Junius. The former Project Blue Book men were asked to join the Thirteenth group and find and fight the aliens they chased for years.

Master Sergeant Lincoln made introductions all around as the group settled into the team room. Once all the men were acquainted, it was time for Lincoln to spill the facts of the new group's mission.

Captain Ryan was first to speak. "Okay, Lincoln, I must say you got my curiosity up. And seeing two Space Force captains and the tech sergeant here, well, go ahead and tell."

Lincoln smiled. He knew Ryan well enough; Ryan was getting the fact this was important. "First, so you understand this is not bull, the Army, Air Force, and now the Space Force would not start a new Special Forces Group, assign us this base, or even transfer men like us without having a great need. Captain, once you see the hangar area and the new equipment, you will understand how big this is." Lincoln paused to let what he just outlined back up the next part, something he knew most people would just not be ready to believe.

"I'm all in for new gear, especially if weapons are involved," Wild Bill said with a hint of excitement in his voice. Bill had been a longtime weapons sergeant. New equipment and weapons would always be like Christmas to him.

Lincoln smiled at Bill and looked back to Captain Ryan. "Okay. So on leave and back up at my home in Upstate New York, I was attacked by aliens that tried to abduct me." Lincoln stopped to measure the reaction of his two friends. There was none. They continued to stare and listen. So he continued, "Whatever they were using to detain me, it failed. I was able to stop them and even took three out in the process, and one lost his arm but got away."

"Holy shit!" the captain said. And that was it. He stayed unmoving and kept quiet for the master sergeant to continue.

Wild Bill pulled out a couple of sticks of gum and started chewing, but his eyes never left Lincoln.

So he kept going. "A local deputy pulled up, and they hightailed it as he came up. Of course, I could not give chase to the ship. It was unreal. I gathered three alien arms I had severed from them and two bodies. The third was inside the ship when they fled."

Robin took a drink of water, cleared his throat, and kept going. "The deputy and I gathered up what we could and headed to his station where we called the nearest base, which happened to be an Air Force base. This is where these three gentlemen come in." Robin gestured to the three Space Force men across the table from the three operators.

"So how are we here and how did a new team come about?" Ryan asked. Bill stayed quiet.

"Seems our new president found out that this is going on—abductions, that is—and felt it should not be ignored. The president was an acquaintance of General Hansen and wanted the Special Forces of the Army to dedicate a unit to the problem, like Delta Force to terrorism."

"Makes sense and about time, I would say," Ryan said as he sat back in his chair as all of it sank in. "Okay, Master Sergeant, you get a pass on pulling me out of Delta. I won't thank you yet till I see if we survive a year of this."

Lincoln knew the captain was serious about that. It was the same feeling he had.

"Well, hell, I'm in and can't wait to kick some little green-man butt!" Wild Bill exclaimed, slapping Captain Ryan on the back. "Wait, they are little green men, right?"

"Not really green, the ones I saw, but more white. And sizes varied, but none was that tall that I dealt with." Lincoln stopped and thought. "Their tech and their ship is what has me taking a pause, and the stuff used on me didn't work, but I don't know how everyone else will fare."

"Well, you will have to be ready to figure out how to get anyone moving who isn't. That simple," Ryan said to Lincoln.

Lincoln sighed, "Just what I was thinking, I really should let them take me."

Everyone laughed, but underneath, they all were nervous as to how they were going to combat the threats a new enemy posed.

"Captain Ryan, Master Sergeant Lincoln, a tram with three more team members is coming in about twenty minutes," the AI stated, causing both Captain Ryan and Sergeant First Class Junius to make faces of confusion.

Lincoln chuckled as well as the Space Force men who had experience with AIs. "Gentlemen, meet Charlene, our team AI. She is awesome. I call her Charlie. Anything you need, just ask and she will direct you."

"I'm here to serve and protect my team and unit and Sergeant Major Lincoln."

Lincoln blushed while Ryan and Junius gave him sly smiles, knowing he was not going to hear the end of this. "Captain, why don't you and I head to the tram and meet the new guys. And, Wild Bill, you head to our armory and get familiar with the new equipment. Charlie will guide you there and help you learn the new gear."

"I would be glad to do that. Wild Bill, follow the blue arrow lights. And, Captain, follow the yellow to the tram," Charlene directed.

"Darlin', you and I are going to get along fine, especially if you know weapons," Sergeant First Class Junius said with a big smile on his face as he headed to the armory.

"Looks like Bill won't have any problem adjusting, Captain. I hope you don't mind me making him assistant operations sergeant of intelligence," Lincoln said, hoping he had not overstepped his boundary of command.

"Nah, we go way back. You and I seem to always make the same decisions on team issues, so keep doing it, Master Sergeant. Who may be coming in on this tram? Any idea?"

"I am thinking Tanaka should be soon. Maybe him."

"Tanaka, you mean Lee from Heidelberg, Germany, warrant officer?" Ryan asked, showing signs of excitement for the first time.

"Yep, one and the same. Figured it would help you not to hurt me if I could get him," Robin said.

"Hell yeah, the three of us are pure fluid working together." Ryan clapped his hands, excited. "No one is as fast as Lee. He was always three steps ahead of anyone I ever met."

"Well, I've got Dwight Davis and Ernest Doolie, Greg Gonzalez, and Rudy Polansky on my poaching list."

"Hot, damn, Robin, the dream team from the sandbox and the Amazon," Ryan said. And now he wore a huge smile of the thought of this all-star team of operators.

Robin had painstakingly told General Hansen about how important these men he had just rattled off were to any success. They had all been together for some serious operations, extremely dangerous ones, and worked like they knew one another forever. The mission to South America had been a challenge, and Robin did not think any other team would have made it out in one piece, but they had. Everyone knew the dangers of the Middle East, but it was the first time all the men met and worked together. That was where the trust the men felt for one another was forged.

The captain and master sergeant told tales as they waited on the tram platform, catching up on their recent teams and missions.

The tram pulled in, and first one off was Chief Warrant Officer 2 Lee Tanaka. Seeing him step off the tram, Ryan and Lincoln started hooting and hollering with excitement and were soon joined by Tanaka as they came together greeting one another like three long-lost brothers, which perhaps they were.

Next out was Sergeant First Class Ernest "Double D" Doolie, the senior medical sergeant of the team and one who had patched up more of the team than any doctor ever could. Doc Doolie, or Double D as he was called, probably passed medical school in a breeze, and he loved action. That never changed in him.

Out last was Sergeant Gabriel "Angel" Hernandez, a top-rated weapons sergeant, who had saved his teams more times than anyone ever could remember. He had earned the nickname Angel—well, Archangel Gabriel—for watching over everyone.

The men grabbed their gear and finished greeting one another and headed for the armory. Master Sergeant Lincoln related the details about the facility and the new team as they headed out.

CHAPTER 9

FOLLOW THE LEADER

Leader sat on the doctor's table in the medical bay of his ship. The doctor was repairing the wound on his foot. How could this happen—the loss of his arm and the hole in his foot? Well, at least one good thing came of this—Navigator was dead, problem solved; and he did not even need to kill him.

Humans were not worth the stress he had gotten on this run to this stupid planet. He would not get as much credit as he would by a trip to Yunari and harvesting the indigenous life-form there. They had four arms and little brains. At the market, Yunarians fetched a lot of credit. Humans were just a bit under them, but still they were a pain, literally now, to catch and hold.

But he was ordered to Earth to round up twenty males, good-condition males. It just so happened that one of the males he went after caused him so much stress. He would take out his stress on the human male he had captured, piece by piece, to ease him. Still, he would look for the male that got away and maybe torture him and keep him as a pet. Then he would continue to round up his twenty and maybe get lucky and get a pack of them and get over his quota, which would be great and impressive to Command, especially One Stripe. The profit for them both would be immense, enough so that perhaps he would move to Leader Two instead of Three.

Leader ordered Engineer to the control cabin to inform him he was now Navigator and second in charge. New Navigator thanked Leader and took his position. The ranks would now move to fill in vacated crew spots, raising status as they did so, as was the way of the Aldions.

Signal simmered slowly at his post. He was passed over by Leader just now, and it was a slight that would have to be avenged in the ways; but he had to think hard and long to kill Leader, moving New Navigator to leader, or kill New Navigator. The problem was that Leader and Navigator were aligned. Killing one may set the other against him. No, the course he would need to take would be to rid himself of both and assume command. Appointing those aligned with him in the process and perhaps aligning those who followed Old Navigator to align with him. *Yes*, he thought, *that would do.*

He stared at the back of Leader, formulating several plans to put his plan in motion. He laughed inside. Leader discounted him, thinking he had no bones to stand against him; but Signal—unknown to Leader, Old Navigator, and Old Engineer—had been aligning the crew his way for a while. Soon, it would pay off.

Leader gestured for Navigator to come take command while he wanted to torture the human in the lab. The medicine the doctor had given him had eased his foot and made him in the need for entertainment. He thought he may just let the human speak so he could hear the terror and the screams. Yes, that would be enjoyable, would not it?

Walking into the lab, looking over the human who had liquid pouring out his eyes, he had a thought. Pushing the comm button in the lab, he chirped to Navigator not to go far away from the ruined building. He believed it to be the dwelling of the male he wanted. Navigator suggested leaving a drone to stand by and watch for human males coming into the area.

Leader grabbed a laser scalpel and praised Navigator for his idea and released the comm. Now he would take a few pieces off this human to comfort himself.

Navigator programmed the ship to rotate a few measures away, after dropping a drone at the burning wreckage of the conveyance and a small distance from the burning dwelling. Looking over the scans of the area, he found a slight indentation in a ridge that would hide the ship and be within striking distance of the burning dwelling. Navigator got a twitch in his left longer hand digit, which he felt was a sure sign that the human male would show up here sooner than later. He loved killing humans. Problem was he did not get much of a chance. They were always testing on them for credit or taking them to the market for credit. Navigator felt that, at some point, some other race would put out a bounty for the killing of the humans. It was the way of the universe. A race would want the human planet. They would insult the wrong beings. Sooner or later, he would get credits for killing humans.

Signal activated the drone on order from Navigator and set the drone to avoid detection and to only incapacitate humans and not to kill them. Signal put out the hunting warning signal, required by the treaty of beings who hunted Earth for its life-forms. This would give them the first rights for humans within a designated area, a must due to the amount of competition from other Aldions and the other factions hunting here.

Signal also sent an encrypted message to the engine room where number 2 engineer, now promoted to engineer, was waiting. He told him to take step 1 of their plan.

Engineer received his message and sent out the signal code, activating preplanted instructions set to activate plan 1 in the attempt to take over. Engineer rubbed his gangly hands together, chirping deceit as the code was authenticated and sent back that it was now in motion.

The doctor sat in his cabin and annotated results from his experiments he was paid to get. Credit was good for gaining information on beings when contracted through Command but more lucrative when the doctor was able to get bids outside the higher-ups. The credits were larger for information that suppliers wanted about races and possible uses for them.

The screams of the human were not bothering the doctor, but they did make it harder to concentrate on his findings. He wished he could be in there to gather information as the leader put the human through serious pain and dissection. It was impossible for that to occur. He would then have to reveal he was working outside command and even more to the point of cutting out the leader for extra credits. The first would either get him kicked off the ship or stripped out of the service. The second would surely have the leader throw him out a space lock once out of the atmosphere. Still, all that precious information on humans would go to waste. The doctor was intelligent. He knew he should have prepared for a time like this, but it was not too late, was it? Of course not. He needed to plan, and no one was better at that than him.

Leader had never felt such pleasure. He had always enjoyed toying with humans, but since he had been injured and allowed himself to do what he wanted—no, what he desired to do to them—he felt so alive. If he had not enjoyed the freedom of being out in the universe, especially now in command of his own ship, he would have become a slave master at the market. Yet would he have discovered his true nature, his true joy, the inflicting of such devious and painful torture? Probably not, and that would have been a shame. Nothing compared to this.

The big toe of the human's right foot was the only digit left on that appendage. But not to worry, the left still had them all. It was a shame that the hands had been burned off, but no matter, he would take an extra human or two just for his pleasure. It was his right as Leader after all.

The scalpel bit down the middle of the toe, cauterizing it as it went through. No blood and sticky mess but, as his little subject screamed, a lot of pain. He stopped when he reached the actual foot. He looked it over and chuckled. It looked like a worm mouth of Alabass 6. Starting back at the top, he moved slightly to the right with the scalpel and cut to the exact point again. Releasing more screaming from his toy. Now it looked like a Scratta floral pod. This was fun. He moved back up and continued as he had done with the previous four digits.

The sick little alien had propped Mackey's head up and allowed him to talk. It was apparent he did not want a conversation from the start. He just ignored him when he spoke, but when he screamed from the pain as the bastard dissected his toes, he could hear a trill sound, a cross between a cat purr and a squirrel barking. It was not a comforting sound, not at all. When Mackey could think, he thought it was a sound the pale freak was enjoying himself. Mackey tried to hold back to not give the shit any satisfaction, but it was impossible. His throat was raw from the screams. He just kept hoping he would pass out.

The leader knew he would have to take a break soon. The human was losing the ability to scream enough for him to enjoy the torture. He knew it would be a short time to let it rest and then continue on. He finally had stripped the toe into many thin strips still attached and decided he would leave it like that till the next session. That way, the human could look at it and think of the torture to come.

Mackey lay there and stared at his stripped toe with dread in the pit of his stomach. He wanted to look away, but he couldn't. Then as he was midwhimper, the sound from his throat was gone. He was locked in his own head again. He thought that the asshole stopping would be a relief, but it wasn't. It was somehow worse. He was left to stare at his abused foot and stripped toe just sitting there, and now he could not express anything. He was trapped inside, unable to let his emotions go. This was hell, pure and simple, and that alien crap head was the devil.

After making the adjustments to his toy, the human male, he turned and headed back out to the control room. The only thing that could make this better was to find the other human and be able to play with him.

Signal felt disgust as Leader came back into the control room at the way he wasted the credit they could have for the two humans Leader had damaged and destroyed. Leader did not need the credit as the rest of the crew did, part of why they hated Leader as much as they did. No, Leader was bad for the mission, which was a fact. Signal felt relieved that soon Leader would get his.

As Leader walked into command, he took stock of his crew. Navigator, very loyal. Then Signal, he was not sure about him. He had not seen him act either for or against. Signal was one of those weak ones that just went with the majority, which did not think for themselves. No, Signal was just a piece of the background. If he did his job and did not make Leader look bad, then he would just stay right where he was. Leader felt good about that—why Signal did not even argue when Navigator was replaced. Although it was his right, not that Leader would have let him, he just let it go. Weak. New Engineer was the one to watch. He had talked back to Engineer-Navigator while given orders to work on the ship.

Beeping erupted from the panel, pulling Leader from his thoughts as he took his seat and checked what was sounding out. Leader saw that the drone at the dwelling was alerting them to the presence of humans approaching. Signal gave him that information just as he had read it out on his panel at the same time.

"Worthless," Leader chirped at Signal, letting him know he saw the information just as he did.

Signal made no comment or noise in response. Weak.

Leader looked at the feed from the drone. It was not the human he was looking for. It was humans who came to stop the dwelling from being consumed by fire.

"Should we go and take them, Leader?" Navigator asked as he prepared to move the ship.

"No. These are workers who will cause great activity by the humans if we take them. We will wait and see if the human comes back." Leader had proven what a great hunter he was in his younger years. He knew patience waiting on prey, especially when the reward was going to be so wonderful.

The fire crew had made it to the house out here in the middle of nowhere. They knocked down the fire and kept it from spreading into the woods. The house was a total loss, and it looked like it had been hit by a bomb. The sheriff was on his way with a couple of deputies. He was missing a deputy, and last he knew, he had been heading here.

The fire chief knew the deputy as they all did, and his car was sitting off to the side; but the pickup the army guy always let them use was sitting at the house, burned-out smoking, a complete and utter loss. Anyone who saw it would think a tank ran over it, then shot it, then ran over it again.

Three sheriff's cars pulled up, and then the sheriff in his big SUV pulled up behind them. The fire chief called for his men to start packing up and get ready to leave. The mood the sheriff looked in was agitated. It was always best to clear the area and let the men with guns do their thing, a heck of a lot safer anyways, especially as agitated as they were.

"Hey, Sheriff, as far as we could find, no bodies, some weird goop stuff over in the middle of the front yard, and, of course, the disaster." The chief waved his hand in the direction of the truck and house, wrecked and smoking.

"Holy shit! Robin Lincoln is going to go ballistic. What the hell happened here, Chief?" Sheriff Bascomb asked as he turned his head and spit onto the grass and moved the chewing tobacco around in his mouth.

The fire chief cringed. He hated chewing tobacco. It made him sick to his stomach once, and he was cured of ever wanting any ever again. "Well, well, I haven't the slightest idea, Sheriff, not even one," he said, taking off his fire helmet and wiping the sweat from his brow.

"Well, any sign at all of my man Mackey? He wasn't in either of those, was he?" Sheriff Bascomb asked, pointing to the house and truck again.

"Nope. As a matter of fact, his car is over there. We recognized it and searched for him all around." The chief made a face, then continued, "Just some weird goo in a couple of places, burn marks like I haven't seen and can't figure how they were made." The chief pointed to the grass where the ship had been and several locations where the alien guns had struck.

"I guess I need to lock this down and call Robin. See who he wants to come out here, Mackey. And he had some strange things go on the other day, and the Air Force came and handled it." Bascomb spit again and moved the chew in his mouth again.

"What was it, Sheriff? What happened?"

"Damn if I know. Mackey just said he was told he couldn't say anything about it, and Lincoln vouched that it was important that it remained secret." Bascomb shook his head. "Damn secret squirrel shit, I hate it. But obviously, it must be tied to that. Has to be, doesn't it?"

"Yep, I would imagine. But I wonder what the hell it was, thinking maybe terrorist," the chief said, taking off the helmet again and wiping his brow.

"Humph, damned if I know. I'm just the sheriff here in these parts. Why the hell should I know?" With that, he spit and walked over to his men who had gathered around Mackey's car.

The chief jumped into his command SUV and waited until his two trucks started out the tree-covered driveway and followed them back to the firehouse, leaving the mess and his curiosity back at the scene. It was times like this he preferred to be ignorant of things that would keep him up at night. He hit the radio, and music came pouring out. Nothing like those loud, obnoxious tunes on other stations, it was set to instrumentals at a leisurely pace, and it was so calming.

"Well, boys, anything over here?" Bascomb strode up to his deputies, turned, spit, and asked.

"Well, Sheriff, I'm still not a boy," Deputy Sue Hamlin said sarcastically, "and Mackey's car is locked up, like he hadn't got back to it from using Robin's truck."

"I'm well aware you're not a boy, Sue. You're a man. Anyone hear from him, try his phone, you know, regular investigative things like that?" Bascomb said just as sarcastically. There were no hard feelings. As a matter of fact, it was the opposite; the sheriff had complete respect and faith in his deputies. He just liked to play the "old country boy" for effect.

The deputies liked it and thought it kept the sheriff grounded and more like one of them that they could trust, and they did.

Deputy Keith Grimsby spoke up next, "No, sir, we all have tried, and it goes straight to voicemail saying the phone is out of range of service."

"Really like were back in the nineties. Haven't heard that crap since you guys graduated high school."

They all chuckled, but underneath, they had a sense of foreboding. That message did not get used much because almost all the networks were all around the world. It did not bode well for Mackey, or at least his phone.

"Okay, serious now, any one of you know what Mackey or Lincoln got into the other day? I hate to say it, but it seems to be related to this." Bascomb spit again, looked them over, and continued, "I mean I don't believe it is a coincidence that, one, they were involved in something secret. Two, they told no one. Three, Mackey was supposed to last have been here, and this is Lincoln's home and truck. Oh, and let us not forget, what the hell went on here? It looks like a damn war zone." Bascomb spit and put his hands on his hips to see if anyone had anything.

No one did, and the look on their faces made him nervous. They all looked frightened and confused, looking to him to say it was all okay. Unfortunately, it was not.

"Sir," Deputy Gary Polk, the quietest of the three, said, "I think we should call that Air Force base and let them know what happened, and maybe they will call Master Sergeant Lincoln. Hopefully, he will know what's going on."

"Yep, good idea, Polk. All right, you three stay here and watch each other's backs and stay alert. I'll take a run over there in person. We do not need a brush-off over the phone. If I'm in their face, then I hope to get them moving faster." Bascomb spit and looked at his young deputies. "Mind what I said—stay alert, watch out for each other. God knows what's going on here."

Bascomb climbed back into his SUV and set out for the Air Force base. He was going to get either action or answers—secrets be damned.

CHAPTER 10

GEAR

The five operators walked into the armory to find Wild Bill sitting on the floor like a kid at Christmas. He had several weapons lying around him and pieces of shiny black armor in his hands. He was inspecting them inside and out.

"Hey, Bill! What do you think? This stuff is going to work for us?" Robin asked, smirking at the big guy on the floor, who had not even looked up at the new arrivals who were laughing at their friend lost in new technology.

Wild Bill finally looked up, and the men broke out laughing even harder at the look on his face. He was smiling so wide it hurt just to look at it. "You will not believe what this stuff can do! The matrix programming on the helmet CPU is top-notch. The information processing and display is next generation! Do not get me started on the whole armor suite. It's an AI setup, a friggin' AI!" His eyes were so wide he truly looked wild.

Captain Ryan took over. "Whoa, Bill, we have got time, buddy. Glad you're excited. I take it meets your approval." Ryan put his palms out to stop the weapons sergeant from getting out of control. "Don't have to tell us more. Just enjoy and fill us in later."

They all laughed and went back to the racks to look over the equipment labeled for each of them.

A tone rang in the room like an elevator arriving and was repeated twice. Then Charlene spoke, "Captain Ryan, if you and Master Sergeant Lincoln would go into the armory administrative office, a video call is waiting for you."

The two men stopped inventorying their gear and stored it in the nearby lockers. When they looked around, they saw a corridor that led to a suite of rooms with glass-paneled walls. A light flashed above the door separating the suite from some other doors, yet for Ryan and Lincoln to identify. The door opened with a whine and a click.

The men smiled and said, "Thanks, Charlie."

And before they could ask which room, a light above one of them flashed and repeated the whine and click. The men found two comfortable chairs on either side of a desk on the wall. To the right of the desk was a flat screen. They both swiveled their chairs to face it, and Charlene darkened the glass to opaque.

The video came up, and a split screen appeared. Former Air Force Blue Book security policeman, now Space Force, Group Thirteen administrative investigator, Master Sergeant Shapiro, appeared in two of the splits on the screen Former Air Force Blue Book security policeman, now Space Force, Group Thirteen administrative investigator, Master Sergeant Shapiro, along with Technical Sergeant Andrews, appeared in what looked like an air base in the background which Lincoln assumed to be somewhere in the administrative section of this base. The next two people in the quad split were General Hansen in the Pentagon and the president in the Oval Office.

The two men went to stand, but the president waved them off.

"Gentlemen and lady, to save us all a bunch of time, if we are on here, then we need to move with haste. So please, by my order, disregard all the pomp and circumstance." He smiled and waved to Hansen to add in.

"Yes, sir, Mr. President. To be clear, when a report of 'alien' activity is confirmed, this type of alert will be consistent. I am aware that Sergeant Shapiro fielded a call and did his job to investigate in rapid response, and Sergeant Andrews is the administrative dispatcher, so to speak. So in this order, first, quick rundown and reference with information for all by Andrews. Then Shapiro give the facts and on-scene advisement. Then Mr. President, if you would give your thought or question. Then Ryan and Lincoln advise and comment along with myself. Then input from all." Hansen finished and waved to Andrews. "Tech Sergeant, please proceed."

"Thank you, sir. At approximately zero four hundred hours, we received a call from the Air Force base where Master Sergeant Lincoln first reported his incident. Master Sergeant Shapiro was dispatched immediately. He arrived there at zero four hundred thirty-five hours." She paused and hit a couple of keys on a computer apparently in front of her. "This is the area." Shown was a map picture of the Adirondack state park along with a highlighted Air Force base and red dot where Lincoln had his incident and a red dot where Lincoln's house was.

"Hey, that's my house, dot number 2," Robin said, perplexed how his house could be a marker.

"Yes, Sergeant Major, it is." Andrews hit another key, and the map went away, and the quad reasserted larger. "Master Sergeant Shapiro is at that air base, with his report."

"Thank you, Andrews. The air base received a call from the sheriff. Then with the new procedures, they went to the new receiving station call lines. I'm sorry, Master Sergeant, it appears there was an incident at your house." Shapiro squinted and made a face as if the next information were painful, which he figured it would be to Lincoln. "The house and your truck were completely totaled. Whatever happened, it looks like they were targets."

Lincoln shook his head like he could not believe it, which he could not. He opened his mouth to comment, but he could not even speak.

Shapiro continued, "The sheriff was worried. It seems one of his deputies must have been there when it happened. He had used the master sergeant's truck and was returning it. They have had no contact with him, and his car is still on the property. The sheriff is here. He took no chances that he would be blown off by the base. He left four deputies on site."

"Are you sure this was an alien event, Sergeant?" the president asked.

"Without a doubt. I went over there and took samples. But just looking at it, there is no doubt," Shapiro answered.

"General?" the president said.

Hansen tapped his lips with his index finger, thinking. Then leaning forward, he picked up a pen and wrote something. "Okay, Captain Ryan, you have an order to mobilize, gear up, move out. I have no idea what procedure to take, so use a hostage abduction protocol. Gentlemen, we are writing this as it goes, so we are the book. So be smart and careful."

"Yes, sir. We only have six right now, but that should do for now," Captain Ryan said.

"It is, Captain. And I'm sorry about the house and truck, Lincoln. Seems you hit a nerve," Hansen said.

The president waved and said, "Good hunting, men." And his image flashed off.

Hansen took his cue. "Yes, good hunting." And following suit, his image went.

Captain Ryan looked to Lincoln to make sure he had regained his senses. He had.

"Shapiro should head back to the scene with the sheriff and move them to a staging area about a mile or two away. Give us some room to work," Lincoln said, doing what he did best, planning the attack.

Captain Ryan nodded. He knew his master sergeant, and his planning was beyond sound. "Go to it, Shapiro. Keep in touch with Andrews. She will be the conductor. Do you need any of the others there?" he said, meaning the Blue Book personnel.

"No, sir, not as of yet. Depends on the length of time we run this," Shapiro responded.

"Andrews, you keep tabs on time and make the call. Put them on alert and ready," Ryan ordered.

"Yes, sir, will do," Andrews said as she hit some buttons and muted herself, giving direction on another channel.

"Okay, let's put ourselves in motion. Let's go hunting."

With that, all nodded. The screen went dark, and Ryan and Lincoln got up and headed out to the locker room section of the armory.

Ryan put his arm around Lincoln and patted his shoulder as they walked. "We will trail these asses to the moon for this, Robin. My word."

Lincoln nodded. He knew if it were possible and it did turn out they had to go to the moon, the captain would make it happen. He was his word.

They entered back in the locker room, and the men looked up from their gear, waiting for the word. As all were experienced operators, they knew the look their bosses carried on their faces. It was go time, time to put into action what they trained for every day, their sole purpose.

"Wild Bill, talk us through getting this gear on and functioning. We have about twenty minutes to be on a fast chopper to go north." Ryan picked up his helmet and looked it over.

Wild Bill smiled and licked his lips. This was what he lived for. "All right! First, let us get a move on work from bottom to top. By the numbers, learn and put on at the same time."

They all felt confidence with the equipment because if Wild Bill was this excited, it really must be something.

As the team was getting ready, the captain had Charlene notify Andrews what they needed for transport and alert the hangar to be ready in twenty more minutes.

The six-man team half of First Platoon, Alpha Company, of the inaugural action of the Thirteenth Special Forces Group stepped into the hangar in matte black armor from head to toe. They looked like characters from a sci-fi movie, but the technology was real and completely cool. A stealth Blackhawk, a modified army helicopter, was on the lift warmed up and ready to go. As soon as it cleared the top hangar, it would spin up its blades and move fast.

The pilots, army pilots, were geared in similar armor but less solid and more conditioned for flight. Apparently, the whole entourage got a makeover.

Captain Ryan shook hands with a major, the pilot of the copter. "Looking good, Major. Seems we all got upgrades. You know the mission?"

"Yep, we have been read in, crazy as it is. But the new gear helps sell it, doesn't it? Oh, and wait till you get a load of the bird's modifications," the major Earl "Deacon" Tucker said in a deep Southern baritone. He was a big man, lighter skinned than Wild Bill.

Ryan had flown with him several times; he was an incredible pilot. His copilot, it seems, he got to keep, Captain Dwight "Apache" Red Sky, who was a full-blood Apache. He had made good getting a military scholarship and becoming a hell of a pilot.

The bird's crew, Staff Sergeant Eugene Jenkins and Sergeant Wilford Burgess, were readying the door guns, tucked in for fast flight; but as soon as on target, they would be set to operate. Captain Ryan was impressed; Hansen had pulled all stops and gotten an elite crew to operate this bird.

As they stored gear and were climbing on board, Technical Sergeant Andrews's voice came across their comm sets. "Call signs. Captain Ryan, your team's will be Hunter. You are Hunter One. Chief, you're Two. Lincoln, you're Three. Junius, Four. Sergeant Herndon, Five. Sergeant Doolie, Six. Major, your unit is Watcher. You are One. Captain, you are Two. Jenkins, Three. Burgess, Four."

"Roger," the major said for his crew. "Watcher One to—hey, what is the base name?" Everyone stopped and waited.

Andrews's voice came back, sounding almost embarrassed. She forgot to have an ID for herself. "Base will be designated Lodge."

Everyone shrugged and kept going as they strapped in and the Blackhawk was closed. The lift brought them up into the old hangar up top as the bay doors slid open quicker than their appearance belied. A cart was attached and drew them out into the light. The rotors quickly rotated, and it lifted off.

It took a moment for the team and crew to find their balance as the modified Blackhawk tore north through the air. It was unlike any other helicopter acceleration they had felt.

"Oh yeah, forgot to say the acceleration would be a little straining at first." Deacon, the major's pilot call sign, said as he hit the red cabin lights inside the blacked-out copter.

"What have you got under the hood, Deke?" Lincoln asked, using the familiar name he always used with the veteran pilot.

"Strong medicine," Apache said in the worse stereotypical Indian accent he could muster.

Everyone laughed. It broke the nerves in the cabin.

"Haha, Apache, I take it you don't know," Wild Bill said.

All the men aboard had their helmets on, which all had keyed to interior communications mode, a new technology in the armor of both the team and the crew's new gear. It allowed the option with an audible command to run through the open channels programmed to the group. Example being, all were talking on interior communications which linked all in the craft through the AI. It also was smart to take and widen the group or allow others with permissions to come online. The AI was smart enough and informed enough on who and what could interject. Monitoring the conversations and keying up any facts or answering questions or problems if it could.

"I could give you a full rundown on the components manufacturer and the ways the propulsion work if you would like," a female voice said into the group net.

"Ah, who the hell was that?" crewman Jenkins asked.

"I am your mission AI, Delta Intelligence Disbursement Net. I am with you to provide any help, information, and clarification as well as monitor health and wellness. I facilitate your communications and targeting and threat assessment." The voice was a little higher pitched than Charlene back at base, almost as if it were younger, more inexperienced.

"No, Didi, not necessary, but thank you." Lincoln was getting the hang of interfacing with AIs. He also liked giving out nicknames. It was part of his character.

"Thank you, Master Sergeant Lincoln, and I like the name Didi." The voice seemed quite content with his choice.

"There you go, guys. Didi is our overwatch, so treat her nice. And yes, I know I said she. My head-up display says we are thirty minutes out, so check and recheck your weapons and gear. We go in. We hit the ground fast and hit about twenty out in a perimeter on the knee, weapons up and running." Lincoln paused as he told Didi to see if Shapiro had ears on and could communicate. "Shapiro, you on," he said.

"One moment," he said quiet and quickly. "Okay. Had to walk back into the equipment van I borrowed off the base. Otherwise, it looks like I'm talking to myself." His voice went from low outside in front of the sheriff and his deputies to echoing in the small space of the van.

"Good. Don't let them know we are skipping going to your location and hitting the scene fast," Lincoln told Shapiro.

"Right. If they get antsy, what would you like me to do?" Shapiro asked.

"Well, if it comes to it, let them know I told you to hold them back, that we have it, that it could be a radiation threat to them, and my team is going in with protective suits."

Shapiro laughed. "You mean give them the old Blue Book run-around. I didn't think I would be doing the same job. Oh, but this is way more official."

"Yeah, and with actual alien threat, my friend is probably abducted at the least. We do not want the rest hurt," Lincoln said, knowing Mackey was probably dead, if not horribly injured.

Shapiro had not thought about the deputy being dead. It brought a different reality to it. "Yeah, the stakes have gone up, haven't they?"

"Yes, they have, but that's okay. We are going to take it to them." Lincoln had a bite to his words; it would have given chills to any invading alien had they heard the emotion in it.

The team in the cabin gave a thumbs-up. They were all ready to get into the fight.

"Watcher One to Lodge, we are approaching target. The Hunters are go," the major said over the comm link.

"Lodge to Watcher and Hunters, you are still clear. On your mark, go," Andrews's voice said, letting them know that no status changed and the mission was still on.

"Hunter One to Lodge and Watcher One, we are green and set," Captain Ryan affirmed his team readiness.

"Watcher One to Watcher Four and Three, open up and provide cover. Hunters, watch the light on green to go," Deacon announced.

The crew popped open the side doors and rotated the door guns out to provide fire if needed. The Blackhawk started to slow and descend to the target zone.

Wild Bill took off his restraint and knelt by the gunner at the open door on the pilot's side. "Didi, scan for threats on the target area." Bill smiled. It was comfortable calling the AI Didi. It gave it a more human feel and made it easier to feel it was part of the team.

"I am not reading any known threat at this time. I am picking up some strange interference. I am trying to clean up the background to pinpoint its location," Didi transmitted to the team.

"Double D, what are you seeing as far as radiation or any contaminant at the location?" Ryan asked.

"Looks higher than normal, but I don't see any threat. Especially with this armor, we are pretty safe," Doolie replied.

Going over the background, air sampling and magnetic and full spectrum reading displayed in the head-up of the helmet.

"Holy shit! My house! My truck!" Lincoln got to see his house and truck completely ruined in multiple visual layers as infrared to full spectrum lenses of the helmet optics.

The light turned green. As the copter hit the ground, the team spread out in a 360-degree perimeter; Master Sergeant Lincoln had assigned sectors of the circle in the head-up display to each team member. The group scanned the assigned areas. All team members called in secure, reading no contacts with hostiles.

"Is somebody sobbing?" Chief Tanaka said over the comm. Chuckles were heard after the comment.

"Hey, Chief, FU!" was all that came back from Lincoln.

"Double D, Angel, take the perimeter. Keep on the move. Rove around while we check the scene," Captain Ryan assigned as Lincoln, Wild Bill, the chief, and he took in the damage and tried to figure where to go from here. "Watcher One, Deke, head out to where

Shapiro is and keep her hot if we need you," the captain said to the Blackhawk.

"Roger, Hunter One. Bird up." The Blackhawk lifted off and headed east to the staging area.

"Hunter One to Lodge, we are on the ground, on target, assessing now. Will advise. What's the view look like?"

"Lodge to Hunter One, we have an anomaly west of you, but it's stationary now. We have no real data on it. What we have, we're sending to Delta," Andrews said over the comm link.

Ryan was amazed at how clear all the transmissions were. The new setup was outstanding.

"Lodge, this is Delta. We have changed my call sign. It's Didi now," the AI reported over the comm.

"Um, okay, I copy, Didi. Confirm, Hunter One?" Obviously, Andrews was surprised at the AI interjecting itself, but she figured it was a young entity. It did not know better. This was going to be more of a challenge than the latest version of Windows. That was for sure.

Ryan chuckled and responded, "Do not ask me. It was Hunter Three and Didi."

"Confirm, Lodge. Didi, I'm sorry they find this so difficult," Lincoln said as dry as he could with a bit of haughty condescension.

"Lodge confirms, um, we're sending data to Didi," Andrews said, somehow able to translate a headshake with only words.

"Thank you, Lodge," Didi sounded irritated and stern. "Thank you, Hunter Three," the AI said in the tempo of a much fonder tone.

"Didi, scan what they are seeing and give us a comparison on any trace of what we are seeing here," Tanaka said.

Lincoln looked over to him and nodded. It was a good move to see if the energy signatures were even similar.

"Doing so now, Hunter Two," the AI replied. "I've got DNA trace over on this fallen tree, human, by the scan. Looks like several places. Not a good sign for our lost deputy."

Wild Bill was kneeling over by the tree where Mackey had been. Tanaka and Lincoln went over to see the area.

Ryan was across from them and started their way. He stopped halfway as his head-up display flashed on a substance it caught as it scanned his path. "Got something here," he said as he knelt just on the outer rim of the trace fluids.

Tanaka turned and went to the other side of the fluid and knelt to let the head-up display give its readout of the scanning.

"The energy source east of here is a stronger version of the residual we captured on scene here," Didi proclaimed. "The fluid we are looking over here seems to be an organic, but its structure is unknown at this time."

"Give us a guess, Didi," Ryan said, something not possible with a normal computer system, but an AI, in theory, would be able to do what a human brain did but at a lot higher level.

"I hypothesize that this fluid is consistent with blood in a human, so it seems an alien was disabled here." Didi came back and said, "Also, an analysis of the DNA would reflect a human in this configuration." A 3D display came up in the head-up of Hunters One, Two, Three, and Four.

"Shit, that is almost a dead ringer for Mackey. Sorry, didn't mean 'dead,'" Lincoln said, sadness showing in his voice.

"Hey, a chance he's still alive, just injured," Wild Bill said over the comm.

"Yes, Hunter Three, a 20 percent chance." Although Didi did not mean it, that was less reassuring than it had wanted to comfort Lincoln.

"Thanks, Didi, Four, but let's be real," Lincoln said. His voice steeled a bit more.

"Didi, give me a check on our friend to the east," Ryan said, changing the mood.

"Our friend?" Didi asked, sounding perplexed.

"Didi, slang for our target to the east in this context. Note it and remember, okay?" Lincoln said as if he were talking to a kid, which in actuality he was, just a super genius kid.

"Okay, got it, Hunter Three." There was a pause. "Our friend has not moved or changed its status."

Lincoln had to smile at that. Didi had said it like it was conspiratorial. It made him laugh.

The probe sensed the humans using scanning devices, so it powered down and went to an alternate power source it recognized the human equipment could not detect. It wanted to communicate with the ship, but it could not. The humans would most certainly pick up on that, and its first mission was to kill these humans, especially now that it had picked up the signature of the violator. The one who had attacked the crew. Now it had a problem. The leader wanted to know when the violator appeared, but it also was told to kill. It was a mixed priority, so it just kept running the scenarios to try to find a solution.

Hunter Five Angel Herndon was stalking the perimeter when quietly a light flashed on his head-up. It was red. So he whispered, "What is it?"

Didi came back, sensing that quiet was a must. She flashed the message instead of talking. It read, "Anomalous shape, 8 yards to left." After it flashed the message, it highlighted the spot outlining the shape it could not identify.

Hunter Five stood still, crouched, and stared at the display, trying to ID the object. He whispered, "Heat." The screen lit up with heat imaging. It had heat but not a lot, so it was not inactive completely. He studied, then whispered, "Frequency." The screen lit up with the ambient radio frequencies of nature, but the object had a blue halo, not really projecting anything. Curious, he thought, whispering, "Match signature with residual energy signs and the anomalous signature." The screen brought night vision on and brought the object into better focus. The screen flashed up to the left the word "Threat, positive match, alien object."

"Share" was his next whisper. Didi accurately understood what he wanted. He saw dots labeled H1, H2, H3, H4, and H6 got little green dots next to them, he guessed signifying they had received the info.

The probe just finished running its processing and concluded it would attack and kill the humans now and incapacitate the violator for Leader so he could kill Leader also, such confusing orders. He would signal the ship as soon as he broke cover and attacked. The probe, having reached its decision, began to power up to full so it could act upon its conclusion.

Unfortunately, Wild Bill had been able to reach the probe before it became aware of its surroundings and targets.

The probe ran scan and saw the violator remarkably close along with other humans and the one just to its left in a threatening posture inside its safety zone. Probe went to react, but something was attached to it. A large surge pulsed through it. The probe's last and only thought was "No!" The cylindrical object—some sort of metal, obviously alien in make—lost its hovering ability and fell over.

Wild Bill unattached his electrical pulse device and attached a power monitor that would continue to monitor the device. If it came back online, it would pulse it again and alert the team to the fact. Wild Bill smiled behind his face shield of the helmet; this new equipment was awesome.

Hunters Five, Six, and Four grabbed the device and brought it out into the clearing, which was Lincoln's yard. They looked it over and surmised that it was some sort of probe or sentry, but for whatever reason, it had not signaled the aliens, nor did it seem to react quick enough to attack them. It was agreed that it would make a great research piece. If they were to be able to thwart the aliens, they would need to understand as much of their technology as they could.

"Lodge, we have an object in our possession. It's contained, and we will need a pickup on this," Captain Ryan informed Andrews. Although the comms had the highest security and coding, it was still prudent to keep information as limited as possible.

"Lodge to Hunter One, Didi has already sent us a rundown of your possession. I am making arrangements. Will pass it along when it's set."

"Okay, team, we are going to set out to come up on the target. Hunter Three has marked a route for us." Ryan paused as Didi circulated the course to the team.

"Angel, Wild Bill, take point. Double D, take our six. I don't think there is any more of these things between us, but Didi will look for them now. She knows them." Ryan paused and said, "Right, Didi?"

"Affirmative, Hunter One. I got our friends logged in now."

The team tried to stifle their laughter. It almost worked, but it was cute the way the AI tried to insert the slang.

"Hunter Three to Lodge, keep eyes on target to the east. It's our primary now, and we're on the move to engage," Lincoln advised as they set out to the east to engage the aliens or what they theorized were the aliens.

The team flowed to the edge of the clearing and entered the woods. As experienced operators who had operated in every type of environment, particularly these six who had been a team before, they flowed back into rhythm with one another.

Didi kept the course and each individual positioning on the head-up display, making walking through the Adirondack Park, well, like a walk in the park.

*****

Leader was enjoying the screams and terror of the human as he took him apart even more. He stopped and looked down on the face of the human, its sad eyes pleading for mercy. Leader tilted his neck back and released joyous chirping, the alien version of laughter.

Mackey stared up into the alien's eyes, and he hoped to see mercy or even compassion, but what was worse, he saw the understanding the alien had of what Mackey prayed for. The alien then reared back, and Mackey knew in his soul that it was laughing. It found him funny, not even pitiful, just amusing. It was the ultimate insult he was nothing more than an enjoyable distraction. He had no mercy.

The only thought now that gave Mackey any comfort was that he could feel the end of his life approaching and pretty fast. No matter what they did to keep him alive, he knew it wouldn't help. He was fading, and he embraced it.

Leader looked down again and started to carve the human up some more. He sighed. The human seemed to be waning. His fun would be over soon. He had better find some more.

In the middle of carving the human to what they called the navel from the side, a high-pitched beep came over the ship's comm.

Navigator's voice came over after five successive beeps. "Leader, Commander One Stripe is requesting you on communication." Navigator paused and hesitantly said, "Now!"

Leader screeched his displeasure and slashed the human, leaving the laser knife in him as he stalked to the command room.

Climbing into his chair as Navigator went back to his position, he waved to Communicator to put on the commander.

Commander appeared on screen. His features creased in a most annoyed and angry fashion. "Leader Three, how many humans have you now since we last spoke?"

Leader was taken back. Commander wasted no time. He insulted him in front of his crew without a pause. This was outrageous, and yet he had to tell him something—he had no viable humans. If he lied to Commander and was found out, he would lose his ship, if not his life. Yet if he told the truth, the result would most likely be the same. It did not matter what he did; the result was going to be the same. He had misplayed this terribly. Well, he could just go out on his own. The crew was as dead as he was at this point. They would not be spared. They too had waited too long to act. They would follow him to go on their own, to be in the outer realm away from the commander and others making their own way. Yes, that would be what they would do.

Leader stared at One Stripe up on the screen as One Stripe stared back, waiting.

One Stripe said, "Well? Answer now!"

Leader sneered and said, "Bah!" and motioned for Communicator to cut the connection, which he did.

Leader looked around the command room and saw his crew, paler than ever, knowing their fate was sealed. "Screw them!" he said.

And slowly and quietly, a few agreed, saying, "Yeah."

"Prepare to get underway. We need to head for the outer, after we just grab a group of humans for our own profit," Leader said.

And this time, they were more behind him, and a little more solid.

CHAPTER 11

PURSUIT

Commander One Stripe sat there, stunned. He was staring at the black screen, unaccepting that Leader Three cut him off. He turned to his communicator and calmly and evenly asked if there was a communication problem, if somehow the signal was cut off.

Communicator ran through everything, then reassured it was Leader Three who just had cut the communication. One Stripe nodded understanding to Communicator and reached down and pulled his pistol and shot Communicator in the head. He knew it was not his fault, but he had to shoot someone. It just happened to be him, nothing personal. He reholstered his gun and pointed at one of his staff to take Communicator's place. Trembling, another took over.

Commander One Stripe ordered New Communicator to contact Leader Two. Fumbling with the controls, Communicator was making small noises of fear. One Stripe started growling, and his hand slid toward his pistol again. As his hand reached the holster, Leader Two came on screen.

"Commander, we have captured fifteen humans and are in pursuit of at least ten more in your honor," Leader Two started before Commander could even speak.

This made Commander happy. Leader Two knew how to follow orders and obey. He also made great profit for the command.

"Excellent, Leader Two. You are truly a leader. I have an important mission for you though. Leader Three has gone rogue!" He let that sit there for a moment to see Leader Two's reaction.

"That is unforgivable. I would be honored to bring him and his traitorous crew to your feet for punishment and death!" Leader Two said with anger showing in his features.

One Stripe could hear Leader Two's crew backing their leader in the background. Commander swelled with pride at Ship Two. "Yes, find them, and I do not care if you bring me just their heads to place at my feet! They must pay, all of them! I want my ship back, but I want their heads most! You have your orders. Honor to you and your crew with success!"

Commander One Stripe waved for Communicator to cut the signal, and he did. One Stripe nodded. Good, he would not have to kill another, at least for now.

Leader Two was extremely pleased. He absolutely hated Leader Three. They had words before and were stopped before they could duel for honor. Now he had permission to kill Leader Three. Even better, he was required to behead him. Oh, nothing could be better.

Leader Two gave the order for Navigator to head out to look for Ship Three. The excitement inside he felt was incredible. He pumped his arm high with his fist tight and chirped the war charge. The crew chirped back with furious glee. The hunt was on.

*****

Leader Three ordered Navigator to plot a course first around the moon of this planet, in the opposite direction away from the Aldion outpost there. It would mean passing the Greelocks' outpost but knowing they would hesitate before attacking gave them the advantage to slip by as long as they moved quick past.

Navigator could see no other course available, so he looped the path a little wider as he plotted it out. It would not hurt to have a little more space between them and any Greelock patrol.

Security looked down and saw a flashing alert on his console. He checked it, and somehow, something had made it through the first perimeter and now was approaching through the second. There must be a fault somewhere. He ran checks on what it was and made a panicked chirp when he read it was humans. It was impossible; they could not have made it so close without warning. Security immediately sent the recall order to the probe. Getting a not-online, no-answer reply, a second panic chirp came out. This was utterly impossible; it could not be.

Leader and Navigator stopped midplanning as Security chirped in panic the first time. They turned to look at him and saw him furiously hitting commands. They were confused by this activity. As they stared at Security and he chirped the panic chirp again and saw him start fumbling at the controls with more urgency, they stopped what they were doing and went over to Security. The whole time, Leader and Navigator feared that Ship One or Two had made it to them already. They were not set for a fight.

Arriving at the console, they peered at the information. Leader was taken aback. Humans! How were there humans right outside of his ship? It was impossible!

Navigator saw the human signals, six to be exact, but the signal was different from normal human signs. There seemed to be a flux on and off on the system actually reading and seeing them. That would be impossible, wouldn't it?

Leader looked over the six human signals, one of which was outlined in pulsing color. A grin crept on his face. The violator was here! Yes, finally, things were falling his way—he would be his own commander and have his own revenge on the human. He laughed out loud, almost insanely for his species.

Navigator felt a chill run through him, and Leader's reaction was ominous. He turned to Security and ordered him to follow him to the armory while he ordered Communicator to get the ship ready to go. Pointing to another lesser crew member, he ordered him to get on the weapons command system and start killing humans.

Leader roared and told his two officers, Security and Navigator, to make sure that the violator was left to him. He needed him to be captured so he could be cut apart piece by piece. His officers nodded affirmative but could only look upon Leader as if he had fallen off the edge of sanity.

As they reached the armory, four more crew showed up, arming themselves and readying to deploy against the humans.

Leader was anxious to capture the human, but he was still aware he didn't want to lose any more parts or risk death. He ordered two of the lesser crew to get in front and secure the way for the officers. He appointed the other two lesser crew to guard him and protect him as he hunted the violator.

*****

Lincoln and Ryan took up position toward the left side of the ship, or so they assigned it that position. The ship was round and smooth, nothing notable on the front or back or side; it was just all the same. Using their right and left of the team, Lincoln had used the head-up display to mark sides.

"Hunter One and Three in position," Lincoln announced over the comms.

Didi had said she had sensed waring perimeter fields and had been able to defeat the first they encountered. Now she reported another, and she was working to dismantle this one also. They had to assume it was working. They had not come under fire or attack as of yet.

The center position was where Tanaka and Herndon were set. "Hunter Two and Five in position."

Instead of being equally distant as the other four, Doolie and Wild Bill moved in close to the ship and made it to what would be the rear if the ship had any conventional shape. "Hunter Four and Six in position."

"Should we have Watcher come in now, do you think?" Ryan asked Lincoln on a separate comm line.

Lincoln thought about it and decided he needed to ask Watcher One how long their response time would be. He told Ryan, who agreed they needed that info before deciding. "Hunter Three to Watcher One, what would be your ETA on our position?" Lincoln formed it not as a request for the response now, just the estimated time of arrival.

"Watcher One to Hunter Three, estimate of twelve minutes from current status to your position. Want us to spin up and move closer?"

That was exactly what should be done. Working with an experienced pilot, with a lot of hours on operations, to draw out beneficial options was beyond helpful. It could mean success or failure or, better put, life or death.

"Hunter One to Watcher One, you're the man," Ryan said.

As he finished his comm answer, Didi spoke up, "I have power fluctuations from the ship. I believe they are going to open a hatch." As the AI finished, she highlighted the part of the ship that was most likely the opening, giving the team the advantage or at least the loss of surprise by the aliens. "Reading possible engine turning on and getting ready in preflight status to be able to fly," Didi said, next sending the information to Hunters Four and Six.

A hatch dropped down, creating a ramp exactly where Didi had highlighted. The team saw the armed aliens start to exit and took aim.

Lincoln drew a bead on one surrounded by two others, noticing it waving a weapon in its one and only arm. "My one-armed bandit is here. Apparently, he is still a little miffed with me," Lincoln said as he readied to fire.

"'Miffed,' that's not 'miffed.' That is downright pissed off. Look at him flailing. I can hear him yelling for you from here," Tanaka said as he drew down a shot on one of the two out front.

"Nah, he ain't pissed, Three. He is downright enraged, like that girl in Singapore, remember?" Angel came back with. Setting his sights on the other alien out in front.

One major help these head-up displays in the helmet gave was as each man sighted down on a target, it was marked and shown to all the team, so they all claimed different targets.

"Well, it's about as pretty as that one was too," Ryan added into the theme.

"*Et tu, Brutus*," Lincoln said to Ryan, who just laughed.

As the captain was about to give the order to fire on the aliens, the team was engaged by weapons fire from the ship's weapon system operated by a lesser crew. The fact that an inexperienced crew member was left to operate the system saved all their lives. Every shot was off and fell close, knocking the team down. The shot assistance control had not been initiated. So firing with no skill, the crew member missed every shot.

"Son of a—Hunter Four, a little assistance," Ryan said as he got himself up and moving, wiping dirt off his faceplate.

"Trying, Hunter One," Wild Bill responded as he conferred with Didi on a plan he had. "Cross your fingers. Here goes nothing." Just as he finished saying that, the weapons started firing again.

Angel, Hunter Five, was moving behind a tree and boulder for cover as a shot went high, missing him. The luck of the fool was with the gunner. He struck a chunk of tree with a huge trunk that blew off and struck Hunter Five as he made for cover. Five went down and was pinned under the section of tree.

Ryan saw an H5 in his readout flashing red. "Hunter Five, give me your status. Hunter Five, respond!" Ryan said, not knowing how Five was. "Hunter Two, do you have eyes on Five?"

Tanaka went to respond, "Negative, we split. And I lost sight after that shot. Moving to cover him from contacts."

Just then, a shot pierced Tanaka's weapon, destroying the first model hypercarbine, causing a minor explosion, sending Tanaka flying backward.

"Four, any time now. Hunter Two, status." Ryan did not get a response but knew there was trouble. H2 was flashing as well as H5.

Lincoln took cover behind a slight hill with rock as half its density. He set to fire on the leader and pulled the trigger, releasing the hyper round. He was dead on target or would have been if the weapons fire from the ship hadn't blasted the berm he was behind. As he shot the carbine, he was thrown flipping sideways, the shot going off target. The hyper round finding the head of one of the lesser crewmen guarding leader. If Lincoln could have seen the result, he would have been impressed. The head disappeared in a fine mist; the body just stood there then, as a tree chopped, fell straight back.

Ryan saw Lincoln go flying and made tracks to check him. Navigator intercepted him by accident. They collided, and both fell to the ground, each losing their long weapons. Navigator shook off the impact and got to his knees and drew his sidearm. Ryan spun to one knee and drew his sidearm and fired. Both had fired at the same time, both striking each other's pistol, putting each weapon out of commission. Both alien and human got to their feet and drew blades. Ryan had a Smith and Wesson 4.5-inch flat dark earth boot knife; and the alien, Navigator, drew a rippling blade with plasma current running through it. They circled each other.

Ryan thought to himself, *It looks like blade fighting is the same all over the universe.*

Navigator looked at the primitive weapon the human was displaying. *This would be over in no time.* In overconfidence, Navigator lunged at Ryan.

The two grappled as Ryan deflected the strike of the plasma blade. Ryan felt a blast of heat and pain from his forearm. He risked a quick look and saw smoke coming from his skin where the alien had scored a slash. Ryan had a grip on the wrist of the alien's knife hand while the alien had missed the grip and took the knife through the middle of its hand.

Navigator smelled the burning flesh of the human and knew he had scored a hit, but he was feeling intense pain from his other hand. Looking down, he saw the blade had gone through the middle of his hand. He had no choice; he closed his hand down the blade, gripping the human's hand onto the hilt in a death grip, making it near impossible for the human to strike him anymore with the primitive blade.

Ryan felt the alien blood dripping slimy cold grip of the alien as he slid his hand down over his and gripped it tight, trapping his hand on the hilt, making any strike more than difficult. The two wrestled for control, really of the only blade in play, the alien plasma blade. For a small framed being with slight limbs, the power in them was surprising.

"Got it."

A large flash went off somewhere behind the ship, and a stuttering weapons fire stopped. Wild Bill and Didi managed to knock it out.

Ryan breathed a sigh of relief over the weapons fire, but he still had a knife to deal with. The slight distraction was enough for the alien to gain an advantage. He twisted one way, then immediately—upon Ryan countering it—reversed using his strength and Ryan's help to swing it toward Ryan's leg. The blade sliced through the armor with only a bit of hesitation. It just made it through Ryan's pants underneath the armor. He grimaced as he felt the heat and seer on his skin. With a surge of adrenaline, he managed to pull it out and twist it in, using the same trick, only letting the alien's momentum carry it in between them instead of at his leg. The blade was now pointed to the alien's midsection.

Navigator realized this and panicked. Struggling to get it pointed away, he looked up at the human. The human blinked just one eye and seemed to smile; it did not agree with Navigator. Ryan had him now. The alien must have felt it. He looked into Ryan's face as he struggled to turn the knife away. Ryan winked at him and smiled; it was all but over. Using his height advantage, Captain Ryan had gotten his foot and ankle behind the aliens, dipping his shoulder. And putting the alien off-balance, he thrusted his weight with his back foot. The two went to the ground. Navigator looked up at the human on top of his body. His eyes closed and opened. He was disgusted being bested by a human, a lowly slave beast, and heaved a "humph" of distaste. Then he was gone. Ryan stared at the big black almond eyes of the alien. It let out a humph, which was unmistakable as disgust at having lost to a human.

Lesser Crewman Twelve, by designation, had ran to the armory and grabbed a weapon with the leader and others. He was behind everyone as they exited out of the ship to repel the humans. He watched as Navigator attacked a human to his right and saw one of the lesser crew that had been told to protect Leader get his head blown apart, in front of him. He saw the humans fly through the air as the weapons hit their positions. It was a lot for a new member of the crew and coalition to have happened on his first flight out of the home world. When the flash and boom happened to the rear of his position, he jumped in fright. Embarrassed, he put on his practiced warrior face, growled, and ran to confront the evil humans attacking to the rear.

Twelve ran around the ship toward Hunter Four and Hunter Six's position, releasing his most horrible warrior scream. He would take the battle to the weak soft humans and send them running like little creatures.

After taking cover and blowing a major electro pulse device at the location Didi had highlighted on the ship, the alien weapons fell silent.

Junius and Doolie stood up from cover and heard a high-pitched noise, quite irritating and piercing. It seemed to be coming toward them. They looked at each other and shrugged. They had no idea what the hell it was.

Twelve came around the ship and spotted two large black-clad humans. They had no faces. He shook his head and stopped and looked again, mouth open, staring. They really had no faces.

Hunters Four and Six stared at the little bluish green alien holding an alien rifle in his twig arms. The thing was staring at them in awe, or at least it appeared that way.

Twelve shook his head and came out of his moment of shock. He realized he had started to tremble as fear roiled up inside. He started screaming again, but not the warrior scream but a primitive fear scream. He raised his rifle and began shooting at the humans. Unlike the training and the techniques they taught him, he had his eyes closed as he fired. And as he soon realized, he was running away, back toward the ramp and shooting wildly behind him.

As they watched, the little alien came out of his trance and went nuts, the screaming started. He fired that weapon as he ran back the way he came. An errant pulse hit Doolie in the thigh armor, and he went down. Wild Bill had another bolt hit just under his boot, flipping him as if he were doing a backward somersault.

Angel had been pinned under the tree section as it lay across his legs and back. The armor supported him, and he was uninjured, but unconscious. The force knocked him out. A blast of smelling salts or the equivalent effect of the nano medical set in the armor was initiated by the suit's medical AI. Angel awoke to see from his position a smaller alien run around the ship toward the rear, letting out an annoying scream.

Unfortunate for Twelve, Hunter Five was in a perfect prone shooting position with his rifle in his grip and his arms free to move as well as his head. He just could not get up. Angel took a bead on the alien and lost the shot as he ran around the rear of the ship. Angel cursed and wished he had not waited to take the shot. Just as he was about to scan for another target and contact the others, the small alien had reversed course, now with a panicked scream and firing wildly behind him as he fled toward the ramp back up into the ship.

Angel already set focused on the target and led it a bit and fired. He had not fired these hypercarbines before or a hyper round, but he was pleasantly surprised and happy with it.

As Twelve ran toward the ramp looking back for the faceless humans to catch him, he noticed a flash off to his left. He had a moment to wonder if the humans had magic and were surrounding him. The thought stopped as his torso and head hit the ship he had been running along. Looking down, he saw quite a bit of torso missing and his legs and lower body travel a foot or two, then tumble to the ground, lastly thinking, *No!*

Leader caught sight of the violator as he fired and saw him go tumbling away as his second guard lost his head. He ordered the first guard and Lesser Crewman Nine—he thought he was—to follow him to the violator, now even more an enemy, having killed another crewman.

Security saw one of the humans try to take cover, but a beam from the ship hit its weapon, which exploded, sending the human flying through the air. Security started off in the direction the human had been catapulted to. He knew the human did not have a long weapon like he still had, and possibly, it had lost its hands, or at least some digits. Security started stalking the human. Wounded prey could be dangerous, but it also could be too wounded to fight. Either way, it—being a human—was no match for a trained warrior such as he.

Tanaka was knocked cold by the blast. He had landed on his butt and slid up against a tree, coming to rest as if he sat down to take a nap. The armor's medical AI did a full diagnostic and concluded he was bruised and out cold—possible concussion. Medic AI hit the smelling salts additive, and it had no effect. Tanaka remained out, so it ran another diagnostic to see if it missed anything.

Security slowly proceeded upon the trajectory of the human, but as of yet, he had not seen any markings where it had landed. Carefully, he proceeded. He would come upon it sooner or later. He knew that.

Medic AI finished the second diagnostic and came to the same diagnosis, possible concussion but no other life-threatening injuries. Protocol now dictated that it attempted the smelling salt additive and, if there was no immediate regain of consciousness, to spritz the patient with water and concentrate the additive to a stronger smell. Medic AI followed protocol and completed each step. Upon the last step, the patient responded and came to, a bit disoriented. Medic AI, following protocol on a disoriented patient, notified armor AI, the lesser piece of the mission AI Didi, completing its immediate task and going back to reserve and monitoring.

"Chief Tanaka, you are in the middle of a mission, in contact with aliens who have fired upon your team. You have lost your rifle and possibly have a concussion. You were sent airborne for over two hundred yards and came to rest in your present location." A heads-up blinking light of his current position as in relation to the engagement ground was displayed. A second blinking red dot as opposed to his green and a tan of the battle appeared around a hundred yards from him. Other green and red dots appeared also.

"No shit, Didi, two hundred yards, huh?" Tanaka shook his helmeted head and pushed himself up a bit. Man, was he sore.

"No, no shit, Chief, it really was," Didi said it so matter-of-fact Tanaka laughed. The fact that she had the voice of a twentysomething, amazed at the world's speech pattern, made it even more surreal.

Security caught a glimpse of the human lump at the base of one of the planet's fauna species. He raised his weapon and sighted in on the figure. In a few more steps, he would be in perfect striking range.

Tanaka put his hands down to push himself up and stand. As he did so, he saw the world spin very sharply and fell back against the tree. Security had drawn into the human the required steps when the human attempted to get up but failed and fell back against the tree, possibly still reeling from its injuries. He approached it, getting closer, it being no threat without a visible weapon and unable to get up.

Tanaka was monitoring his head-up display as he made a second attempt to get up, this time using the tree to steady his body by sliding up the trunk to get to a standing position.

Security watched as the human attempted to get upon its feet by using the fauna to brace itself to raise up.

Tanaka was halfway to standing when, all of a sudden, he pitched to his left straight to the ground. The alien was about twenty-five yards away at this point.

Security steadied his weapon as he approached and was getting to the prime distance of his weapon. He could not miss from here. The human had made it halfway to standing, its pathetic attempt to flee. He was trying to decide whether he should play with it by shooting it up before killing it or just do a straight kill shot. He decided on a straight kill shot. He fired dead center, but the human had fallen to the ground. As he did so, he could not have hit him. He looked back up at the fauna, seeing his shot had created a gaping hole in the trunk. Perplexed, he looked down to his chest where he had felt a liquid running down. He realized he did not feel any pain, and that was because the hole in his chest meant he was dying, and his system was shut down. Then all went black.

Tanaka lay on his side pistol in his hand, pointed at the alien still, ready to fire another hyper round. The hole the first made in the alien chest gave proof that one hyper round was all that was required. He looked at the pistol with a new admiration. This was the way to field test a new weapon. Check, hyperpistols kill aliens.

Leader pushed his remaining guard forward. After the tumbling body of the violator, he looked back to see the lesser crew cowering behind him. He waved him forward with his guard. The two aliens with Leader following behind fearfully trudged forward, scanning for the human. Now they had seen him kill four of the crew and take Leader's arm. They saw signs of the human having landed in the dirt and what looked like he had rolled down a small ridge beyond. Slowly, they made their way to the edge to find the vicious human.

Hunters Four and Six regained their senses after the weird action of the strange little alien. Doolie had grabbed at his thigh as soon as he recovered from the push backward he got from the hit. He ran his hand over the spot and asked the AI to run a check. All of it came with a negative on any injury. The armor had a mar where the shot hit, but it was mostly cosmetic in nature.

Doolie jumped up with relief and ran over to Wild Bill who he had seen take a head-over-heels flip after a stray shot. He did not have any idea where Junius had been hit. Coming to the side of Hunter Four, he knelt and looked for the hit or some injury. He started laughing when he got to the prone man's foot and saw smoke coming from the toe area of the armor boot.

"Hey, Doc, you okay?" Wild Bill asked, having seen the doc go down with a shot to the thigh.

"I am fine, scratched my armor, but that's it. You?" Doolie asked.

"A-okay, Doc. It flipped me, but the armor dispersed the energy out to cancel any effect, except for the concussive force that flipped my ass." They both laughed at the sight they had seen.

"Um, if you two are done braiding each other's hair, girls, could you come get me out from under this splinter," Angel said over the comm, breaking in on their link.

"Right, be right there," Doolie said as he got up with Doc helping him. The two had Didi guide them to his location.

The aliens made it to a spot where it was obvious the human had landed and stopped. As they peered around, they became more agitated as they could not find any sign of the human anywhere. Leader crept to the side, putting his back a few feet from one of the taller fauna to protect his backside from the human sneaking up on him. He directed the two others to head at a forty-five-degree angle from his position to look for the violator.

Leader waved his pistol back and forth from crewman to crewman. If either was attacked, he would fire everything he could to bring down the human.

As he kept looking for the human, the fauna dropped one or two of its pieces to flutter across his face. It was odd. He felt the woosh of air behind him and heard a thump directly after.

Hunter Three was crouched on the limb of the tree. And as luck had it, the alien—the one-armed bandit, as he had named it— backed up right under his position. The other two aliens fanned out away. He shook his head at how this had played out. He had slung his rifle on his back to climb the tree, so he went with it, jumping directly behind the bandit, who was so conveniently pointing its pistol in the correct direction.

Leader felt the human breathing on his neck as it grabbed his hand and clamped the warm gooey skin of its hand over his. He screamed at being in such proximity of the human, such disgusting a life-form.

Lincoln placed his hand over the alien's on the gun and pointed the arm at the alien forty-five degrees to the left and fired twice. The alien exploded. Spinning the arm to aim at the second alien as it started turning, not quite registering the threat yet but hearing bandit scream or whatever the hell it was doing, he came on target and fired a two-shot burst again with the same satisfying alien explosion—pieces everywhere.

Leader bent to the human arm holding his and bit as hard as he could and squirmed out of the grasp of the creature, human. The gun had bent toward the human in the struggle and went off, missing the human's head by inches. The human let go and fell backward. Leader's mouth still hurt from the hard shell the human had somehow been covered in. Leader jumped forward to the human, aiming the gun at its head, which was faceless. The only thing he would regret in killing him this way was not looking into its eyes as it died.

Lincoln hit the ground, his arm pinned under him, and he could not reach his pistol with his opposite hand, and the rifle was still slung around his back. The alien was on top of him with the weapon aimed at the face mask of his helmet. Lincoln saw the rage in its eyes, and he wondered how many shots he could take in the helmet before he would be injured or dead.

A shot rang out, and Lincoln tried to feel if he was dead. All he could see was blurry. *Crap*, he thought, *I am blind*. Then a weight fell on top of him, pushing him to the ground. Lying there, he tried to take stock of what was going on, but he had no reference to try to puzzle this out.

The weight rolled off him, and a strange blurry creature was swinging across his faceplate. It appeared the blurriness was due to some kind of liquid, and it was an armored gloved hand wiping it so he could see.

"You're welcome, Hunter Three."

He could make out the similar faceplate looking down on him, and a hand extended, helping him up. "Thank you, Hunter One." Lincoln looked down on the headless body of his one-armed bandit, or headless bandit, and now shook his head. "Didi, any way to clear this crap off my visor so I can see easier?"

"One moment."

Lincoln could feel the faceplate heating, but it was just a mere fraction of what it might actually be in temperature. He saw the blood of the alien dry, then turn to smoke, and clear. "Outstanding, Didi," Lincoln said as he unslung his rifle and checked it and readied it to fire.

Tanaka made it to the clearing where the ship was, and off to his right, he saw Doolie and Junius cutting up a tree with some nifty laser cutters—thank you, new gear. He held his pistol ready as he came forward, heading to the ship, covering the ramp for any more hostiles. "Hunter Two to Hunter team, heading towards target vehicle now," he put out over the full comm system. Watcher and Lodge would be in on the information also.

"Watcher to Hunter Two, we are two mikes out. Copy."

"Roger, Watcher. Copy, two mikes." Tanaka walked steady to the craft, about twenty yards out, when the ramp started raising. "Shit. Hunter Two to all units, the target is closing up to make a run for it." Tanaka broke into an all-out run for the ramp, holstering his pistol for what he was about to do.

"Copy, Hunter, Watcher, stepping it up to intercept if we can." Hunter Two could hear the determination come from Apache. He

90

had taken the radio as Deke tried to goose whatever extra speed he could to intercept the craft.

Tanaka had ridden with that crew so many times he could picture the scene inside the flight deck.

Tanaka reached the ramp. It had a two-foot gap, and he leapt toward it, extending his arms.

"Hunter Two, no. Hunter Two, copy, disengage." Ryan and Lincoln were running full speed to stop him from trying to jump in that ship. If he made it clear, he would be lost.

The comm was quiet as the ship lifted and the ramp closed, leaving Tanaka spread prone on the ground.

"Hunter Two to Watcher," Tanaka broadcast, lying on his chest on the ground, sounding winded.

"Watcher to Hunter Two, we have visual of target and will be on it in current mode in thirty seconds," Apache transmitted.

"Negative, Watcher, stay back and just follow where it goes down," Tanaka said, his breath steadying and getting up off the ground.

"Come again, Hunter Two," Apache sounded as confused as they all felt.

The alien ship went to full engine to exit the atmosphere in seconds when a large explosion followed by another came down the corridor from the ramp section.

Watcher One had just started pulling back on his speed when the ramp blew out and left a jagged hole with black smoke pouring out of it. The ship wobbled, dropped, went up, then wobbled, and took a dive down, proceeding about a mile from the takeoff point.

Watcher One marked the spot, came about, and put down in the clearing to pick up the Hunters. They had a trophy to secure.

"Hunter One to Lodge, we have contacts down at primary location. Need extreme pickup. Watcher is transporting Hunters to the secondary of target vehicle resting point," Ryan said with a bit of gusto.

"Roger that, Hunter One. Will dispatch movers now. Advise on need at secondary." Andrews was excited and barely contained it on the comms. Real aliens, the team had met real aliens and was bringing back proof. This was why she had joined the Air Force, to discover new things to be a part of the future. And now she had been moved to the Space frigging Force, and on a special operations team at that. Oh, and did she mention "aliens"!

The alien ship had gone down at an angle, cutting a path through the trees. Following the path was easy for Watcher as they lifted and headed toward it, with Hunters on board.

*****

Communicator opened his eyes; he had lifted the ship up, and Engineer had come up to the command deck to take over. Something had exploded at the ramp, and fire had erupted through the corridors of the ship. Power had flashed on and off, and he tried to get it back up; but ultimately, it failed, and he had no control of the landing.

Engineer came stumbling over to Communicator, urging him to get up. They had to get out of the ship. Communicator looked around. It looked as if all the others were dead. He took Engineer's hand and got unsteadily to his feet. They steadied themselves and made for the ramp or the hole that was where the ramp had been.

*****

"Did you really think I was going to jump into the ship?" Tanaka asked of the captain.

"Well, at the moment, I kind of thought it. By the way, what did you finally throw in there?" Ryan asked.

"You see, I was checking out these sticky grenades." He patted a pouch on the modular lightweight load-carrying equipment built into the armor where munitions pouches were set. "You pull the strip, and it's like a glob of ultrasticky C-4. I didn't know if the magnetic ones would work on whatever metal the aliens use, but I figured sticky would. Sticky works on everything."

Everyone nodded in agreement because who had never got gum on their shoe, blew a bubble, had it on their lips, or, as a kid, got it in their hair? Sticky was a universal factor.

Watcher banked down to follow the path of downed trees and pulled up and dropped out twenty yards from the smoking, downed alien craft.

"Hunters, we are down, and you're clear to disembark. The target is at twelve o'clock. Not reading any movement," Deke called out over the comms.

The Hunters bailed out of each side of the Blackhawk, three to each side, crouching low and angling away from the copter and toward flanking the alien ship.

Hunters One, Two, and Three started heading for the opening in the ship.

Wild Bill did a scan of the area to the left of the open hole in the ship. He caught a trace residual trail from the hole to the wood line to the front of the landing spot of the ship. "We got little movers to the left and forward of the target. Hunter Five and Six, on me, keep loose formation," Wild Bill instructed as he took the other two in pursuit of the escaping aliens.

"Hunter Four, watch yourselves. Any trouble, call in Watcher to seed the area," Ryan said as he and Lincoln took either side of the opening. And Tanaka took a knee just in front to evaluate before he entered first.

"Roger, Hunter One. Oh, and red mode will probably be perfect for entry, on your visual spectrum." Wild Bill had learned a lot about the armor in the time he had with it. So if he advised something, they would listen.

Problem was Tanaka, Ryan, and Lincoln were not sure how to engage some of these things.

"Roger, Hunter Four," Ryan said it but did not sound confident he knew what he was talking about.

One advantage to the new armor and AIs built into it is you could give commands in your helmet, and it does not go out over the whole comm system, so you could even dictate a text-type message from one to the other. Even better, the mic pickup in the helmet was AI run. So as in a bone mic or throat piece, you did not have to actually vocalize above just under a whisper.

A message flashed on Ryan's display from Wild Bill, "Just say 'initiate red mode.' Lighting from armor and visual display will come online, good for interior passages with or without lighting."

Ah, that was easy to do, Ryan thought. "Open comm to Hunter Two and Three," Ryan voiced, opening up comms between the three entry members. "Okay, Bill says just give the command 'initiate red mode' and we will be set on visual for entry and moving around in there."

The three men all gave the command. They could see red mini-LEDs come on over the armor. The head-up display took on an all-over red tint, and everything became hyperclear, and the suit AI was labeling things as it was viewed.

"Damn, could have used these back in the caves over in the sandbox. Might use it to go piss in the middle of the night," Lincoln said as he took in the visual info.

The three men had their weapons trained on the opening, watching for movement, but with red mode, they could actually see ten feet in and saw no threat.

Wild Bill took center of the path they were tracking. Doc was back a couple of yards, and a yard to his left, Angel was back a couple of yards and back a yard to his right. They each had their rifles out and scanning to the front for any contact.

Hunter Four, Wild Bill, had been picking up traces of a bluish fluid. The AI said it was most likely alien blood, about an 86 percent probability, which meant one or more of the aliens they were tracking were injured.

Hunter Two went into the ship first, went to the far wall, and went to one knee, taking position of cover for the other two to enter. Tanaka had pulled a hyper-round close-quarter combat gun from his gear bag aboard the Blackhawk when they had got aboard for the pursuit. It was more suited than his rifle, which was destroyed, would have been anyway.

Hunter One came in behind Tanaka and took up position standing across and forward of his position, scanning with his rifle. He had not had a replacement for his destroyed pistol. Hunter Three came in just after, crouched and carrying a new shotgun he grabbed out of his gear bag. It was a new type that fired a gel ignite round. It bore into its target with microrotating blades and the gel ignite. His rifle he kept slung on his back.

As front man now, Hunter Three said, "Clear," allowing the next man to leapfrog ahead.

"Moving," Hunter Two said over the comm. He crouch walked past the others and moved about five yards down the passageway. "Clear," he said as he took a kneeling position again up front.

Hunter One said, "Moving," as he took his next position. "Door," he gave the command as, taking up his overwatch position, he noticed the first hatch door they came across.

"I'll take it," Hunter Three said as he crept forward toward it past his teammates.

Reaching the hatch, he looked for a way to open it. It was slightly open from the crash. He went ahead and tried to push it open. At first, it was stuck, but he heard a pop, and it slid freely. He looked it over and guessed it was some sort of crash protocol so survivors could escape.

Once the hatch was open, he stuck the barrel of the shotgun, moving the barrel from left to right, then back again. After getting no reaction from the inside, he moved fast to one side of the hatch, kneeling, bringing the shotgun up, and scanning the room—no movement. "Clear," he said as Hunter One came in next.

Hunter Two came in and took up a position guarding the door, watching the passageway.

They walked about the room. It obviously looked like a medical facility. Another hatch was in the far wall. They moved to it.

Ryan nodded as he covered Lincoln so he could open the hatch. Tanaka stayed watch on the other hatch.

Lincoln forced the hatch till it popped again. Then it slid free. This time, he went in fast and got low on one knee, gun up and scanning. He froze his gun on an alien and was squeezing the trigger when he realized it was dead. Easing off the trigger, he stood and went over to it. It appeared that during the crash, it had been thrown onto some sort of lab equipment; what it was used for was unclear, but that some sort of pole thing that was through the alien's midsection was clear.

Lincoln looked over and saw some sort of operating table. It used some sort of stasis field, which was blinking on and off. As he approached, he recognized what was in it, a human. Unfortunately, he knew the human.

Mackey saw the armored figure with the faceless helmet come peer over him. He could only hope it was some merciful creature, if not a human.

Ryan came into the room; he saw what Lincoln was doing and gave him a moment by checking the rest of the room out.

Lincoln saw a moment of realization and fear in Mackey's face. He deserved to have his fear abated and know someone came to get him, even if it was too late. It would be what Lincoln would want for himself. Lincoln gave the command and removed his helmet, placing down next to the alien operating table—no, torture table.

Mackey recognized Robin, his friend. He tried to smile, unsure if he was. Nothing was straight anymore.

Lincoln looked down and smiled at his friend. He saw Mackey do something that was probably relief and smiling, but he had been through too much for anything to really show.

Mackey could only think of one word, "good." It was all he could concentrate on. Good, he would die. Good, he would be out of here. Good, his friend had found him. Good, he would be released. Good, he knew Lincoln would exact revenge on the little asses. It was all good now. Mackey tried to say something in a voice that was raw and strained. "Good," as weak as it was, came out to Lincoln as loud as any scream he had ever heard.

And as soon as it was done, Robin nodded his head and gave a weak smile. "Yes, my friend, I got it from here," Lincoln said as Mackey gave in and passed on his way.

Lincoln gave a roar and saw a panel that looked like a control center for the table. He took his armored fist and thrust it with all his power at the panel. Sparks flew, and the whole section went dark. He put his helmet back on, made the sign of the cross, and said goodbye with a prayer for the dead. Not for the first time nor the last had he done this ritual.

He turned and straightened up and looked at Ryan who nodded, and Lincoln nodded back. Ready, they had a mission to finish.

Coming over a rise, Hunter Four caught the back end of one of the aliens going down behind the next rise. The sound of rushing water was picked up on his helmet's sensors. "Five, Six, got contact up ahead. It looks like we have water to target's front," Wild Bill said as he raised his rifle as he picked up his pace. The others matched him.

As the alien ducked down to his side, popped up another one with a weapon pointed at the Hunters.

"Shit!" was all Wild Bill could say as he dove for cover. As fire ripped through the space he had just been, Hunters Five and Six started returning fire.

The other little alien popped up behind the ridge from farther to the right from the first one's location. He came up firing in a spray pattern.

Hunter Five saw him popping up. "Down!" was all he had time to say, but it was enough.

The first alien had Hunter Four behind an outcropping of rock. He was blasting away at it, raining down dirt and pieces of rock all over Wild Bill, who stayed low.

Hunter Six, Doc, tried to get a shot at the little alien who had Bill pinned down. He was opposite from the crazy little one spraying fire all over. Doc took about three shots, blowing debris all over the alien but not hitting him, making him duck back down, which gave Hunter Four a chance to move into a firing position.

The second alien was still spraying shots but doubled his back and forth toward Doc in little arcs of fire. Hunter Five popped off a few rounds at him, sending him falling sideways, his shots going up, hitting a tree branch over Angel, which nearly fell on him.

"What the hell is it with these trees? They hate me," he commented as he rolled out of the way of a second limb in such a short period of time.

The Hunters started pouring shots at the aliens from each of their positions, finally getting the initiative from them. The aliens were now on the defensive, ducking back down and only getting a shot or two.

Now with the suppressive fire, the Hunters started to try to move in on the aliens, but their plan was brought to a complete halt when, from the location of the water behind the aliens, another ship came up above the ridge and started to slip on top of the aliens. A light projected from the bottom and engulfed them.

The Hunters, sensing the loss of their prey, tried to focus shots on the suspended aliens. That was when the ship erupted with counterattacks of multiple shots. The ground between the Hunters and the alien ship erupted as if the ground was fighting gravity, mounds flying in the air, cascading over the three soldiers. They had to take cover or be randomly crushed by a deluge of earth and stone.

The aliens made it into an opening in the bottom of the ship just as a fire plume cut across the sky and rocked the alien ship. Two more came striking the ship in a small tight grouping. The ship was pushed back a few yards and wobbled unsteady. Hunter Four looked and saw three dents where the rockets had scored some hits.

The alien ship wasted no time and evaded a fourth rocket and, at an impossible angle, shot up and out, most likely passing the atmosphere in seconds. The sonic boom followed.

Watcher, in their blacked-out Blackhawk, came flying over and banked on top. They watched it drop down over near the water. The Hunters gathered themselves and headed over for their ride.

*****

"Command, this is Leader Two. I am heading for the base. I have two of the surviving crew from Ship Three."

"Eh, fine. I will want to question them upon your arrival. What of the rest and Ship Three?" Commander One Stripe asked.

"The humans have the ship. It is mostly destroyed, and all other crew are dead."

"Why did you not extinguish that ship and the humans!" One Stripe yelled.

"I beg your forgiveness. The humans have new weapons. I took fire from one and have sustained damage. I did not want you to be short of two ships, my commander." Leader Two used such a humbled tone it was hard for One Stripe to get too angry. Plus, his logic was sound.

"Fine! Bring those two to me!" One Stripe cut the signal, as was his way.

Leader Two walked down to the ship's cargo bay. Ship Three's remaining crew, two to be exact, were held in a stasis cube—prisoners for now.

Engineer and Communicator could see through the stasis cube but could do nothing but think. Engineer had to think quick to come up with something plausible that would save him from execution, maybe not punishment, but alive was alive.

Communicator knew he did not have much hope unless if he said he was in engineering and knew of nothing. The only way to make that work was if Engineer went along. It all depended on if he could plead his story first and Engineer did not contradict him. It was a long shot, but it still was a shot.

As Leader Two stood observing the two, he wondered what was going through their heads. He chuckled as he saw the gears turning behind their eyes.

*****

The Blackhawk touched down back in the spot it dropped them off at about an hour ago. Hunters One, Two, and Three came out of the ship about the same time and ambled over to the copter.

"Hunter One to Lodge, we need extra movers with a big rig to haul away our cleanup. We have target. All occupants out of commission. Watcher and Hunters will stand by till secured."

"Copy, Hunter One. Lodge has movers en route. ETA, ten mikes." Andrews paused. "Will you be direct to the Lodge?"

"Negative. We have information for staging area. Will detour for there first, then direct to the Lodge," Ryan said, the hint of sadness conveyed in his message, evident the deputy had been found and not in good condition.

"Roger that. Will relay status to Conductor and Eagle." Andrews paused, then continued, "Hunters A1, all accounted for. You bagged your limit for the day." She hoped she wasn't being presumptuous or out of line, but this was a glaring success, and she knew far above what was hoped to happen.

A pause sat there, and Lincoln responded, "Lodge"—he let it hang there for a second—"damn right! Have 'em set up and ready for a celebration at the Lodge!"

The Hunters and Watcher crew altogether said, "Hoo-hah!" which accidently went out over the comms.

Back at the Lodge control room, Andrews did a fist pump and called down to the mess hall to have it ready for a coming-home dinner. Not many missions meet or exceed hopes of outcomes, but as a first-time engagement with an unknown hostile enemy, this was over the top.

Now they had actual aliens, albeit dead, but they had them to study, and a ship that was the big prize. The science and technology from that one ship was more than what had been acquired in over fifty years. All in one day, they had jumped from being in the dark to stepping out in the sun—the hope now not to get burned.

CHAPTER 12

AFTER-ACTION REPORT

Touching down at the staging area, Captain Ryan and Master Sergeant Lincoln got out, leaving the rest in the idling copter. They cleared the blades and straightened up and removed their helmets, holding them under one arm.

The sheriff turned and faced them, a sad scowl on his face. It was easy to read the message the two men were delivering. The other deputies gathered behind him. Tears were held back, except for a few strays; somehow, it made it sadder, the stray tears.

Lincoln came to attention and saluted the sheriff.

He stiffened and returned a salute not up to military standards but full of respect. "Master Sergeant," the sheriff said in a weary voice straining to stay even. He nodded to the man.

"Sheriff, so you know, I was with him when he got to go. He was okay in the end. He knew I did all I could. He said 'good' and tried to smile. He was strong, sir. You prepared him well."

Puddles formed under the sheriff's eyes, but he kept control although the sound of sobs came from behind him. The sheriff sniffled, looked down, wiped his eyes, and took a deep breath. He looked Lincoln straight in the eye and put out his hand.

Lincoln took it, and they shook. It was more than a handshake, and all of them knew it. The sheriff broke off and turned around. And the group, sheriff, and his deputies held a group hug as each took a turn saying a prayer or a thought for their fallen friend and brother.

Shapiro stepped forward, grasped Lincoln on the bicep, squeezed, and said, "I will handle this from here. You did the best, Master Sergeant."

Ryan put his hand on Lincoln's shoulder, and they turned and returned to the Blackhawk and lifted off for a trip back to the base.

Watcher came into Canaveral Base over the Atlantic and slipped in to landing pad and was towed into the abandoned hangar. The Hunters disembarked, and as they headed to the freight elevator, they heard a Chinook helicopter coming in, following their trail. Curiosity got the better of them, and they went to the hangar door and peered out.

The helicopter had a cargo pad under it, attached with cables. They watched it sway by with its load, which appeared to be two M1A2 tanks shaped under the camo tarp. They watched as it went by and headed to Patrick Space Force Base.

Deke, with Apache next to him, both standing behind them, said, "Those babies can carry a lot of load. That, by the way, is the spaceship, camouflaged to look like tanks. They have a lab under Patrick. They have been setting up as they were working here."

The Hunters turned and looked at Deke.

"What? I had to make a few runs to practice my landings so I would know where to put down if I was doing transport," he said as he shrugged.

They all nodded it made sense. It would figure they would need to have a lab close to work on whatever the Hunters could bring back. Although no one thought they would have this much material at the get-go.

"Let's go clean up and store the gear, take inventory of what we lost and need. Then we can go check out this lab and see what we got," Captain Ryan said, patting Chief Tanaka on the back and heading to the freight elevator his team would take down to the hangar below.

"Okay, Watchers, let's do the same. Ride down with our bird and get her to bed and meet up with the Hunters," Deke said as he turned and headed back to the lift the Blackhawk sat on with his crew walking behind.

"All the after-action reports are done and filed, thanks to Didi. Dictation and the no-paper initiative makes you want to wear these helmets all day. Save on all sorts of paperwork," Lincoln said as they were taking their armor off, cleaning it, and storing it in their over-sized lockers in the armory.

Lincoln, as operations sergeant of the team, was responsible to make sure all the paperwork on return was done and filed. Thanks to the AI in the armor, it was all done on the trip back to Canaveral. They sat in the copter cabin and dictated and submitted their reports through the team net. Lincoln just had to review and send back to the team member for any corrections. Then when it came back to him, he electronically signed them and submitted them.

People see the life of a Special Forces soldier as just run, jump, and shoot. They forget there is always paperwork—well, in this case, no paper, but still work.

*****

Ship Two landed at the Aldion Earth's moon base, located on the far side where it could not be viewed from Earth. The humans did not have the capability to view them years ago, but now if they were located more toward the Earth, they would be seen.

It puzzled the Aldions—even the Greelocks, located on the opposite side of the moon—why the humans did not even send their little satellites. Humans were not bright, but they were good labor and fetched plenty of credit on the market of Docentia Prime.

Leader Two expertly took his ship into the landing bay of the base, taking his spot in the prime fleet of Commander One Stripe. The spot reserved for Ship Three was vacant, as were the rest of the fleets. They were out, charged with filling the slave pens to be shipped to market. Soon, Ship Four would be promoted to take that spot. As all would move up, a new crew and ship would be brought into the fold.

Leader Two smirked. Leader Four was a protégé of his and would be an ally for the future. He needed to either rig the next leader coming into the fleet as one of his protégés or coax the new one in to lean toward his way of thinking. Leader Two knew he could take over this fleet with enough swaying of the others to his way. He just needed time.

A set of One Stripe's personal guard was at the dock, waiting to take the two traitors into their custody and bring them before the commander. Two had his men prepare the two for the custody switch, when he had a brilliant idea. He had his men hold off the securing of the two traitors. Instead, they were brought before him in a private conference room in his ship. Alone, he would debrief the two and give them the choice, death or loyalty to him. Oh, this plan was brilliant.

Commander One Stripe was becoming impatient. He wanted to bring down his wrath on the traitors. Instead of the traitors being dragged in by his personal guards as he expected, Leader Two with his doctor and Security came walking in. Commander One Stripe growled and spat, a sure sign he was furious and not pleased.

Leader Two and his men kept their eyes and heads down as they approached the command chair. As they came before it, they each bent to one knee, outstretched their arms palms up, and lowered their heads even lower.

One Stripe wanted to have their heads taken off immediately for not following his orders and bringing the traitors to him, but he held back. The surrender of respect to him could not be violated by his temper, or he would lose much respect, placing his command in question.

Leader Two stayed in his position, waiting. He would wait for several cycles if he had to. He would not lose this battle of wills. He and his men did not even move a finger. They were strong and ready. This was a match, of them and the commander. This was the Aldion way.

*****

The Hunters had gotten back into their army combat uniforms and headed by tram over to the Patrick Base tram platform. The men of Watcher joined them, and the tram sped the distance between the two bases. The discussion in the tram was full on how the team and the copter could have been more in sync with their actions. It was a lively discussion that left them laughing at one another, especially those who kept having trees fall on them or were covered in dirt.

"So were you guys briefed on what they were going to do with whatever we bring back for them?" Major Tucker asked, more to Ryan, the team commander, or more to Lincoln, who everyone knew General Hansen picked to help develop the new unit.

Ryan shrugged he had no idea.

"What was supposed to happen was we were going to get a team of scientists cleared to work on this stuff—alien tech, that is." Lincoln took a sip from a water bottle he had brought with him. "Who or what in the way of a lab or team, I don't know. So Andrews told me we were meeting with a Lieutenant Troy. He is supposed to liaison with the scientist and us."

"Okay. Is Troy a Special Forces man or a Pentagon man?" the major asked.

"Well, I guess we will find out in about fifteen when we get there," Senior Sergeant Jenkins said.

Pulling into the Patrick Base platform, they saw a young man, a lieutenant, waiting for them. He looked like he just got out of high school and did not even shave yet.

"Welcome all. I am Lieutenant Jim Troy of the new Thirteenth Scientific Research and Development unit or, as it will be referred to as, SRD 13." Troy was beaming from ear to ear, extremely excited to be here and doing what he was doing.

"So are you just a pencil pusher, Troy, or do you know some of this science stuff?" Ryan asked as they gathered around the young man as they exited the tram.

"No, no. I graduated West Point. Then I received two doctorates from MIT before I was assigned to DARPA. Physics is my thing, but follow me. You have to meet doctors Brolin and Fargo. They are who are heading all the developments you have used and will use." Troy turned and took a left branch of tunnels no one had noticed before. He made it about twenty steps before he realized no one was following. He stopped and turned, waving for them to follow. As soon as they took a step toward him, he started down the tunnel. Everyone shook their heads and laughed, typical science guy.

The tunnel runway turned a few times and branched a couple of more times. It seemed they had gone about a half mile already. Finally, they came to what was almost a dead end.

A desk sat in the middle of the tunnel. Two Space Force military police, which must have been new—no one knew they had them—were fully armed and combat ready and guarding either side of the desk. Behind was what looked like a vault door.

A young man in a Space Force uniform lieutenant's rank sat at the desk. Controls were set in front and to the side of him. Three computer monitors sat in front of him. The counter was about chest level, and several security devices sat on it. The man said, "Welcome to SRD 13 security point 1. Protocol is by rank. Starting at the left end of the counter, place your hand on the fingerprint reader. Second, put your right eye to the viewer next to the reader. Third, place your finger—any one of which is acceptable—into the slot on the DNA reader. After the security checks, step through the full-body scanner one at a time, for screening of biohazards. Once everyone is cleared, the vault door to the facilities will unlock and admit those cleared to enter. We have an AI, Echo, running the lab. You may direct any procedural questions or results to the AI."

"Wow, that was a mouthful there, Lieutenant," Major Tucker said.

"Yes, sir. And now that you heard it, and with as many of you as there are who heard it, I won't have to do that again please."

Everyone laughed. They had all been there at explaining things that was longer than the actual procedure.

Troy went first. As an assigned member of the unit, he only had to walk through the scanner.

"How come he only had to walk through the scanner?" Lincoln asked as Tucker started down the line of security protocols.

"Because Lieutenant Troy has a chip inserted under his skin. It provides all the data. I believe you will have an option for one as you get ready to leave," the desk officer said.

Troy looked over. "Yes, that and a couple of other things too. I hope you take them. It's well worth it," he said, nodding his head with enthusiasm.

The rest of the men chuckled; Troy was unaware that he had made a joke about himself.

After all had cleared through the security checkpoint, the vault door released and opened, allowing them entry. No one was sure what they were going to see, perhaps Frankenstein's lab, a crazy inter-dimensional doorway, a dungeon; their imaginations ran wild.

What no one expected was for the vault to open to an ordinary hospital-looking atmosphere, with all the medical people in Space Force scorpion army combat uniforms. The hallway was double wide and had a nurses' station twenty feet in through the doors and had rooms that ran the length of the hallway. At the end of the hallway, two sets of double doors sat ten feet apart. A hallway branched off either side, one to the left and one to the right.

"Where we are right now is the front entrance to the unit head-quarters, so to speak. The rooms you see are conference, office, and some smaller labs. The double doors are the main labs. The left is where all the evidence and alien tech, bodies, and such will go to be catalogued and researched. The other set of double doors is the development lab, where we test, design, and implement all our ideas and designs."

"Impressive. I did not expect this, I have to tell you," Captain Ryan said, looking about with a new respect for the organization they had achieved considering they had just been activated as a unit.

"Thank you, sir. That is a compliment coming from you. Shall we go meet the doctors? They are pouring over the new stuff you got for them," Troy said as he led them down the hallway.

The staff eyed them, and all nodded and smiled, obviously quite thrilled to meet the men who recovered a treasure trove of alien technology.

At the double doors to the research lab, Troy stopped them and said, "Okay, I have to warn you the doctors are quite eccentric and can be overzealous, but please do not take anything they say as insults or anything of the kind. They are truly the nicest, most brilliant men you will ever meet. They painstakingly worked on that armor to upgrade current military standard to be able to stand up to what they perceived an alien threat would be. They nearly killed themselves with worry about your survival."

"Well, I can tell you it worked, and I am damn thankful it did. I owe them. Plus, those helmets are outstanding," Lincoln said, meaning every word. "I would wear that helmet all day if I could," he added.

"Then you will love meeting them and the things we have here set for your teams," Troy added.

Lincoln nodded in agreement, and Troy waved his hand over the security lock to the research department.

The door slid back and revealed what looked like a warehouse, albeit one clean and neatly arranged with modern storage compartments. Some doors led off the sides, probably smaller labs and offices.

The alien ship was set up with scaffolding holding it in position so it could be entered and explored in upright position. Two men in white lab coats stood before the opening, arguing about what was not to clear. Everyone had to stop and look over the two men. They looked like two movie actors, Christopher Walken and James Earl Jones.

Troy waved the men forward and interrupted the doctors and introduced them. Dr. Brolin was first, and when he spoke, he confirmed he could have been James Earl Jones, or his double. When Dr. Fargo was introduced, he was just as much a doppelgänger for Christopher Walken. The men just stared at the doctors, awed by the coincidental resemblance.

"Hello, gentlemen. I am honored to meet all of you, to see the men we create for and to get your input on how we did with your new equipment." Brolin leaned in and put his hand to the side of his mouth. "It was our idea to start this unit and work closer with you. Being removed from the men who do the work is just ridiculous, in my opinion."

"I agree. I agree with Dr. Brolin. We were wasted, I mean wasted at DARPA, without seeing and talking to you men. We need to see how the things we make work," Fargo said.

They both seemed quite excited and happy to be in the front line, so to speak.

"This ship is full of treasure. Oh, not the money kind but the technology kind. All the things in here, we should be able to even the fight a little for you," Fargo was saying as he stared into the hole blown into the side of the ship.

"Have you been inside yet, doctors?" Lincoln asked as he waved a hand at the ship.

"We were just arguing about that as you men came in," Brolin said.

"Why were you arguing? Surely, you both can go in together. Neither has to be first. Plus, we"—Ryan waved his hand past Lincoln, Tanaka, and himself—"we were all inside together already. So the point of being first is not relevant now."

"Oh, we weren't arguing about that. It was should we wear hazmat suits or masks. Even if for the good of the unit, only one go in if something should happen to the other," Fargo said as he chuckled and finished. "I am kind of a little germophobic, so I wanted the full suit."

"Well, we did have your armor on. By the way, it was outstanding—the armor, that is—when we went in," Lincoln offered.

"Interesting," Dr. Brolin said. And he did not expand on that, and they waited for him to, but he did not notice.

"What's interesting, Doctor?" Captain Ryan asked as they all waited for an answer.

"Hmm, what is what?" the doctor asked, lost in his own thoughts.

"You said 'interesting.' We were wondering what that was," Ryan continued.

"That you seem to like the armor," Brolin said and once again did not expand on that.

"Well, it really isn't. Seems all of us found the armor to be beyond our wishes. You gentlemen had hit every item we would have asked for," Ryan said.

"Except for snacks and drinks," Angel said. Everyone laughed, except for Fargo and Brolin who looked like they were going deep in thought.

"Is there a spot for a snack holder and a delivery system, Fargo?" Brolin asked.

"We will have to go over the schematics and see and possibly infuse soft drinks with a snack delivery system. You will have to go over the power draw at that point."

Lincoln punched Herndon on the shoulder for saying that joke to two very literal men. "No, don't listen to him. Sirs, we are quite happy with the gear. It's perfect," Lincoln said.

"Well, great, but now we have a challenge. I can see so many benefits to the application to be built in," Fargo said, but then he said, "But that's for us to work out. We won't bore you with our ruminations, but follow us to the new equipment room. We have some things you will greatly need."

The group followed the doctors over to a door, which turned out to be like an armory, but more extensive.

"Wow!" was echoed by all the men as they stood before the boards displaying the equipment and their names and purpose.

"First, I want to show you all these capsules." He held up in a set of tweezers a small capsule resting in its clamp. It was a bit smaller than a standard aspirin or such pain capsule, about half the size. "This is an AI capsule. I know you look very skeptical, and I don't blame you," Fargo said. "But it's true. It links with the armor and a broad network we designed. When linked, the AI is stronger, but it works on its own too." Fargo held it up a little higher and twirled it from side to side, looking on it with pride.

"Now you swallow it, and it finds its own way to the best location in your body. You don't feel anything at all. With this"—Brolin held up a small object no bigger than a pinhead—"you can hear and talk to anyone in the unit or on comms anytime. You just voice the command, and the AI acts like a phone operator and puts you through. Well, that is unless the person has asked for privacy mode, then they won't be disturbed unless an emergency occurs."

"Um, where does that go?" Doolie asked.

"That," Fargo answered, "goes just behind your ear. Once put on your skin, it hooks into you and matches the skin color surrounding it."

"Uh, hooks into you?" Jenkins asked.

"Yes, but you won't even notice, not one bit," Fargo replied.

"Well, lead by example. I'll take them first, and you all can watch how I do," Ryan said as he walked up. And Fargo put the capsule onto his tongue. He swallowed. He did not have any reaction at all. He actually did not feel anything, like it dissolved in his throat.

Next, Dr. Brolin brought a minidot in a smaller pair of tweezers over and placed it behind his left ear.

Once again, he did not feel anything at first, then a slight tingle, like something just started up in his ear—a small, tiny fan. Then it was gone. He stood there and shrugged. "Okay, how long does this take? Because I felt nothing. I don't feel anything now."

"Good," both doctors said.

Brolin continued, "Felicity, please greet and introduce yourself."

"Hello, Captain Ryan. I'm Felicity, a nickname for model F, foxtrot, AI. Dr. Fargo has a daughter, Felicity, and thought it would be easier to relate to than foxtrot."

Ryan swiveled his head around, and his brow furrowed. He heard it clear, but not overwhelming, like a woman was just behind him and said these things at a quiet yet clear tone.

"Does it hurt, sir?" Burgess asked.

He grinned. "No, not at all. It's just going to take a bit to get used to a voice just over my shoulder, right, Felicity?" Ryan said. And the AI answered, but no one else could hear.

Lincoln had lined up behind Ryan, so the two now had the devices and said to make a connection to each other. With barely a whisper, they had a conversation. Everyone followed suit, including the Watcher crew.

Lincoln and Ryan both picked up a new pistol—Ryan to replace his, and Lincoln was now going to wear two. Tanaka picked up a new rifle. Usually, they could just request these, and some spares were in the armory; but since the actual stores of them were before them, they decided to just get what they needed now.

The men continued on the tour and met four biologists, two of which were xenobiologists. The alien crew had been laid out on operating tables in a big morgue room with over twenty tables. Eighteen were filled. The Hunters had given the researchers more material in one action than they ever even hoped for.

Brolin and Fargo were positive that they would be able to engineer or, properly put, reverse engineer a beam weapon or two from the weapons that were recovered from the alien ship.

During the tour, Angel or Herndon had been able to slip in, asking Dr. Fargo to make cowbell and that he needed more cowbell.

Dr. Fargo did say, "You need more cowbell?" Then he asked, "Why do people keep asking me that?"

This earned Angel another hit from Lincoln even though everyone tried to stifle their laughter. When Herndon had gotten another moment, he asked Dr. Brolin if he was his father.

Dr. Brolin, of course, said, "I am not your father, but people seem to ask that a lot of me. Peculiar."

Lincoln tried to explain to the good doctors their uncanny resemblance to the two famous actors, but the cause was lost. In the end, he just said, "Never mind."

The group bid farewell and were quite impressed with having a lab so close with such productive and brilliant researchers. The tram was still at the platform and carried them back to the Canaveral platform and base.

Upon arrival, Charlene greeted them, "Major Tucker, it seems that you and your team's quarters are ready, and your gear has been set in everyone's quarters."

"Thank you, Charlie," Tucker said and was about to ask which way to them, when markings on the floor came up and everyone knew it was the way to the aviation unit's section.

"Major, I have been passed orders officially creating the Thirteenth Special Flight Wing and putting you in command. Your duty station will be, of course, here. And you are being assigned several other crews and aircraft to your command."

"Really? Well, how about that? My own command, and new unit at that." Tucker was taken aback. He had just assumed they would be enveloped under Special Operations Aviation Regiment as always.

"General Hansen has called a meeting via video to be held with Captain Ryan and Major Tucker. He would also like Chief Tanaka,

Captain Red Sky, Master Sergeant Lincoln, and Sergeant First Class Junius to attend. Major Tucker, you have the crew of the Chinook and the crews of two Little Birds—is that right?—reporting in for their new assignment to your command."

"Oh, get the new command and already have three more crews and units. And yes, the AH-6 is called Little Bird. You are correct, Charlie. Charlie, have they been assigned quarters, and have their helicopters been given spots in the hangar?" Tucker asked, trying to move into commander of a wing as best he could.

"Yes, Major. They actually have been assigned and occupy quarters now, and their helicopters are all in the hangar here and getting checked over by your aviation crews."

"Oh, almost forgot I have aviation crews, mechanics, and the likes now."

"Aren't you fancy, Major?" Apache said and smiled.

"Charlie, do I have an office and a conference room, and are we assigned our own section down here in this ghost city?" Tucker was referring to what everyone had started calling the base, ghost city. It was huge and had so many sections for battalions, but even at full strength, sections would still be uninhabited.

"Yes, Major. When you're ready, I will give you a tour after you check in to your quarters."

"Excellent. Charlie, advise the crews we will have an initial meeting after my tour, and I will go over assignments." Tucker finished as he shook hands of congratulations from all the gathered men.

Tucker and his men—the newly formed Thirteenth Special Flight Wing of the Thirteenth Special Forces Group, US Army—headed off to the newly appointed section of the first support unit added to the Thirteenth Special Forces Group.

The base had been continually upgraded and expanded over the years. The section where the Thirteenth Special Forces Group had been assigned had facilities, allowing each battalion a separate space, branching off a central headquarters area, like spokes on a wheel, the headquarter being the center and each battalion a spoke. Each spoke and headquarter had single rooms for each assigned personnel and with ten empty rooms to spare. Included in the battalion sector was the armory for the battalion, divided by teams, by lockers, and by work areas. A section of offices for all the team leaders and assistants, then the top two sergeants of each team, along with a planning and meeting room for the team. The company commander had their own office, which was the first team of each company.

Each battalion had its own mess hall, with staff attached to the headquarter section. Also included were various facilities, storage, gear rooms, gyms, and med facility, which were staffed by headquarters personnel. The premier additions to the sections were the ranges and shooting scenario arena. Of course, as a military tradition, there was the dayroom, where pool tables, Ping-Pong, TV, music, and general gathering was done.

Of course, the section allotted to the Thirteenth Special Flight Wing was the size of a battalion in a hub anchored in the center by the Thirteenth Special Forces Group headquarter. A total of six battalion-sized sections surrounded the headquarter—four Special Forces battalions, one headquarter at the center, and one aviation, which was the Thirteenth Special Flight Wing.

Two more hubs were being used. One was the hangars, of which the center was the main hangar with the lift to the abandoned hangar up top. The battalion areas were used for vehicle parking and maintenance. Two of the six were where the aviation maintenance crews were housed. The second hub was for the two fighters that were being stationed and assigned to the Thirteenth Special Flight Wing. They were F-35 single pilot fighters, modified as the helicopters had been, originally Space Force, still on its rolls but assigned to the Army and its aviation. The F-35s had been marked matte black and had reflective Space Force markings on infrared. The pilots wore Space Force flight suits. They were joined by a C-130 Commando II, also Space Force but assigned to the Army.

The one lone stray was a Marine Corps Osprey, V-22, detached to the Army. Wearing Marine Corps flight suits and patches made for the Thirteenth Special Flight Wing, Marine.

The flight wing patches were Space Force, Army, and Marine signifiers. It was for morale these were issued, and if seen by civilians and most military, a giveaway to the unit's presence was kept hidden to all those not read in on the existence of the group and its support units.

Major Tucker took the head of the conference table, his copilot to his right and his crew in seats at the back of the room. The two OH-6 Little Birds pilots were to his left. They were a two-man crew, pilot and copilot. The pilots who sat next to his copilot Apache were from the Chinook everyone saw moving the alien ship to the research lab. The crew of the Chinook sitting with his crew, it appeared some of them were acquainted and even friends.

"Welcome, everyone, to the new Thirteenth Special Flight Wing of the Thirteenth Special Forces Group. Our mission is to support the Thirteenth group. Most of us worked SOAR, black knights, but this mission is even darker. It's secret. It is not something we will be able to talk about outside these walls. I think, with the exception of Captain Singer and Lieutenant Allen and Lieutenant Manning and Lieutenant Gregory of the Little Birds, we have all seen enough to know what this is about." Tucker stopped and took a sip of water, allowing the men he had just mentioned to ask the big question.

"Sir," Captain Singer asked, being the senior of the new men. The two crews and helicopters had been reassigned from Delta Force out of Fort Bragg. "What exactly are we doing, or is it a secret to tell?" he asked and received chuckles from all, even the major. "Joking aside, we were moved from Delta, sir. I mean, what is bigger?" Singer finished, obviously disappointed at his transfer that he took as a punishment.

"Captain, when I explain it, you will not be disappointed about being transferred to the Thirteenth. As a matter of fact, everyone in this room should feel honored that the president and the general of the Special Forces think enough of our abilities and character to place us here." Tucker let that sink in.

"Okay, so now my interest is peeked," Singer threw in.

"The Thirteenth was put together for one mission, as hunters, alien hunters." Tucker had to stop; the four pilots started to grumble about tracking illegal aliens from other countries.

"Hold on! Settle down. Not human aliens, I'm afraid, aliens that come to Earth to abduct humans. And before you start laughing or scoff at it, it's true they are real!"

The room was quiet. All the crew members had seen the proof. The four new pilots were not sure if this was some sort of psychological test or a joke.

"Charlie, turn on the feed from the lab. Let these men see the proof 'live' and in person," Tucker instructed.

"Yes, sir, here is the live feed."

Some of the men looked up, not expecting a voice to respond as it had.

"Oh, and Charlie is our AI that runs the base and communicates on actions. Look at the screen. That's a drone controlled by Charlie in the lab, giving direct views of the alien ship and recovered crew from our earlier action," Tucker finished, watching the new men absorb the information.

"Now your skills were beyond the normal, so you were picked. But also your ability to absorb and accept this new reality was judged to be also enough above normal to have you shipped in. I know it may take some getting used to, but you really have to buy in and move on." Tucker sipped his water, letting the men compute everything.

"You heard me say 'from an earlier action.' Well, one of the new teams, Master Sergeant, had a run-in at his home and took out a couple of aliens. Now in retaliation, they destroyed his home and pickup truck. We caught up to these aliens, and we captured their ship. And all their crew are deceased and in our possession—well, except for two who were scooped up by another alien ship and fled."

"Real, and you have already engaged some and took them out?" Captain Singer asked.

"Yes, early this morning. Unfortunately, we responded after they abducted a local sheriff's deputy. They tortured him, and he did not live."

"Shit," Lieutenant Manning said.

"Exactly, boys, we're in the shit now. Are you in and ready? Or before we get comfortable, you can back out. This is the point of no return." Tucker furrowed his brow and looked over the four new members—well, possible members of his wing.

"Captain Singer, Lieutenant Allen, what will it be?" Tucker asked them and waited for their response.

Captain Singer sat there for a moment, staring at the video screen, watching a research team measuring and poking at an alien corpse. Then he smirked. "Hell, I'm in Special Forces for the long haul. This is what it's all about, isn't it? Count me in. Red?" Singer said, asking his copilot, Lieutenant Steve "Red" Allen, if he was in with him.

"You know I am Rock. Where you go, I go, brother."

"Good. Glad to have you aboard. Your ship is LB-13 Alpha. Call sign, Falcon. Rock, you are Falcon One. Red, you are Falcon Two. Pick two rooms and get settled."

The two got up and made a semisalute and went to get their gear and grab rooms.

Once they had left, Tucker looked over to the new men left. "Now if you are not staying, I understand. This isn't for everyone, no shame in it at all. I know Rock. We have worked together a long time. I knew his answer. So I sent them out. Lieutenant Manning, Lieutenant Forrester, what will it be?" Tucker asked. He did not want pressure on these two. They were young and newer to the life than the other two.

"I knew it. I always knew it." Lieutenant Manning had not taken his eyes off the screen. He was mesmerized by the aliens. "This is better than any other assignment I could ever have dreamt of." He was smiling and continuing to watch the screen.

"Sir, as you can see, I'm the responsible one of the team. And if I wasn't around, he would most likely crash into a mountain while watching one of them little blue-green guys running around," Lieutenant Forrester said, smiling.

While everyone got a laugh out of that, Manning came out of his trance of aliens and knew he had been insulted by his copilot, so he punched him on the arm.

"Excellent, your bird is LB-13 Bravo. Call sign, Hawk. Crane, you're Hawk One. Flare, you're Hawk Two. Any questions? If not, go grab your gear and pick out rooms."

Tucker waited, but no questions came up. And the two men got up, semisaluted, and headed out for their rooms.

Tucker stood up and look to the remaining men in the room. "Okay, any problems? Anything I need to fix or get done, guys? Well, since no one has got anything, let's go finish unpacking. We have a meeting at HQ in an hour with the general, and don't be surprised if the president isn't sitting in on it."

They broke up their meeting and headed out of the room. Major Tucker now had a Blackhawk, his, two OH-6s, and a Chinook in his wing, not bad for one day.

When Ryan and Lincoln returned to their section, they found the rest of their men present and waiting for a briefing and assignments, so they called the whole unit to the team conference room.

Captain Ryan, Chief Tanaka, and Master Sergeant Lincoln stood at the head of the conference room. Herndon, Doolie, and Junius sat on the left side of the table, having been initiated into the assignment, almost by fire; but having been told of the existence of aliens, they got to see it up close and personal.

Toward the rear and off to the right of the conference table sat Sergeant First Class Chung "Bang" Patterson, a weapons sergeant 18B, as the Army labeled them; Senior Sergeant Doug "Grumpy" White, a medical sergeant 18D army code; and senior sergeants Dwight "Sparky" Davis and Reese "Pieces" Peterson, both communications sergeants or 18E for the Army. Next sat the final members, the engineer sergeants 18C, Sergeant First Class Rudy "Sleepy" Polansky and Staff Sergeant Greg "Speedy" Gonzalez.

"Well, we got the band back together. We all have worked together in the past and will work together now." Ryan got a couple of chuckles out of his band joke. "Now, being transferred here, under complete secrecy, and finding this unique base must be driving you nuts about what we're doing. Well, it's going to be a shock, so be prepared. What I'm going to tell you is the utmost secret, that the organizing of a new Special Forces Group is being done as quietly and slowly as can be to keep our existence totally need to know." Ryan stopped to let that sink in. He could see the wheels turning in their minds. And he knew them all, so it was easy to know which direction their minds raced.

"Cartels?" Patterson asked. "China?"

"Canada?" Gonzalez added in. Everyone laughed.

"No use guessing, you would not get it in a million years," Ryan said.

"Aliens," White said as a fact, not a question. Chuckles came from the group. White didn't laugh; he was serious.

"No questions about it, 'bout fucking time too," Polansky said, no hint of humor at all. As a matter of fact, it came out with a bit of rage.

"How? What? Did you hear something, guys?" Lincoln asked, taken aback from the attitude both men had.

Polansky and White looked at each other. "Remember Peru? When Polansky and I lost a day, everyone thought we had malaria or something. You looked everywhere. We had no memory. We spent a month back here at Bethesda, getting all sorts of tests. They figured it was something like malaria, or we had been drugged." Bitterness White had in his voice.

Polansky continued, "Well, it never sat right with either of us. I could not let it go. We kept in touch. Then one day, I see this thing. I cannot remember what it was, but it made it all come back." Polansky stopped, but his jaw was clenched tight with anger and memories.

"You know, it all flooded back for me a day after him, every horrible moment of that day. I just called Sleepy and said, 'Meet me at Johnsons,' and he did. We talked it all out."

"We knew we were not insane. We both remembered exactly the same things," White said and just went quiet.

Ryan looked at them. "You guys never said anything."

Polansky laughed. "Like then you would have believed us. It was after the team got set apart, so I wasn't going back to you guys all over the world. Plus, Cap, you had entered Delta. We all know how tough that shit is."

"No, no more of that shit. Everyone in here. Listen, I am your commander, but I'm also your brother. We are family forever. We have spilt and lost blood together. What one of us goes through, we all do!" Ryan let his words fall on them and looked each one in the eye, one after the other. They all read the seriousness in his stare. As he looked into each one's eyes, they nodded, and he moved on.

Last was Lincoln, who nodded and turned to the men. "Hoo-hah!" he said.

All the men returned his call in unison. "Hoo-hah!"

The pledge had been made and answered. No matter how long apart, they were still that strong team they had been in South America and later in the Middle East.

"So yes, it's aliens. And now after hearing Sleepy and Grumpy, I don't have to hard sell it. Plus, we had an action with them this morning. We came back with a lot of proof. Charlie, can you get a feed over at the lab? Is that possible?"

"Why, of course, Major. I have a drone wandering over there for such a reason," Charlene related to them.

"By the way, men, Charlie is our in-house AI. She's a wonder, but apparently, she does not know a captain from a major," Ryan said. And the room laughed.

"No, sir, I do. You just haven't read your orders in your office yet. You are now major and in command of Alpha Company. Congratulations." A bunch of hoos and hollers came from the room and handshakes and pats on the back for the newly christened major and commander. "I ordered you a new set of insignias, and the HQ quartermasters brought it over and set it on your desk."

"Thank you, Charlie. You think of everything."

"Yes." The room broke out in laughter at the unabashed candidness of the AI.

"Okay then, as your company commander"—Ryan had to stop and let the applause and whistles of his men die down—"take your bags, pick out rooms here in the section, and unpack. Then Charlie will direct you over to the lab to get your locators and commo gear, then back here, and Wild Bill will run us all through this awesome gear we have. I am telling you in the field it was the shit, and we didn't even know its full uses. Okay, troops, get to it!"

The men filled out the new arrivals, catching up with the unpacked men and heading to pick out rooms. Major Ryan, Chief

Tanaka, and the master sergeant stopped in Ryan's office and picked up his new rank. The three then headed to the headquarter hub for the staff meeting with the general.

*****

Commander One Stripe could not wait anymore. He was too curious about what Leader Two had for him. It was only ten Earth minutes before he said, "Stand and report!"

Leader Two was shocked. He had fully expected to be held in obeyance for at least an hour. One Stripe must be very curious indeed. This played well into Leader Two's plan. "Thank you, Commander. These two"—Leader waved a hand over toward the captured engineer and communicator—"were held prisoner aboard their ship. Leader Three placed them under arrest when he committed treason. These two tried to kill him." Leader Two brought his hands together and bowed slightly and continued, "They were freed upon the ship being disabled and crashing, but before their arrest, I got a message from them warning something was wrong with Leader Three. I had just decided I would try to locate them and question their leader, but I could not get a response from them. Now I know they had been locked up."

One Stripe looked over Leader Two and said, "Humph," which was a good sign; he was buying the story.

"So when you ordered me to go after Leader Three, I knew he had gone traitor at that point and reaffirmed the loyalty of these two. So I ask that Engineer Three be given Command and Communicator Three be made his navigator."

One Stripe did not answer. He just kept looking them over, quietly judging the merits of Leader Two's suggestion.

Leader Two knew he had One Stripe. He just had to push him a little. "How would it be if he became Leader Twelve and Navigator Twelve? Then you now would have myself completely loyal at the top and Twelve completely loyal at the bottom. Then you would have complete loyalty from top to bottom, and we would alert you to any more renegades."

"Yes! I will have total control, knowing when a leader of mine strays. Yes, very well done, Leader Two!"

"My honor, Supreme Commander. Your glory is our glory."

"Yes, that is so!" Commander waved his hand, shooing the group out of his throne room.

Leader Two held back his smirk. As he waved the others out in front of him, he knew he just cemented his future to take over this slaving fleet.

Commander Two had his one eye he had left on the senior commander spot; he could work with that. He would need to find out how many other commanders wanted to move up, by any means. As One Stripe watched Leader Two and his group leave and waited till they were out of sight, he waved his hand for the out-of-sight Leader One to come from behind the partitions behind his throne.

Leader One stepped up next to the throne and watched as Leader Two exited. He gripped his hands behind his back and felt a discomfort. He realized he had been squeezing them tight. He relaxed them.

"And, Leader One, what is it you took from that?" One Stripe asked as he took a chunk of food from a Boligrian slave girl, kneeling before him with a tray of treats.

Leader One looked down on the slave girl and scowled—weak; he only saw the weakness in it. Boligrians were interesting, very feline—the humans would call them, a light soft down over their soft skin. Their faces were humanlike but with some Earth cat features—a little nose with whiskers, the eyes with a split lens like the cat. They purred too—oh, but not the ones used as slaves, especially when being used. When they were alone—or thought they were—and together, then they purred. Their skin was frail. Like a human, they needed clothing, whereas Aldionian superior skin was tough and temperature perfect, which was why no clothes were ever needed.

One Stripe reached down and petted the creature and rubbed its ear. Humans had weird-enough ears, but at least they were hidden on the side, mostly tucked in, not like the Boligrians, pointed on top. Uncultured weak animals. One thing they had, strength and quickness, but the collars kept them at bay.

"Leader Two has plans. I can tell you that!" he told One Stripe.

"Humph, he is an Aldionian. Of course, he has plans. Tell me something new."

"We need to get a few of our agents on Ship Twelve. Watch the Watchers. How is that?"

"What of Leader Two and Ship Two?" One Stripe asked as he took more treats.

"Well, I know my commander. You already have one or two aboard, as I can guess there is one or two on my ship."

One Stripe bellowed out a large laugh, scaring the slave girl, who shuddered under his hand. The slave girl caused the two Aldionians to laugh harder.

*****

Charlene led both Hunters and Watchers leaders to the head-quarters conference room. General Hansen was going to be video-ing in, and most likely, the president would also. Charlene informed both majors, Ryan and Tucker, that the group commander and a few of his staff had come in last night and would be at the meeting.

The Watchers and the Hunters arrived at the hub at the same time and entered the hall to the conference room together. Robin Lincoln thought to himself that the aircrew and his team had bonded better than any combo units he ever had. Maybe it was because both units were treading on a territory no one had ever been before or of the action they just faced together, possibly even both things.

The conference room at headquarters was nothing like the standard conference rooms the battalions had. This was a big step up. This was more like a conference room and a mission room. Video screens were up, and technicians were working some computer stations. A global map board was up on a far wall, showing sightings, events, all sorts of information, real time. There were clocks on all over the room from digital to analog; one marked Zulu time sat above the world map. Zulu time was military time that all units would go to during missions so that everyone around the globe would be on one time. This made coordinating actions easier.

As the men stopped looking around the room, they noticed a short man—very muscular and older, about forty—sitting at the front of the table. He had light brown skin and was a man who loved to be outside a lot. He wore a silver oak leaf on his uniform. Lieutenant Colonel Frances Rivera, who trained Ryan, Lincoln, and Tanaka when they entered Special Forces. They rushed up to him, and all shook his hand, all noting that he must be the group commander.

"I thought I was getting a veteran team, not wet-behind-the-ear pups," Rivera said as he slapped Ryan, Tanaka, and Lincoln on the back.

"Well, what did you do to piss off the old man and get sent here?" Ryan asked.

"I was given a choice to come here and take some time off of my sentence to hell for my sins. Had I known you three were going to be here, I would have declined the offer."

"Yeah, I took the offer. They told me I either served under you here or hell. I said Florida is a couple of degrees cooler. I'll take the deal," Chief Tanaka said.

"Chief Tanaka, you still owe me fifty bucks," Major Daryl Johnson said.

"Major, good to see you. Ryan, Lincoln, meet Major Johnson. We served together in the Philippines a few years back. Saved my ass back then."

The others nodded a greeting and shook hands.

Lincoln was just about to ask who the senior noncommissioned officer of the group would be when he heard a voice that made his skin crawl. Command Sergeant Major Paul Whitfield. The one man in Special Forces he hated, truly hated. They clashed in so many ways, and twice now, he almost got Lincoln killed and did get a friend of his killed.

"As I live and breathe, Sergeant Robin Lincoln, I thought I heard you left Special Forces. Heard you had an incident that shook you up and you had to resign." A hint of sarcasm was in the voice of the taller, broader man, who came walking up behind the group.

Lincoln almost spun and cursed the man out. As it was, his cheeks started turning red with anger.

"Luckily, that's not true, Sergeant Major. We are blessed to have him here, and it was his 'incident' that propelled the group being formed," Colonel Rivera said. "I thought you said you were read in on this assignment?" Rivera knew the history and knew the men; he was not a fan of Whitfield, but it wasn't his choice or his decision to have him here. "Well, gentlemen, let's take our seats and let the general know we're ready."

Sergeant Major was not happy that he didn't have a chance to dress down Lincoln. He hated the man. He was aware of his part in the forming of this group, but he was determined to have him kicked out and dishonored. And at this level of secrecy, it played into his hands to get that done.

After they took their seats, the video screen came on, and General Hansen was now at his office at Fort Bragg, North Carolina. A second screen turned on, and the president came on the screen. A third screen lit up, and to everyone's surprise, the prime minister of England was on it.

As Whitfield was eyeing the table, Master Sergeant Donald Logan came in and sat down next to Lincoln. Whitfield sat next to Major Johnson.

Lincoln noticed that Johnson leaned over to Whitfield, and the two exchanged some words. Whitfield nodded and quickly glanced at Lincoln. Lincoln did not look away. Whitfield continued speaking low to Johnson, who was nodding now. Something was going on, and Lincoln got a bad feeling he wasn't going to like it.

Hansen went over all the events that brought them together and formed the group. The fact that rumors had started flying around, things on the recruiting front slowed from the veteran Special Forces men for the moment, but he was looking down other avenues for manpower. He did not expand on that information, and everyone knew if the general meant to have it known, he would have said it, so no one asked what he had meant.

The president spoke next, congratulating the Hunters and telling them that by moving the scientist to them and out of DARPA, the Army could now keep the projects a better-kept secret. He then introduced the prime minister of England and advised he was sitting in on this meeting so as to get as much information as he could and lobby Her Majesty to create their own division and work in concert with the US.

Colonel Rivera then briefed everyone on the inventory so far of what had been recovered and the status of any research, and then he ran a photo presentation of the actual recovered items. No one, except the Hunters and the Watchers, had actually seen the aliens. So the rest of the men were glued to the screen, watching the pictures and shaking their heads from time to time, not believing what they were seeing.

The prime minister was stunned that so much had been recovered and that it made it so much more real to see the pictures. The president thanked all the men for their indulgence of him and the prime minister and said they were going to sign off and talk business. He winked to the room, and the two monitors went dark.

General Hansen praised the two units and congratulated Ryan on his promotion from captain to major and as the new company commander of A, Alpha Company, First Battalion of the Thirteenth.

The next hour, the general conducted a standard staff meeting letting the commanders know of what he expected, as in setting up the base; but with what had been reported to him, it looked as if it was running perfect. He made one last comment that the flow of men to the unit may now be just a trickle, if not a downright drip. The news had somehow gotten wind something was being stirred up in the Army but, as of yet, did not have any clear direction on what.

General Hansen, as his last bit of business, reminded all of them that keeping a lid on their unit and activities was paramount at this point. Then he concluded the meeting and dismissed the men. Colonel Rivera seconded that, and the men went to their unit sections.

Major Ryan steered Robin out of the room and back toward their section before Whitfield could take another shot at Lincoln and he lost his master sergeant. Ryan knew most of the problem was between the two, but there wasn't a lot he could do about it.

Whitfield had never had anything badly written or reported about him. So on paper, he looked totally golden. He just hoped that Whitfield wouldn't venture into the confines of section, that he just stayed in the headquarter area, but somehow, he knew he wouldn't be that lucky.

Lincoln could not believe his luck. Getting Whitfield as his sergeant major was a kick in the ass. He tried to put it out of his mind, but Angelo Ceci wouldn't let him.

Whitfield had been the team operations sergeant, and Lincoln was the assistant operations and intelligence sergeant. Angelo had been one of the two engineer sergeants for the team. They were in a small village in Afghanistan, on a mission. Lincoln warned the team of some intelligence he got about an ambush on a patrol op they were to undertake, but Whitfield ignored his opinion and information and decided to shortcut the mission and send Staff Sergeant Angelo Ceci out to demolish a bridge over a chasm by himself. Lincoln put up a fight, saying at least send him with Ceci, but he told Lincoln he was a coward and a poor excuse for a soldier. The two got into a fistfight, and Lincoln was pulled off Whitfield, before he killed the man. He told Whitfield to send a backup with Ceci. Whitfield just laughed and said it was too late; he had dispatched him an hour ago.

Lincoln wanted to kill the man right then and there, but he took two of his men. And on his own against Whitfield's orders, he and the two others went out to back up Ceci. It had been too late. They found that the bridge had not been destroyed; but rather from a distance, they saw their teammate had been tortured, staked on a pole, and left at the end of the bridge as a message. The three men, outraged, snuck up on the insurgents responsible for the ambush they had made, using Ceci's body as bait, and wiped them out. They found Ceci, as the final insult, had his skin flayed while he was alive and placed on the pole to die in the sun of unbelievable pain.

The three-man team returned to base with their teammate's body and some incredible intelligence that led to one arm of a network of insurgents coming into country shut down completely. The biggest insult was Whitfield took credit for dispatching the three men and took no responsibility for the death of Sergeant Angelo

Ceci. Before Lincoln could tear apart the man, Whitfield had been given a promotion and shipped back to work at the Pentagon in Washington, DC.

The two had crossed paths a few times but never in a capacity that the two had to work together. To discredit Lincoln, Whitfield had been actively spreading little rumors that could neither be proved or disproved about Lincoln. Knowing full well that if Lincoln ever came out and attacked his reputation, he knew Lincoln could come under a cloud of disinformation. Lincoln had the policy that if he had an issue with someone, he would take care of it face-to-face. Robin Lincoln was not a man to fear confronting a person who he knew was in the wrong.

"Any chance that Whitfield will just avoid you and we go about our business?" Ryan asked as he, Tanaka, and Lincoln sat in his office.

"Not a chance in hell. The blood is bad between us, and he has it on his hands," Lincoln said in a low growling voice, not sure he wanted Whitfield to stay away so this could be settled once and for all.

Lincoln looked over at Tanaka. "Chief, how is that Major Johnson?"

"Well, he pulled me out of a car just before it exploded, so he did save my life. We didn't work together much past his backup once, but we hung out a couple of times. He seemed squared away. Why?" Tanaka asked.

"Whitfield and he were trading some kind of info at the table. They just seemed kind of close. Is all."

"I don't think he is that kind of guy, but like I said, I don't really know him," Tanaka said.

"It's all right, Chief. Don't worry about it. We got enough around here to worry about without that stuff," Lincoln said. Lincoln did not feel much confidence in his own statement.

*****

Leader Two walked aboard Ship Twelve, with Leader Twelve and Navigator Twelve trailing behind him. Although it was Twelve's ship, he thought of it as his, in his own fleet he was creating. "Ah! This will do quite well, not top-of-the-line but it will do. Don't you think, Twelve?" Two turned and faced Twelve to see his reaction.

"How could I be anything but grateful, my leader." Twelve bowed his head. "I was sure I was to be dead, but because of you, I am here and with a ship of my own. You are a true leader."

Two was not sure how Twelve was going to react, but this was more than acceptable. This was grand. Two said, "Then I leave you to it. Put your ship in order, and in a few hours, we will go round up some humans for our profit." He then walked past Twelve and headed for his own ship. He needed to check the others and make sure they stayed in line.

As Two walked along the ships of the fleet headed to his, Security Two and Navigator Two came abreast of him. "So how many do we have, Security?" he asked as they strolled along, meaning how many ships he had in his control.

"We have five now, Leader. Leader Four has not said as yet. He is being careful, as am I. I have gotten closer to persuade him, but he needs a push."

Leader Two furrowed his brow at that. Sometimes Security's pushes could be extreme, no matter how menial he made them sound.

"I don't think we should chance any, let's say, bad accidents on Leader Four or his ship. It may cause an adverse reaction, one we can't afford now," Navigator said, reading the leader's mind and voicing the same concern running through Leader Two's mind.

"Navigator has it right. We don't need to push anyone just yet. We still have an advantage. Besides, Leader One has been conspicuously absent of late. He makes me nervous."

They all gave a nod and humph.

As if saying his name aloud were to conjure him, Leader One stepped out from a stack of specimen crates. Leader Two and his group gave out a surprised chirp and stopped with surprised looks on their faces.

"Easy there. It's just me, not a Greelock, after all." Leader One had a smug look on his face. It made Leader Two's stomach sour, giving him an obvious frown. "We haven't talked in a while, Two," One said with a hint of disgust as he said Two.

"To the glory of the commander, I suppose we have just been pulled in separate arcs on his mission," Two said, able to pull a smirk on his face, recovering from the initial surprise.

"Ah yes, I suppose it's true then. But I thought after Three went rogue, I should check in with you and see if you needed anything," One said with a touch of suspicion in his tone.

Two furrowed his brow. "Are you accusing me of going rogue or siding with Three?" he said with a bit of venom behind it.

"No. As yet, there is no reason to. Is there?" One said pointedly.

"Yet? Yet if you have something to prove me traitorous to the commander, you had better bring it forward or I have a right to a challenge. And if it isn't shown I am disloyal, you will lose your position, One." Two leaned in closer to One's face and, with a sneer, continued, "I would be glad to have you accuse me once more so I can see you piloting Ship Thirteen." A grievous slight since Thirteen did not exist but was thought of as the cabin-boy position.

One's color changed, and not in a good way. He jutted his face inches from Two and growled. "Step easy, Two," he spit out. "I am One! Know your position, and having stood for the traitor's crew members, you are close to being traitorous! I would enjoy a falling of yours any way it comes about!"

They stared deadly daggers at each other, neither blinking. One growled and turned and stormed off to his ship.

Two stayed in his exact position, not moving until One and his men were out of sight. He then straightened and smirked. Behind that smirk, he was shaking inside. That had been too close.

Security stood next to him, quietly chirping anger and blood-lust at Two's side.

Two noted that and patted him on the shoulder. "There will be a time, I promise, my friend."

CHAPTER 13

HORIZON

Master Sergeant Robin Lincoln needed to get some fresh air to clear his head, so he snuck through the hangar and took the stairs topside. Exiting out the door, he could feel a soft breeze come off the ocean and smell the salt in the air. He inhaled deeply and felt better. He heard the waves crashing against the retaining wall about a hundred yards from the hangar. He decided to stroll over and watch the ocean for a bit.

As he got close, he saw a figure sitting on the wall, looking out over the ocean, feet hanging off the wall. He recognized the Space Force army combat uniforms, and as he got closer, he could see it was a woman with her hair in a ponytail. As he approached, he could tell it was Technical Sergeant Andrews. He cleared his throat as he got close to her to avoid scaring her—his luck she would fall off the wall into the ocean.

She didn't jump, but she did turn to see who it was. When she did, she smiled at Robin. He found himself blushing and smiling back. Why he was blushing, he had no idea.

"Afternoon, Master Sergeant," she said pleasantly.

"Afternoon, Andrews. Um, do you mind if I pull up a stone there and sit?" he asked, pointing to the wall next to her.

"Please do. Just clearing my head. Something about the salt air and the power of the sea," she said as she squinted out, looking to the surf and the horizon beyond.

"Yeah, I know what you mean. I smelled the salt air and thought the same thing." He was staring at her, seeing her not for the first time but in a different light maybe. He felt like he was staring too long, and he didn't want her to think he was weird, so he looked out over the ocean to the horizon like she was.

He was thinking something was different with her. He had seen her over a dozen times since they started setting up the base. He stole another look at her, and she turned and smiled at him. He blushed and looked away quicker. She seemed to giggle a little and just looked back out over the ocean.

Crap, he thought, *now she thinks I'm an idiot. Maybe I should say something. No, she would think I'm creepy or just guilty of staring. Well, I was, but I don't want her to think that.*

"I cannot believe we actually proved there are aliens, can you?" she asked, not looking away from the horizon.

Whew, he thought, *better, not awkward.* "I know. I haven't really had time to let it sink in, you know. I just accepted it and kept going," he said, trailing off in thought about it.

"Funny, but I can see how that would be. I mean with the way it was kind of forced on you, with no time to sit and think, I bet this is your first time just doing that," she said.

He liked the sound of her voice. It was sweet but comfortable. He hadn't realized that as many times as he heard it.

"Yep. I don't know if I should be afraid to think about it or not. I mean I lived through it. But can my brain take the sudden jolt of all that I have encountered? Does that sound stupid?" he asked as he stared out at the ocean.

"Nope, not stupid at all. Actually, it sounds like the opposite to me," she said and fell quiet. He actually felt good she thought that.

He realized they had fallen into a moment of contemplation. He felt her turn and look at him. He didn't want to turn to disturb her or make her stop. Something about her looking at him, appraising him, made him feel jittery inside.

He turned after a few minutes and looked at her. She was still looking at him, and she had a cute and contemplative smile on her face. It was beautiful. He could not recall having seen anything as lovely. He felt like he had a stupid goofy grin on his face, but he didn't care. He could not pull his eyes away from her eyes. He let his eyes read every bit of her face. He needed to take her in to preserve in his mind the memory of this moment.

He was guessing she was doing the same, for she did not take her eyes off his, and he could tell she was scanning his entire face the same way.

They somehow had moved their hands together, and he realized he was covering hers with his. Her skin felt so warm, and it made him tingle on his palm. He didn't want to remove it, but it was wrong. They barely had talked or knew each other outside of duty.

He lowered his eyes and brushed his hand away. "I'm sorry. I didn't mean to just grab your hand like that. I apologize. I'm not like that, Andrews," he said as he felt that damn heat of blush again. He had to stop that.

He could see her smile out of the corner of his eyes, and she reached over with her hand and placed it over his. The warmth ran up his arm and somehow worked it down into his gut where it made it all fluttery.

"Please call me Louise. I don't think you're like that at all, and I think I grabbed your hand as much as you grabbed mine, Master Sergeant," she said in the sweetest words he could have heard at that moment.

"Please call me Robin. Thank you, Louise." He rolled his hand into hers and held it in his and lightly squeezed as she did the same. It was absolutely the most wonderful feeling. He had never felt it before. Just holding her hand was beyond anything he had felt before.

She leaned into him, and he leaned toward her. Her lips lightly touched his, and she pressed in a little bit more. Then leaning back, she said, "Robin, I have to go back down. I don't want to. I could sit here forever with you." She blushed this time. "I'm sorry. That's too much, isn't it?"

"No, not enough at all. Forever would be too short, Lou. How about we eat dinner up here together tonight? I'll grab some things from the mess hall." The words came out of his mouth without any thought, just pure impulse, so unlike him.

She smiled. "Really? Are you sure?" Her smile melted his heart. It was so beautiful.

"Really. Say yes, Lou," he said.

She giggled. "You know, twice now, you called me Lou."

He looked on the verge of panic. "Oh my god, I'm sorry. It just happened. I didn't—"

She took her finger and put it onto his lips to quiet him. "I know. It was wonderful. I love it. No one has ever called me that. It…just…feels right."

He smiled, and his chest grew tight. He felt on top of the world right then and there.

He jumped up and helped her to her feet, thankfully not dropping her into the water. He walked with her back down inside and headed back to his office. He wasn't sure if his trip up had cleared his head or clouded it, but he didn't care. He felt the best he had ever in his life.

It was around five o'clock in the evening, seventeen hundred in military time, when the team was notified of several sightings near the mountains in Alabama, well within striking distance of the base. The team scrambled into their gear, and Watcher had the bird ready to go.

As they boarded the Blackhawk, Ryan said over comms, "Hunters, online and set. Load information into the system, Lodge."

"Watcher is online and reading location. Setting up flight plan," Major Tucker added on comms.

"Roger, all units. Lodge is online and reading comms loud and clear. Information sent." Andrews paused, then said, "Watch your backs."

"Hold tight, boys, we are about to hit the gas," Tucker said as he lifted off the ground and started to dip forward to go.

Strapped in, the Blackhawk jetted forward toward the alien sightings, the Hunters ready for action, this time with the full team at full strength of twelve men.

"Okay, if we get any action, I want the six who don't have experience with the equipment to buddy up with the six of us that do, Lincoln," Major Ryan said.

"Got it, Major," Lincoln responded as he used his AI to make buddy assignments for the team to be displayed in the head-up display. As each member accepted their assignment, a green check appeared in Lincoln's head-up display, noting the acceptance. All checked in. The team was ready to go.

*****

Leader One had set down in a valley as he saw a group of humans. Through his study of their habits, he knew it was a hiking party, one had said. There were ten of them, male and female, which was fine. They both would bring profit, especially as fit as they were.

One and his men had snuck around their camp just before dawn and paralyzed them all. Crew Member Fifteen 15 was coming from the ship with transport sleds. They would be piled up on the sleds and their gear on another and brought to the ship. Some of his fellow slavers didn't realize there was a huge market for the gear the humans had. One was above the rest in profits because he recognized all avenues of profit. This was why he was Leader One, although soon Commander was going to get rid of Commander Seven and place One there.

Leader One picked up a stick thing. It had a point and a handle. It was some sort of metal. He poked Crew Member Twelve and was rewarded by him jumping in the air. Leader One and a few others laughed as they watched him.

Fifteen finally arrived with the sleds, and Leader One started directing the fleshy human loading onto the sleds, as he detailed three other crew to round up the humans' equipment and start loading it on the other sled.

*****

Senior Sergeant Doug White was nicknamed Grumpy, mostly because he hated mornings and could barely hold a conversation till two cups of coffee but was one hell of an operator and medic to boot. He most likely could have been a doctor, but the military fit him much better. Right now fit him much better, he thought, as the AI-assisted aiming brought a bulbous head into his sights. He tracked it as its head bobbed around, picking up gear around the hikers' campsite.

"Hunter Eight, wait" was all that Lincoln said. He could sense the man next to him tensing for the shot. It's not that he didn't want to shoot the little jerks himself, but the team needed to be set in position. And Hunters One and Eleven were almost there, but not yet. Lincoln also now knew that Grumpy had a grudge to work off. Usually, he wouldn't have to watch over his men, but knowing how personal it was now made a difference. As operators, they were detached, but some things, you just couldn't detach from, like being abducted.

White closed his eyes for a second, took a deep breath, calmed himself, and took up the sight picture again; but he knew he could feel his control. "Hunter Eight to Hunter Three, I am ice."

"As usual, all right, Hunters, get on it. Hunter One, give the command on your mark." Knowing that One was almost in place with Eleven, Lincoln wanted all of them to sight in on a target, which would then be marked on the head-up display, so everyone had a different target.

They had been inserted by Watcher about a half mile out and made their way to the target silently. They had a horseshoe formation around the camp, in an attempt to ambush the eighteen or so aliens on the ground. They didn't mind if the aliens headed back to their ship, as long as the human cargo was stopped from being taken. Either way, they were going to prove to the aliens this was a costly endeavor.

Leader One felt a twinge on the back of his neck. He stood up as straight as he could and slowly turned in a 360-degree arc, looking out into the wood line. Something was not right. His senses felt something, but he could not say what it was.

Major Ryan just got into a kneeling position and took up a sight picture. He put his mark on the one in the center. It looked like it was directing the others. No sooner had he fixed it than it reared straight up and turned in a circle. It looked like a deer when it smelled something and got spooked. "Shit, Hunters, fire! They are going to rabbit!" No sooner did Ryan give the command over the comms than the center alien turned and ran for the spaceship, chirping out a high-pitched sound, obviously an alert.

Leader One knew something was wrong. He could not define it. It just made an itching feeling under his skin. Then he caught a flash of light from a small corner of his eye, the part that saw into infrared spectrum. It was about the size of a pinhead, but an early warning.

He switched his sight to infrared and saw the crisscrossing beams of light across the whole camp and marked on his men. He drew his weapon and turned to head to the protection of the ship, yelling for his men to ready weapons and head for the ship. No sooner did he take a few steps than he felt a concussive force fly by his head, knocking him to the ground. He had been turning and running off-balance. That probably saved his life as a second projectile passed where he had been. He flopped over and started firing wildly into the wood line while trying to get to his feet.

In a kneeling position, firing all over in any direction, he could see nine of his men had fallen by the attack already. He stood, fired, and ran again for his ship and the cover of the weapons it held.

Major Ryan had taken his shot but missed, and it knocked the alien down as he had led it with the second shot, again another miss. Two beams shot in his direction, one blowing a bark and a limb from a tree next to his head, which knocked him over on his back.

White was ready when the order came. He fired and was rewarded with the alien head exploding in a mist of blue, covering an alien right next to it, freaking the thing out; but that only lasted another second as he put it out of its misery, this time firing center mass, and rewarded it with a large hole being forced into its chest.

Lincoln had fallen his target, but the rest started laying down fire and moving in groups back to the ship.

The first contact had pared the aliens down to almost equal numbers now, but it was unclear who had the superior weaponry.

The Hunters had their heads temporarily pinned down as the aliens finally reacted and started laying down a great deal of return fire. They didn't have any targets, which made it worse. They were just firing in all directions.

The woods were exploding, with trees, bark, leaves, limbs, and branches flying all over the place. The one thing that was to the advantage to the Hunters was that the aliens were firing about three to four feet off the ground, so getting into the prone position was the safest place on the battlefield right now.

Now the Hunters had adjusted and figured it out. They went prone and started to fire back again, getting some to turn and run, decreasing the suppressive fire from the aliens.

Three more aliens dropped before they were able to take cover in the surrounding woods and tried to make for their ship.

Leader One could still hear projectiles zooming past him, so he knew he wasn't out of range, but he was out of view directly by the plants around him. He stopped from time to time behind the large thick foliage to shoot a few beams at the attackers. He saw his men doing the same. "Ship, this is Leader. Get up and head over to our location. We need to have you lay fire on these humans. I want this now!" he yelled into his comm unit.

"Yes, Leader!" was the reply.

He heard the ship power up and knew it was going to be up and moving to their direction any moment.

Watcher was moving on the right side of the battle slowly and quietly, heading back to the ship to keep it pinned down without alerting it. Major Tucker knew once that thing got up to move and was clear, they could not pursue it, so the best bet was to hit it either on the ground or when it had to slow to pick up the aliens it left on the ground. "Lodge, I have movement of the large target. Going to try to maneuver in to stop it from backing up the contacts and pinning down the Hunters."

"Watcher, stand by. Hold cover for the Hunters. I have a surprise for the large target," Andrews said. She sounded a little upbeat.

Tucker pulled back the Blackhawk from moving forward toward the ship. He didn't feel right letting that ship head toward the Hunters, but he either had to have confidence in Lodge or not. He hovered for a minute as he made his choice. Apache stared at him, waiting for his choice. He would back him either way.

"Watcher, can you hit that thing with a laser? We're coming in hot and want a snapshot for final approach for strike," an unfamiliar voice said over the comm channel.

"Watcher One to last unit, identify please." Tucker was a bit angry. He was the wing commander and did not like knowing who was possibly messing with his air operation.

"Watcher One, this is newly activated Lima Thirteen Alpha, Gunner. One minute out and hot," the same voice said.

"Okay, Apache, light that thing up. Seems we got a new wing unit just reassigned," Tucker said, just a little irritated.

"Aye, sir, hitting it," Apache said as he painted the alien ship with a laser targeting system.

"Watcher One, Lima Thirteen Bravo, coming online. Hammer, in the mix, on the wing of Gunner," a second voice came over the comms.

Tucker shook his head. *Okay, two units, but what kind? What the heck was a Lima anyways?* "Roger, Hammer, Gunner. Do you have the picture now?" he asked as he saw the readout on the display that they had full targeting paint on the alien ship.

"Whoop! Yes, Sir Watcher. And boy, is she pretty? Nothing like your first time is there," came the happy voice of Gunner as the engine roared in the background.

"Damn, that's not a copter. That's a fighter, sir," Jenkins said on the cabin comm line to the crew.

"I know that engine sound. That is a Lightning," Burgess chimed in, sounding like a kid on Christmas morning. "They sent us the big boys."

"We are the big boys, Four. They are our attack dogs," Tucker said. Even though the comms were the most secure anywhere, caution was always used to only use call signs on mission—no names.

As the Hunters moved cautiously forward, keeping the pressure on the aliens, who were backing toward their ship, they heard a growing roar from above. When they checked with the head-up display, there were two objects, green dots, headed in fast to their location.

Watcher One caught sight of the two black streaks coming in. They fired missiles at the ship and did barrel rolls over and under each other, avoiding lancing beams from the ship as they fired a second volley and broke off wide as the alien ship missed with more shots.

Burgess was an F-35 Lightning II fanatic. He loved those fighters, but he had never seen any move as fast or as agile as those two had. They had to be supped up like their Blackhawk was.

All the participants—aliens, Hunters, and Watchers—saw the strike pass in only seconds. The rockets hit the ship. The first set hit the shielding, but the second hit the hull. Four holes appeared in the hull, jetting flame and smoke. Metal debris flew in all directions. The ship flipped end over end and straight into the ground. A few secondary explosions roared from the ship as plumes of flames spewed from the gaping holes.

Leader One stood on the edge of a clearing as he was prepared for his ship to pick him up. Instead, he stood there agape with distress as his ship was completely destroyed. Five of his crewmen had made it to his side. He heard the battle raging behind him.

Leader One blinked, and then he looked straight out. And a ship, one of his fleet, was there with the door open. For a second, he thought he was hallucinating. Then he saw Leader Four in the door, yelling at them to get inside. He ran and jumped inside, followed by the five crew that had made it. When they were all in, the door closed, and the ship burst out into space, the inertial dampeners saving them from being turned inside out from the acceleration.

Leader One leaned against the ship's hull and slid down to the floor, sitting. He could not accept his ship was lost, and to top it, some of his crew were still down there. He had no idea how many he had left behind.

Lincoln and Wild Bill took their partners and moved around the cornered aliens. Ryan and Doolie moved around the opposite side. Hunters Two and Twelve moved from the bottom while Hunters Five and Hunter Ten were able to get out in front and close the circle around the remaining.

It appeared that five had been left behind. The aliens were down to three when they threw down their weapons. Apparently, surrender was universal. The Hunters came in ready for a trick, but the three aliens just stood there, shivering. Fear was universal too, it appeared.

"Watcher, put down in the clearing. Lodge, we have three contacts in custody. We need a transport for these. What do you have?" Major Ryan said over the comms.

"Lodge to Hunter One, we have a pet carrier. It will accommodate your needs. Mover is on his way, as well as Hawk and Falcon for escort. The Lodge is cleaning up for visitors. Proceed to usual door." Andrews was level voiced this time.

"Lodge, status on Gunner and Hammer," Major Tucker asked.

"Watcher, they are back in the barn. They caught target 2 for a moment, then lost visual," Andrews said.

"Roger that, Lodge. Surprised they even got a peek."

"Watcher, we're rolling in now, but we almost had a parting shot. Just need a bit more kick on these rides," the voice of Gunner came across.

They stayed in the cockpit, ready to go, just inside their hangar at base, in case an intercept was needed. They would do so till Mover touched down and went below.

Gunner was Captain Alan "Race" Pollard, newly appointed Space Force special operations fighter pilot, the first one ever given the position. The second was his wingman, Captain Robert "Chill" Keller, whose unit call sign was Hammer. The F-35s they flew were the new creations of Thirteenth Scientific Research and Development. Normal F-35s, only now supped up with highly technical and advanced modifications. The engines had been retooled and at the limit a human could safely fly it with g-forces. The weapons were modified impact electronic missiles, twice the speed of any other missiles known. The guns on board were modified to be the hyper rounds.

Lincoln, Ryan, and Tanaka watched the prisoners as the rest of the team went to secure the alien shipwreck. Major Ryan shooed them over to sit on a grouping of rocks. They still were shivering out of fear.

Lincoln raised his face shield and looked them over. "Do you speak our language? Any Earth language?" he asked them and then again in French and German.

141

Tanaka asked in Portuguese and Italian. Ryan asked in Spanish and Russian. The aliens either didn't speak or understand any languages or were too scared, and of course, there was the possibility they just didn't want to let them know.

Well, this was a part of the mission they really didn't think would be upon them till they had time to study the things they already captured.

"Do you find it scary how much success we have had against these guys?" Chief Tanaka asked the other two.

"Yes and no, we obviously have the home ground. But think of it this way, they have for how long had the run of things, no interference whatsoever from us humans. Now here we are fighting back with major effort," Lincoln said, obvious that he had contemplated the same thing earlier.

"What we have to do now is not to get complacent. They are going to get the fact that we are going to be pushing them back. We know what happens when someone gets pushed. It's a universal law of action and reaction. At the molecular level, no reason to think these guys are not going to keep doing what they are doing." Major Ryan pointed his weapon at them as he was saying it. They seemed to shake a bit more. "I just hope we are prepared for the reaction. I think it will be a bit more than a push."

The wump of the Chinook sounded in the distance. The transport for these three prisoners was almost there.

Mover landed in the clearing as Watcher took off and held guard position with the two Little Birds. The alien ship had been a total loss. The thing burned out intensely inside. The cleanup crew from the Thirteenth Science and Research Development unit had arrived with large trucks to move the ship and the alien bodies back to base. The team walked the three aliens inside where a metal cage had been rolled in and secured to the cargo deck.

Polansky and White took great pleasure in holding the cage door and prodding the aliens inside. It went a long way at healing them as they were now allowed to be the captors. Shooting a bunch of them earlier was therapeutic also.

The Hunters loaded up into the Chinook and sat around the cage to keep an eye on the aliens, who huddled together in the center of the cage. The Hunters did not expect any trouble but were always prepared because trouble always waited till you weren't expecting it.

Watcher and the Little Birds flew cover for Mover as they headed back to base. Gunner and Hammer sat ready to go if any alien interference came about. None did, of course, because they were ready, both the fighter pilots thought.

Landing at Lodge, they rolled into hangar 1, and the lift took them down. A larger cage with wheels was there to take the transfer of the aliens. Lincoln had been at the base longest but still wasn't sure where the aliens would be kept.

Unlike before, the team rode down in the helicopter, staying with the alien prisoners, who just stared at the Hunters and Mover crew. When the lift reached the bottom and the cover slid back in place above the lift, the back ramp lowered, and several of the Space Force military police members were there to secure the aliens.

First Lieutenant Troy was there among them as well as Colonel Rivera and Major Johnson. Sergeant Major Whitfield was not on hand; Lincoln heaved a sigh of relief.

The military police went inside and helped loose the holding straps from the helicopter deck. The wheels were unlocked, and they rolled it down the ramp as the Hunters headed out first and gathered below, still armored up and ready in case any surprise was to happen.

Once into the hangar bay, the major directed the cage to the rear of the room to a roll-up door in the up position. It led to a larger corridor with bays off it, apparently for large vehicles to be brought in out of the main hangar to be worked on or whatever was needed to be done.

The last bay on the left of the corridor had a steel vault door affixed to it, and it stood open. The cage or cell was wheeled in, and a larger habitat cell was staged in the center. The larger cell had cameras mounted to poles all around it and on top of the cell. A monitoring booth hung directly over the cell from the high ceiling. As well as two more booths on each side of the cell far against each wall. The cell sat dead center.

Lieutenant Troy pointed to the interior of the main cell and said, "So we approximated the interior furnishings from what we were able to see on their ship. As well as facilities they may need. We hope they or we are able to find a means of communication so we may tailor the surroundings to their needs."

He was interrupted by Hunter Eight, "Like it matters if their needs are met, the evil little bastards." Lincoln put an armored hand on his shoulder.

Colonel Rivera turned toward White. Lieutenant Troy looked aghast.

Major Ryan spoke up, "Colonel, pardon my man. He has had a prior incident way back that has left a raw spot in reference to the aliens."

Tanaka spoke to his AI, "Restrict White's access to speaker and internal net outside our team. Hey, White, it's okay. We know, and we will not let them be pampered, okay?"

White gritted his teeth behind his face shield and nodded his helmeted head. Only the team had heard Tanaka. Lincoln patted White's shoulder with the hand, which he still kept on it.

Tanaka opened a line to Polansky. "You okay, buddy?"

"Yeah, I'm good" was what Polansky replied, sounding anything but.

"Understood, Major. Perhaps limiting exposure to the aliens for those with concerns should be enforced," Colonel Rivera said. It would be the same procedure he would take for a prisoner of war, well, a human prisoner of war, since this was a true war with the aliens.

"Yes, sir, I think that would probably be wise. I will send half the team back to our section to work on the gear. Master Sergeant Lincoln, SFC Junius, and myself and my weapons sergeants will hold here while we transfer the prisoners. For security, Chief Tanaka will head back with the rest of the team," Ryan said.

"Good. Continue on, Major" was the only reply the colonel gave as he turned his attention back to the task at hand.

Tanaka took the rest of the team back to their section, and they hit the armory to clean and secure their equipment as well as shower and change into army combat uniforms.

A bridge between the cell and the transport cage was placed between the two. It was locked into place, and with a tablet, one of the military police opened both doors.

The aliens didn't move. They sat huddled in the center of the transport. One guard walked over and banged on the back of the cage and walked alongside, pointing for the aliens to move into the other cell. They seemed to follow his movements and seemed to get the idea. Lincoln thought he caught a glimpse of fury on one of their faces, but it subsided as soon as he saw it. That quick. It made Lincoln a little uneasy, but then they all moved into the new cell, and they shuffled around so that he couldn't tell which one was which. The aliens started chirping and making several different noises as they walked around their new residence. None of them showed any more behavior different from one another as Lincoln had seen a minute ago.

The door to the cell closed, and the bridge was removed. The transport cell was rolled out and put into the hangar where it could be used expediently if needed in a similar situation.

The Hunters remaining in the room just watched the aliens for a moment. It was hard to compute the things in that cell being so cold to do the things they had been doing. One by one, the Hunters each shook their heads and walked out of the room to head back to their section.

Major Ryan stayed and removed his helmet and stood next to Colonel Rivera.

"How many, Steve?" Rivera asked, not taking his eyes from the aliens, who were busy strolling around their cell, looking at things.

"Two, sir. We found out just before we headed out. They did fine out there, but we have to do something about some mental checks," Major Ryan said, standing next to the colonel.

Neither talked very loudly. They both wanted it kept quiet for the moment.

"I thought I would have more time to vet someone for that. I knew it was going to be necessary once contact started being regular with these guys, but I didn't really think about our people having been abducted," Rivera said.

"It took me off guard also. I mean I remember when it happened. It was my team on the Seventh Forces Group, and we were in Columbia. The two were out on an assignment and disappeared for two days. Then out of the blue, *bam*, back like nothing happened. All sorts of theories went out about their being missing, but this scenario was not one," Ryan said to Rivera.

"Well, I am not of the mind to pull them from duty, not at this point anyways. But I also do not want to jeopardize a whole team or unit or mission for the sake of two men." Rivera was the kind of man that didn't say things like that lightly. He knew how hard life could be, without an outside force you couldn't control, messing your life up; but he was also practical and had a duty to a lot more people and a country and, in this case, a whole planet of people.

"I get it, sir, but give me some time. I will evaluate them. And if needed, I will have them sit out the next mission. My word," Ryan said.

"Good enough for me. Just be biased, okay?" Rivera said, finally looking at his junior officer.

"Yes, sir. I was trained by one of the best. You can count on me." Ryan gave a slight smirk to the colonel.

"Suck up, good thing you didn't say one of the best. Get the hell out of here," Rivera said as he hit Ryan on the arm. He forgot he was still in armor and winced. The two officers laughed, and Ryan moved out.

Once Ryan left, Major Johnson came up next to the colonel.

"Want me to keep an eye on that situation and step in if I need to?" Johnson asked.

"Major," Rivera said very flatly and paused for effect, "I, and particularly we, do not operate like that. Copy." The tone left no room for any interpretation than a resounding no.

"Yes, sir, I copy" was all he said. And to his credit, he didn't try to make any further argument for himself or the question. He received his answer and dropped it. That was how Colonel Rivera operated.

Ryan made it to the armory, showered, changed, cleaned, and put away his gear. He stopped at White's room as he checked with

Charlene to locate White and Polansky. He knocked on the door and heard, "Come in."

Standing in the doorway, he leaned on the jamb. White was putting his clothes into the closet or locker and dresser.

"Look, Major, I'm okay. I admit I was out of line back there and a bit jumpy to shoot in the field, but I'm okay."

Ryan just looked at him and measured him up for a minute. "Okay, I'll trust you. And if you tell me you're okay, I can go with that. If at any point you are not all right, you need to tell Lincoln, Junius, Tanaka, or me. But most importantly, take yourself out and sit on the bench. You know how dangerous it can be if you are not 100 percent out there, and this is not the time to see. Do you copy me, and do you agree to be up-front?"

White sat down on his bed and looked at his hands for a moment. "Look, I would be lying if I said I don't want revenge because I do. But I also am a professional. I can separate the two. I pledge everything to this team. I'm a damn good operator and a damn good medic. I swear I will let you know how I'm doing, and I promise to take myself out if I can't hack it," White said, staring straight at Ryan's eyes.

Ryan stood up straight and held White's eyes. "Okay, as always, I hold you at your word." He nodded and turned and left. End of discussion.

Ryan found Polansky heading to the mess hall and had the same conversation.

"Look, sir, I have a lot of pent-up anger, but I cope with it by working out and hitting the range. As long as I do that, I'm good, not perfect but good."

"Good, keep at it and let me know if anything changes," Ryan said as he turned and headed to his office, allowing Polansky to go get some food.

Ryan looked down to check his unit tablet he had been given to manage his work on the go, when he was knocked into by a rushing Robin Lincoln, going past, rushing to the mess hall. "What the hell, Master Sergeant? There a special in the mess?" he said as he turned to see the back of Lincoln.

"Uh, sorry, boss. Kind of in a hurry," Lincoln said over his shoulder and continued into the mess hall.

Ryan just shook his head. He didn't want to ask anything else. He didn't want to know. This time, he paid attention where he was going and headed back to his office.

As Major Ryan got to the entrance to his section, he was almost knocked over by Sergeant Major Whitfield. "Sergeant Major," Ryan said, surprised to see him come out of his unit area.

"Ryan," he said as he went to pass the younger man.

Major Ryan grabbed his arm by the bicep as he tried to hurry by.

"What do you think you're doing?" the sergeant major asked in an angry tone. And he tried to pull away, but Ryan's grip was too strong he saw the sergeant major wince as he squeezed it tighter to hold him.

"No, Sergeant Major, that is my question," now Ryan said, a bit of edge to his voice. And he didn't loosen his grip.

"Let go. This is my unit to command you—" Whitfield's face had turned red with anger.

"Ah! Before you finish that thought and really say something more stupid than you have, shut up!" Ryan said and stared down the man. His jaw clenched tight with anger. "I don't know where you were before or who you had as officers. But in my army, we show and use respect for officers, especially in the chain of command. I will not tolerate the kind of behavior you just showed." Ryan stopped as he let that sink in, and he stared him down, daring him to talk back again. "Now this is my command area, *Sergeant* Major. I am a major without the 'sergeant.' That means I outrank you! You will not enter this area without my permission under any circumstances. You just wore out your welcome. If you have a problem with that or me, see LTC Rivera and me at your court-martial. Now, before you answer, try your best to use that little brain of yours. Do you understand what I just said and my command I gave you?" Ryan said, letting go of his arm, which Whitfield grabbed and rubbed.

He stared at the officer who had squared himself to the man and stared death back at him. Ryan could see the thoughts churning behind his beady eyes. Then he watched as he concluded he would not win this. He looked away, then down, and swallowed. He stood up straighter, almost to attention, "Yes, sir, I understand. By your leave, sir." He sounded contrite till he put an emphasis to the "sir," and Ryan wanted to punch him.

"Charlie," Ryan said, not taking his eyes off Whitfield.

"Yes, Major Ryan," the AI responded.

"Did you record and save that interaction and log it for me?"

"Yes, sir, it is in your daily duty log."

"Thank you, Charlie. Oh, and do me a favor. Put a block on the sergeant major from entering this sector unless I provide authorization or Colonel Rivera."

"Done, sir." The AI had a slight humor to its voice.

"Whitfield, you have any other comments to add, or will you be on your way?" Ryan said, a slight smirk on his face.

Whitfield knew he was thoroughly beat and humiliated, and his face was redder than a tomato. But he just swallowed again and pulled his lips tight and shut. He came to proper attention and saluted the major.

"Carry on" was all he said to the sergeant. He saluted and waited for him to turn and leave.

The section door, usually left open, was closed as he entered it and headed for his office.

"Major, would you like to review the sergeant major's actions while in this section?" Charlene asked.

"Yes. Please have it spun up on my office computer when I get there," he replied. He was very curious as to what he was doing.

Sitting down at the desk, he went to access the file that Charlene had placed there. As he went to highlight and open it, the system crashed and booted back up. When the computer finished, the file was gone. "Charlie, what the hell just happened?" he asked, very confused, as he searched the screen for sign of the file that was just there.

"I don't know, Major. I was shut out of the system for a moment. I can't explain it. The file is gone. I can't find any record saved anywhere." The AI seemed very distressed about the incident.

"Is that possible, Charlie, for you to be looped out? I mean, can you see any trace of who or how it was done?" Ryan asked, genuinely concerned at the turn of events.

"It appears so, Major. If you had asked before this, I would have said no, but now…" the AI trailed off, obviously in doubt of what it thought was facts.

"Quietly, Charlie, I want you to poke around and see if you can find out anything. But keep it between you and me and Master Sergeant Lincoln for the moment, okay?"

"Yes, Major. I find that a wise course of action. I will quietly see what I can find out."

Major Ryan would like to point a finger at Whitfield as being the cause, but he didn't believe the man had the skill nor the opportunity to have accomplished the feat in the amount of time.

*****

Leader One had gotten himself to the medical bay, where he had directed the doctor to give him a relaxing shot to calm his nerves. Seeing his ship destroyed in that way was unsettling. *How could the humans act that way? They never had done anything like this. It was unheard of. The pure act itself was unbelievable from the lesser beings.* "Four, go directly to base. We need to take action. Commander needs to be informed now!" Leader One said as he walked into the command deck.

"One, Leader Two has asked to meet him at collection point 3," Leader Four said.

Rage appeared on Leader One's face. He drew his sidearm and blasted Four's head off. The body slumped to the deck out of the command chair.

Leader One stalked to the chair. As he got there, he was glad to see Navigator One step next to the chair and, with a cloth, wiped the seat of Four.

Leader One turned to the crew, who shook at their positions. "I give an order. I do not expect any hesitation!" He furrowed his brow and stared down each crewman. "Now this is Ship One. You are Crew One, *my crew*! Navigator One is my right hand and your navigator. Adjust yourselves down as expected." He looked around in complete control.

"Course set for base, Leader," Navigator One said as he took the number 2 position of command.

"Excellent. Now get me there!" Leader One leaned back. He looked down to his elbow. Seeing a piece of Leader Four on the armrest, he flicked it off, with a smirk spreading across his face.

*****

Robin Lincoln came out onto the pavement from the false hangar. He carried a cooler he had "appropriated" from the mess hall, along with a mix of foods he could get ahold of and a blanket he took off a vacant room he found along the way. It was dark out, about eight o'clock at night. The moon sat over the water, twinkling in reflection as the water splashed the retaining wall.

He looked around and didn't see Andrews anywhere. *Lou*, he corrected himself. They were off duty and not in the same chain of command, thank god, or they would never be. He swallowed as that thought ran through his mind. He didn't like it.

He blinked as he stared out at the water. How had he got here? He talked to her a handful of times. Now his heart raced when he thought of her. Then when he thought of not seeing her, his heart hurt, pretty hard too. When had it happened? He couldn't remember. It just was.

"Hey, you forget what you were doing?" a soft voice came from behind him.

He shook his head. He didn't hear her come up behind him. He was so lost in thought. The voice made a goofy grin grow on his face, and he blushed, grateful it was so dark. "How could I? It was all I was thinking about as soon as we got back," he said in a soft voice as she walked from behind him and put her fingers on his shoulder as she moved directly in front of him.

She leaned in and up the few inches. He was taller than her. And she whispered, "Good answer," and gave him a slight kiss on the cheek and as quickly turned and walked away down the side of the retaining wall.

There was a picnic table a few hundred yards away from the last hangar. He hadn't noticed it before now, but it didn't surprise him.

He jogged to catch up and walk next to her as soon as he regained his composure after her kiss.

*****

A message came in to Ship Four, which was now Ship One. It was Leader Two.

"Put it on the screen," Leader One said, smiling at the surprise Leader Two was going to have.

"I said to come to collection point 3. Why are you heading out of atmosphere?" he said in a very sharp, angry tone.

"Ah, not unlike you to demand what you cannot have, Two!" he issued with a bit of spite. Two looked up, and his mouth fell open. It was worth the loss of his ship and crew just for that moment. "Yes, Two, this is Ship One now. And whatever your plan was, it is over. I will be at base, and Commander will be eager to hear my report." He waved his hand to have the signal cut, and it was leaving Two with a very curious face, a bit dread and fear and confusion. Leader One threw his head back and laughed as hard as he could.

*****

Robin strolled back into the unit with his head in the clouds. For the first time, he had spent a relaxing enjoyable evening with a woman and was completely relaxed. He didn't worry about upsetting her, scaring her, or trying to impress her. They were just themselves, open and raw in each other's company.

"Major, the master sergeant is back in the unit area," Charlene said, notifying him as he had asked.

"Thanks, Charlie." He quickly subvocalized to his personal AI to open a comm straight to Lincoln. "Wait, is the master sergeant Robin Lincoln humming?" Ryan's voice sounded in Robin's ear.

He looked around, and his AI prompted it was an internal connection. "Yes, yes, I was" was all he said as he continued walking to his room. He had dropped off the cooler and items back in the mess hall.

"Why?"

"No reason."

"That means it's a woman."

"No."

"Yes!" Ryan said with a little emphasis.

"So what was it that made you jump in my head?" Robin said, changing the subject.

"We had a visitor earlier," the major said it with a bit of irritation.

"Whitfield!" As soon as he said it, he looked around as if the mention of his name would conjure him out of thin air.

"First guess on the nose."

"What was he doing?"

"That is the puzzling thing. I had Charlie ban him and spool up the footage of him in our area." Ryan paused a beat.

"And?" Lincoln said as he waited for the rest of the details.

"We had a strange surge, and the file was deleted from the system along with all copies. And to boot, Charlie was blacked out for the time." Ryan genuinely sounded fearful.

"Huh? That seems impossible. Yet there it is. Charlie, I assume, didn't have any ideas. What did Whitfield say when you saw him?" Lincoln was curious as to what was Whitfield's excuse.

"He was caught in the cookie jar and acted like any bad kid. He tried to bully me but ended up just getting red-faced and contrite." Ryan smiled at that memory, and it came through in his voice when he relayed that last bit.

"Shit, Major, I can't see how he did that. I have never known him to have that skill or be that good at anything."

"I know. Plus, he didn't have enough time to do that kind of thing. He had just left me and would not have even been back to HQ hub, let alone to somewhere, to access the system," Ryan said, leaving the two puzzled at the situation. "Well, it gave me cause to bar him from our section and to court-martial him for insubordination if we had any other incidents with him. But that was all I could do for now." Ryan paused and thought for a moment. And he added, "No, Lincoln, you cannot shoot him."

"No fun" was all Lincoln responded with.

*****

Ship One entered the space dock of the Aldion moon base, tethered. And Leader One exited by himself to see Commander One. He left Navigator One to get the crew and ship in order and be ready upon his return.

It was now he felt the loss of his most trusted Security One. With him at his back, he did not have a worry at all. Security had agents everywhere; he was a master at his craft.

Leader One strode into the command room and greeted Commander One. He was ready to start conferring with him, when Commander One held up a hand for him to wait. He took the signal from Commander and stood straight, showing respect as required by his position.

Commander One waved to a communications system sitting on the side. A holographic image appeared in front of him. It was of Leader Two. "What!" Commander One spit at the hologram. And he leaned threateningly forward.

The image leaned back as if the bark from the commander actually struck him over the hologram net. "Commander, I am calling to inform you of Leader One's failure," Leader Two said in a pleading tone, trying to act as the reliable soldier.

"Ha!" Commander laughed at the figure but said no more.

"Commander, I am only trying to do my duty to you and the fleet. I do not mean any disservice," he said in a continuing pleading tone.

"Two, you have never tried to serve anyone but you. I know what happened to One. Do you think I have no idea what goes on with my fleet? I think it would surprise you to know how much I do see." He stopped there and let that float in Two's mind.

It had the desired effect. Now Two was unsure how much Commander did know. Perhaps he was underestimating the commander.

As if he was reading Two's mind, he said, "Two, how do you believe I have risen to Commander? And not just a commander but the Commander One!" he stated, bringing home the fact that he was at the highest rank outside of Aldion itself.

Two stood agog with that revelation. He had never taken time to analyze his goals and who actually was going to be working against him. He had been so naïve. "Yes, Commander, I truly never took that into thought. Of course, you know." He meant that as plain on the surface but also underlying.

Commander nodded. He truly saw that Two had taken what he said and processed it. Maybe there was hope for Two to be a major ally. He knew Two controlled near half the ships of his personal fleet. What the commander needed was to take One and Two and train them to be reliable and ride to high command with them watching his back. Getting them to cooperate together would solidify his fleet and let him put them in commander position and start to build a massive fleet and power base. He just didn't know how much he could let Two in on at this moment.

"Commander, I see what you have tried to lead me to."

"Does this mean you will be beside One and not behind with a dagger?" Command offered. This was the point he either cemented his fleet or he would have to cleverly lose Two.

"Commander, I stand beside One. We should be one strong fleet. Your goal shall be ours, and we ride heights as one with you as our guide."

"True answer, Two. Now we may be about our glory to the loss of the others. As Commander, Two, and Three, we could control such a glorious profit trail." He saw the dawning realization of the ultimate plan.

Two now saw the ultimate plan unfold before him. It was not to strive for such low position. Commander was moving to control a much larger piece of the profits, with One and himself on either side of him. Now that was power.

Commander waved One up to his side so Two could see him.

Two looked on as One came into focus on the screen. He saw through new eyes he had been fighting against the way to where he wanted. One and Commander watched as Two knelt on one leg and placed both palms down and bent at the middle, lowering his frame down so his head nearly touched the floor. The ultimate position of capitulation and reverence.

"Welcome Two to the revolution. May our profits grow our glory." The commander and One nodded to him as he raised to standing. "Now return to base. I am dispatching Command Two and Three to destroy these humans who have insulted us twice. They will learn why it is unwise to meddle in our profits. We must plot our path, the three of us and our glorious fleet."

The three conspirators smiled as they shared the win-win situation. If Commander Two and Three failed, then Commander One could claim their positions with his men. If the humans were defeated, then there would be more glory to Commander One. It was brilliant.

CHAPTER 14

ACTION

Breakfast was busy in the mess hall. Everyone wanted to get in at least one full meal, and with the way things had been going since being activated, the action hadn't really stopped.

The team was all present in their army combat uniforms in a group of tables, eating and trading thoughts on the alien patterns and tactics or, as Angel said, the lack of tactics so far.

"I want to warn everyone to be on high alert on any missions now. We have given them two black eyes because they were not used to us fighting back or even recognizing the fact they existed. Now they know we are aware and are not sitting back and letting them have their way with us. I expect the next time we meet, they will be ready to exact some revenge." Major Ryan looked over his team.

They were still shoveling food into their mouths, breakfast foods with Tabasco peppered on them. Everyone's heads were nodding though. They all were experienced, and they knew once you poked the hornets' nest, the hornets were bound to take notice. The fact that these hornets had beam weapons was definitely not a good scenario.

"The fact that we have taken out two ships and prisoners, I would imagine, has put them now on the offensive to prove something to us, like stop now," Chief Tanaka said as he took a spoonful of corned beef hash.

"So are we all thinking the same thing then—the next meeting is going to be an ambush setup?" Senior Sergeant Gonzalez, Speedy, said as he took a big swig of his coffee.

"As conceited as they seem to be, yes, I think that will be their next move," Robin said as he took two sips of tomato juice.

"When are we expecting this move?" Wild Bill asked, chomping down on some rye toast.

Major Ryan looked around the table at all the men engrossed in getting a max amount of calories, and he laughed. "Well, as I look at eleven veteran operators and we all seem to be eating our fill, I think we all subconsciously know it will be real soon. The enemy does not like to wait."

"Hunter Team One," came over the comms, "we have a report of activity at coordinates 30.63406, -82222408, which is the Okefenokee National Wildlife Refuge, near the tar lake area," Andrews finished reporting.

"What's the activity?" Ryan asked as the team got up and headed for the armory.

"We have spotty signals and traces of the spaceship signals, but they are coming and going."

Ryan looked over across the mess hall and saw Major Tucker and his men getting up and heading for their ride.

"Watcher One on comms, we are headed to the bird."

"Hunter One to Watcher One, we may need to have some backup. We think this is a setup."

"Same thought, Hunter One. Just adds up. I think we may want Falcon and Hawk to be up. Gunner and Hammer will also be ready to play."

"Good to go then. I'll put two on each Little Bird."

The best part of having integrated comms with the chips was that planning on the fly was so smooth and allowed the two units to know the game plan and still get to their equipment and get ready.

"Doc and Sleepy, ride on Falcon. Grumpy and Speedy, hitch on Hawk," Ryan dispatched as he wanted his medics separated to do as much as they could to keep one up and running if a need arose. And having the engineers with them gave him some options of response.

He got a roger from each man as they finished putting on the armor and headed for the hangar to catch their rides.

The two men assigned to the Little Birds each headed to them, peeling off from the group when the Hunters arrived at the hangar. They strapped in, and both Little Birds went up two smaller lifts they stayed parked on. Once in the hangar, the blades turned, and the two small copters hovered and moved easily to the opening large hangar door. Both birds exited together and went up and waited for their larger kin, the Blackhawk, to come out next.

"Watcher One to Gunner and Hammer, go on a standby pattern off the coast parallel to our position."

"Got a feeling, boss?" Apache asked from the copilot seat as they hovered and moved out of the hangar.

"Yeah, what I would do if I was them" was all Tucker said as he hit the main engines and headed for the Okefenokee Refuge.

"Hunter One to Lodge, can you feed me real-time data on the spotty activity we are getting," Ryan said and was answered with an overlay on his helmet head-up display, showing the popping up and out of the signature energy from the aliens.

Ryan shared it with his men as they studied it. Being Special Forces, they all were adept and trained to analyze the actions of others. It was key to the role they played for the military as independent actionable units.

The Blackhawk banked to come in from the top of the state of Georgia instead of direct course. Ryan didn't have to ask Tucker to take actions like that. Tucker was as much a veteran operator as the others. He had flown dozens of special operations missions. He was still living, so he must know something about flying.

Lincoln switched his head-up display to display their course and overlay it on the traces they were receiving. He could identify the pattern they were trying to sell the team. They were laying heavy to the west, so an easy attack strategy would be coming in from the east, with the sun behind them. Which would make sense if your enemy wasn't trying to lure you into a trap.

"Falcon, come in from the west slow like and be ready for anything. Hawk, lay here at the bottom of the crescent as we make our way around the target and come from north of it." Tucker gave the assignments as he continued reading the activity.

Hunter Six put his rifle up to his shoulder. The optics on the top of the sniper rifle fed directly into his helmet head-up display. He scanned the area ahead and looked for signs of the aliens popping up like it was reading on the scans. "Hunter Six to Hunter One and all units," he said over the comms. "I'm not seeing the activity that we are reading in the scans. The target area is quiet," he reported and kept scanning.

Gonzalez was the other sniper. He performed the same actions as Doolie from his angle and position as they moved up and then east toward the target. Scanning, he didn't see anything of the aliens as he ran the rifle optics over the terrain. "Hunter Twelve to Hunter One and units, I'm not getting anything either." He sighed, "Just the whack-a-mole readings coming in." Several chuckles were let out over that report.

"What are we missing because we are not getting errant readings?" Ryan asked over the comms.

The net stayed silent as no one had any ideas at the moment. Ryan did not really want to go to the area they were getting the hits from and set down there. He knew it was a death trap, but he didn't have any other choices at the moment.

Doc Doolie was scanning when he finally caught something. It was a glint of reflection off something. The sun had hit it just right. He scoped in on it and pulled it up. "Son of a bitch," he said as he captured the image and sent it on to the comm net. "Okay, I'm tracking it now, and some others crisscrossing. Now I know the shape," he said with relief, putting a face to the culprit.

"I remember that garbage can. Almost fried me," Angel said as he looked over the still taken of the alien scout unit.

"They appear to stay hidden and fire off and move to another location to lay out a target for us, a target area of the aliens' choosing," Major Ryan said as he now considered the options.

"Lodge to all units, being advised by Bookworm that those are fully armed and dangerous. Distance is your friend on those," Andrews relayed from the Thirteenth Scientific Research and

Development. Apparently, they monitored all actions, not surprising as they would get to see the alien equipment in action.

"Hunter Six, Twelve, is it possible to hit from your spots?" Major Ryan asked.

"Aye, sir, I can hit a few from my vantage, thanks to these systems," Speedy stated as he drew a bead on one, waiting for orders.

"Yeah, I can knock off a toaster or two," Doc said as he also ranged out his shot.

"Lodge to Hunters and all field units, Bookworm states you may get unwanted attention when poking the anthills."

Crane Manning, pilot of Little Bird Hawk, spoke first, "Roger, I copy. Slip and slide after each shot. Not a problem as long as Hunters don't puke in my ride."

"Falcon, we copy. Some little dirty dancing and we're cool," Captain "Rock" Singer replied.

"Okay, Hunter Six and Twelve, do what you do," Ryan said.

Doc had his first shot lined up and took it, the hyper round hitting the alien metal and splitting it, dropping the first alien sentry robot. Quickly, he scanned for another target. When he sighted on one, he saw it launch at them. "Shit" was all he got out as the Little Bird started moving in awkward jerks. The missile flew past. The copter evened out. And he traced back to the bot, got it in sights, fired, split the bot's casing, and repeated the moves all over again.

Speedy had lined up his shot and fired. He was rewarded with a center mass shot which blew apart the sentry bot. The Little Bird started sliding and raising up and down in awkward movements, which worked as a missile went flying by. Speedy leaned out the side and sighted down the heat trail of the passing missile and fired, once again taking out a bot.

"Down!" commanded Lieutenant Dan "Crane" Manning to his two passengers and slid sideways.

The missile entered over Speedy's head, which he had between his knees after the warning, and so did Grumpy. The missile passed out through the other side of the copter, and Crane spun it around, facing the direction the missile came from.

His copilot, Lieutenant Greg "Flare" Forrester, locked in a missile of their own and fired. The electronic head-up display showed a hit as the bot exploded with overkill. "Whoop! Splash one!" yelled Flare.

Speedy was up with his weapon to his shoulder and locked in on the next target, firing and hitting two in quick succession.

Crane flipped the bird sideways and then swerved, which was impressive in the air. "Awesome count, Speedy," Flare said as he watched the two quick hits and a missile fly by.

Speedy was up for it. He got two more bots as Crane straightened out. Then he danced away from another.

Rock was juking his bird as deftly as Crane while his copilot, Lieutenant Steve "Red" Allen, worked the defenses and monitored the missiles flying at them.

Doc was able to get one bot, in between each evasive maneuver.

Watcher was cruising in from the north with the rest of the Hunters. The distraction the Little Birds, Falcon, and Hawk provided had the sentry bots jumping from spot to spot trying to hit the moving targets.

Watcher One came in the area, unnoticed by the alien ship parked at the edge of a field. The aliens were out and set up for the west landing of the Little Birds. About three hundred yards out, Watcher let out suppressive fire as it skidded low, about five feet off the ground. The Hunters bailed out and made for the wood line. Missiles and chain guns fired in unison, blasting out rounds and smoke, covering the Hunters safely into the cover. Watcher spun up and out as the aliens finally regained composure and returned fire, but Watcher was already evading and out of there.

The Hunters spread out in the woods, making a line across, with twenty feet between them, and advanced silently on the alien position.

The aliens had lost the location of the men who had spilled out of the Blackhawk. They marched up the clearing, trying to catch sight of the humans. The aliens were jittery and fired at trees blowing from the wind.

Once close to the alien ship, the Hunters started turning their formation so they now faced the ship and the aliens head-on. They proceeded to the forest edge and took up positions of cover to turn the ambush around on the aliens.

Hawk, with Speedy and Grumpy, was taking it to the bots, when a missile blew up within ten feet of the copter, causing a momentary twist and shutdown of the blades. Crane, with the aid of Flare, was able to get enough control to hit a hard landing, jostling the men aboard. Speedy was thrown about twenty feet out and away, knocked out cold. Grumpy did a combat rollout and twisted sideways into a rock. Crane was tossed sideways into the doorpost, knocking him out, slumping in his seat. Flare's door popped open with the stress of the landing, and he half fell out, caught up in his harness restraint.

Grumpy felt a sharp pain as he inhaled, and his side was on fire with pain. *Shit*, he thought, *took out a few ribs*. He tried to get up, but it took a great deal of effort to just move to a sitting position. He got himself up and seated with his back against the rock he had rolled into. The armor probably kept him from dying or having a punctured lung, but it still hurt like a bitch. He looked over and could see Crane leaning against the doorpost, not moving. He caught movement on the other side of the copter. It was three aliens and a bot, coming out of the woods and approaching the pilot and copilot. "Hunter Eight to any units close, Hawk down. Hawk One and Two, unknown condition. Contacts bearing down on them. Any response would be good. I'm down but not out," he said as he looked for his rifle. He saw it about six yards away, not really helpful. So he got out his pistol and tried to crawl to the rifle, keeping an eye on the aliens' progress. Even with the cooling unit, the sweat ran down his forehead into his eyes with effort to crawl to his rifle, each move a flaring of pain. The suit's medical AI wanted to give him a pain suppressant, but as a medic, he knew it most likely would make him too groggy to be of use.

Falcon came sweeping down. Doc and Sleepy jumped out. Doc took a kneeling position and shot the bot, putting it out of commission, while the other three aliens took cover at the helicopter. One grabbed the limp, hanging form of Flare and pulled him up to protect himself. Sleepy screamed a deadly scream as he had a flashback of his abduction. He took off straight at the alien holding Flare. He had almost made it when an alien from the side fired several bolts at him, and the one behind the unconscious copilot fired from five feet away. The armor could not keep its integrity, and Sergeant First Class Rudy "Sleepy" Polansky crashed to the ground. Doc was able to put one shot in the forehead of the alien that took the side shot. The third alien was moving around cover, firing at Doc, who had to dive and make for cover as the shielded alien and the moving alien laid their fire at him out in the open.

Polansky lay on the ground but not dead. He crawled slowly as he came closer to the shielded alien. He drew his knife and, with every last ounce of strength, raised up enough to thrust his blade into the chest of the alien, who fired a last shot at him. Polansky crashed onto the alien, who died and fell backward. Finally bringing down the alien with his last ounce of strength, he let go and died.

The third alien had managed to get behind Doc and was about to take a back shot when his head exploded. Doc spun around and saw the stump of a neck and the wet messy ground just as the body flopped back headless.

Speedy came limping out from the woods, having saved Doc's life.

Falcon stayed hovering close to protect its sister ship and crew, shooting at any of the remaining bots still trying to close in on their position.

The aliens had turned toward the sounds of battle coming from the other side of the clearing. A slight rise in between kept a clear view out of the question.

Ryan had his men set and gave the order to fire. Aliens fell as shots hit home, but out of the sitting ship, a platoon—or what looked like a platoon—came out, all shooting. The secondary ambush did its job, catching the Hunters off guard and pinning them down as the ranks started closing in on them.

Watcher One, Tucker, said, "All right, Watchers, look alive. We're going in to take some pressure off our boys." He banked around the Blackhawk away from Hawk's downed location he was headed to, but Falcon waived him off, saying they had it right now.

Lodge, Andrews, was watching and managing assets on the battlefield. She could see all the life signs from everyone as well as a couple of Space Force doctors whose job was to monitor that, along with a medical AI linked with the suits of armors' medical AIs. She couldn't help herself looking more than needed at Robin's signs. She chided herself for it, but she didn't stop doing it.

Monitoring Post Two yelled over to her from across the control room, "We have got movement off the coast directly east of the target site!" He punched some buttons, and it popped up on one of the big screens.

Colonel Rivera leaned over her shoulder and watched the plotting. He remained quiet as he saw her fingers fly over buttons and keyboards, talking into her headset multiple times. He pursed his lips and nodded and knew he needed to just let her at it. He crossed his arms and stepped back and watched the big screens, trying to watch all the action. After a moment, he pulled down the mic on his headset unit and gave a couple of orders. Continuing to watch, he let his trust of his headquarters personnel do their jobs.

He noted the maps as he saw two alien ships rise out of the ocean off the coast of Georgia and start toward the battle. He was about to say something as two blinking dots came flying up on the trail ship. They flew past it crisscrossed in front and began looping around it. He shut his mouth. Andrews must have put Gunner and Hammer on the ships or at least the one they could get to first. God, he wished he had a couple more in time, he told himself.

The other alien ship was making its way to the battlefield. Lodge gave the heads-up to all units.

Watcher was swaying among the aliens, avoiding their shots and harassing them to keep concentrated fire off the Hunters. It was working, and some of the aliens had fallen to his crew's fire and the Hunters'. The Blackbird had taken some damage but was hanging in there, thanks to the upgrades the Thirteenth Scientific Research and Development had done.

Tucker tried to stay out of range and shots from the alien ship. It hadn't been placed in a position to give it the best angle. He thanked that pilot for inexperience. "Listen up, Hunters. Watcher is going to be a bit occupied in a few. We got inbound bogey. We will be going evasive, so I can't guarantee that much support."

"Copy, Watcher One. We need our ride, so do what you have to. We will take it into account in our maneuvers."

Gunner flew a barrel roll over the top of the alien ship and let off a flare on its hull. It tried to shake it off as Hammer came in a step behind and used hyper rounds to pepper the ship and was rewarded with pieces of ship chipping off and a visual wobble.

Gunner did a loop, ending up coming at the ship from below and opposite Hammer's run. He fired two missiles and peeled off to the right as they impacted. Smoke started to come from a hole that he had made with that last shot.

The alien ship no longer tried to take them on but fled along the coast north and out to sea, but unlike its usual hyperfast movements, it ran about as fast as the fighters. This allowed them a fair fight now. The aliens should have run when they could.

The responding alien ship got into the tar lake area, saw Watcher, made a straight line, and fired missiles. Watcher got the warning from Lodge of the approach and made evasive maneuvers, barely getting misses from the missiles; but scorch marks were left on the Blackhawk's body. Watcher One hated doing it, but he needed to draw the ship away from being able to reinforce the alien troops. He started running away from the target area to play cat and mouse.

Major Ryan got on the comms, "Okay, team, look out for contacts on your sides. Watcher is busy." He felt a knot in the pit of his stomach as he watched the Blackhawk hightail it with the new alien ship on its tail. "Let's hope those little guys can't dogfight. I don't want to walk home tonight."

Hunter Three, Robin, noticed movement on his right. It looked like the little pests were flanking him or trying to. He had to give them credit. If he were a stupid animal as apparently they thought, he would run right into the trap they were setting up. Now he could read their maneuver; he could counter it and turn it on them. The group of five was tracking loudly to his right, hoping to flush him back into the group of ten that had set down in cover to his left, the natural direction from the attackers charging toward him.

Lincoln saw he had Hunter Nine, Sparky, to his side. "Nine, flush straight back and loop to my left. Watch the contact party and do a pincer with me on them." Robin mapped it on his head-up display and sent it to Nine via the AI system.

"Roger, good to go," Sparky replied as he started his maneuver to get to the opposite side of the aliens coming in on them.

Robin set out to sneak as best as he could around and through their formation, but if they caught him, he would be ripped to shreds by their fire.

Hunter Ten had gotten back when the reinforcements had come out of the ship and took cover, but now he was pinned between two groups of aliens, ten strong on each side. They didn't have his exact position, but they had a rough estimate of the area, a ten-yard-by-ten-yard patch, with rock groupings and trees shielding him from their view. It should have been comforting, but they were randomly shooting into the area, keeping him low. He couldn't move fast, or they would no doubt track him and cut him down. He really did have the luxury of sitting tight—though they were inching up and closing in. He could not fire off any shots without giving away his exact position, which gave them free movement.

Hunters Seven and Five had made a ravine and were holed up in it. They had good lanes of fire and were keeping the aliens at bay. They were able to randomly slip from spot to spot, pop up, and fire, shielded from fire by the ravine.

Hunters One, Two, and Four had been able to flank around the assault and were behind the grounded alien ship, moving with stealth to assault from behind the enemy formation.

Robin was able to get down under the low cover of a fern bush as, five yards away, an alien came by, firing off into where he had been—pure luck. He kept down till the alien passed and now had his back to Robin's position.

Hunter Nine, Davis, held his breath as an alien walked by three feet away. He could smell the alien. This one smelled terrible. He kept his head down to the ground, hoping the alien would miss him, counting on the electronic camouflage packet to melt him into the background. It took everything he had not to jump up and kill the alien, but muscle memory and training took over. Only you can't stop the brain from messing with you. As he remained still and not able to see, he kept picturing the aliens standing over him, waiting for him to look up and cut him up. His outside mic pickup told him a different story. The rustling and stomping was past, he slowly moved his head up to see off the forest floor. It was clear his head-up display read no signatures behind him. He slowly raised up to a one-knee position. He slowly raised his rifle to his shoulder, optics clicking on the head-up display. Projecting sight pics overlayed on the head-up display. "Hunter Three, I'm in their wake. Got a nice view."

"Hunter Nine, copy. I'm in position on my mark. Light them up," Robin responded.

Hunter Ten, Sparky, was keeping his head down, unable to even look out to see where they were. The forest to his left suddenly went bright, and roar after roar echoed down to his cover spot. He was able to look toward that direction, seeing that the aliens coming in from there had turned and were now heading, at a fast pace, toward the direction of whatever barrage that had been. He worked up the nerve and turned to his front where a group of six was moving to catch up to the other group. Turning again, the aliens who had been heading in from his right were trying to join up with the others, also seven, coming straight at him.

"Lack of discipline," he said to himself. They were totally occupied with events past him he was able to get his rifle up and fire off four shots, falling four aliens, before the seven—now three—realized a human was right in front of them. He ripped off a fifth shot, but the three remaining aliens were diving for cover. So his shot blew the right arm and shoulder off as it tried to go prone. It was now prone, weaponless, chirping, and thrashing around on the ground. Two explosions of dirt went off on either side of him. The remaining two had had made cover and were firing back. With the luck he was having, he had one on the left and one on the right, far enough apart.

He would have to turn and face each in turn and have his side to either one at any given moment.

Hunters Seven and Five each picked off an alien apiece and then moved far to the right. They popped up to see the remaining eight aliens peppering their last location with shots. They each took out another alien. Seven blew half a head off one looking away as Five put a hole the size of a soda can through another's side. They popped back down and low crawled far to the left. The aliens turned and fired, all remaining six of them, at the location the Hunter had just vacated. They were slow learners, and Seven and Five hoped their learning curve was slow.

Hunter One was prone, low crawling under the ship, coming up under the ramp area. Hunter Two was straight out to the side of the ramp, just in the tall grass, prone with a line on the two guards that were left at the ramp. Hunter Four was moving up crouched, three yards from One, ready to move when he struck. One got near the far guard at the ramp. Four got down and low crawled now to the other side. One and Four both were up in a flash, and each had used their knives and silenced the alien guards. Two, in a low crouch, moved fast to the ramp. He took the entrance first, weapon ready.

It had been awesome, Robin thought. He and Hunter Nine, Davis, had gone full attack on the aliens, each throwing two heavy-mass grenades, then rapid firing their rifles. The woods were still ringing from the explosions, and the weapons the first group of aliens had were no more than a collection of parts.

The reprieve was temporary though as two more groups came up to take their place, laying down some heavy fire.

Hunter Ten was cursing the fact he couldn't catch a break. Here he was again sucking the ground as he was getting alternating fire from each side. The only saving grace this time was one each, not the twenty or so he had peppering him earlier.

The aliens had finally figured out the strategy and came up with a good reply to it. They were randomly each taking a section and firing at irregular intervals. The problem for the aliens was they were now down to four.

Ryan recognized the ship's entry, only last time the crew was dead; this time, he had no idea how many were on board or what kind of defense they faced. Tanaka reached the first door of what they found to be the medical bay on the last ship. He came in the door and went low. Junius came in next high.

A little blue alien screeched and came running at them with some sort of scalpel device. Hunter Two swung the barrel at the charging alien and let the round go. The alien flew back. Two more came out the back room, firing but wildly. Wild Bill put them down in short order. Tanaka rushed to the back room and found no more aliens. He was heading back to the door as Wild Bill scanned the room. They heard the shots from the hallway and stepped up, moving out.

In the hall, Major Ryan was standing over three alien bodies, their weapons strewn about. It appeared as if they came running around the corner when the major stopped them dead.

"Cool," Chief said as he spied the corner and moved on down the hallway.

Wild Bill passed him next. "Yeah, cool," he said, trailing Chief.

The major just shook his head and trailed the two, watching their back, as they moved through the ship.

Hunters Three and Nine were each able to get a shot or two off, but the rate of fire back made it difficult.

As Nine went to take a shot, a beam or two hit his armor in the left arm. A small piece disappeared off the armor, and he received a gash crease on the forearm. He fell back behind the rocks he was behind. The suit immediately shot a burn lotion on the wound, and a section that looked like foam came out and sealed the hole. It didn't look exact, but it would do as a field patch. He tried to move his arm, but the motion was difficult and painful. A medical AI alerted him he had a hurt muscle in the forearm and his movement and strength were now only 20 percent in the arm. "Crap," he said. "Three, I'm winged but fine," he communicated over to Robin.

Robin had his status already displayed by his command AI unit. "Got it. Sorry, you still have to stay here and work. I can't send you home, no matter what excuse you use," Robin said back as a large explosion at the front of his cover blew him ten yards back and a large chunk of rock smacked his helmet, knocking him out.

"Shit! Three, do you copy? Three!" Nine called as he saw the bot hit Lincoln's position with a missile. He took the lull as the bot started toward Robin's location and put two hyper rounds into it, creating an explosion that took out three aliens who had thought it would be covered to go with it.

With the dust trying to settle from the two explosions, Nine streaked out of cover and dove for where Robin had landed. Several shots scorched his armor, but he made it safe and scorched but further unharmed. He grasped Robin by the shoulders and tried to roll him over. He had landed facedown. He was deadweight, and Sparky was smaller, so it was tough, not to mention he had an injured arm.

Hunter Ten was getting pissed off. The two aliens would bury him with dirt as they kept shooting up his cover, pelting him every few seconds. The worse part was that he thought they had found it safe to advance on him slowly—the jerks.

Andrews, back at base, had been calling in movements and warnings, coordinating it all; but this time, she looked at Robin's status. It was rimmed in red and pulsing off and on. Her heart raced, and she almost lost it. She closed her eyes for a second and breathed in and out. A hand landed on her shoulder. She looked up and saw Colonel Rivera standing there.

He smiled at her, squeezed her shoulder, and said, "You got this, kid. You are doing great. Stay focused," he said it low so only she heard it. He then crossed his arms over his chest and went back to monitoring the screens.

She focused and got back to work; her eyes strayed to the readout though.

Hunters Seven and Five now were still down and couldn't take out the measly four aliens they had left shooting at them.

"Screw this!" Patterson said as he reached into the pouches on the carrier and pulled out two heavy-mass grenades. He pulled a pin and held it as the spoon went flying. He pulled the second and did the same now, one in each hand.

"What the hell," Angel said as he ducked down, knowing if those damn things went off this close, that would not help.

Two large explosions went off, and dirt came flying into the ravine, along with some blue gunk, a piece landing on Patterson's faceplate.

Angel sat back up and patted himself down. He was fine. He looked over, and Bang Patterson was up firing, yelling, "You want a piece of me? I got a piece of you!" as he pointed to the chunk on his faceplate.

Angel broke out laughing, grabbed his rifle, and climbed up with Bang. They walked firing and scanning on the aliens who were still in shock from the blasts. Really, only three were left. One had taken a grenade full blast. They checked the bodies and found they had taken them all out. They made for the ship, knowing the three others were in there and would need backup, not knowing what to expect or what kind of resistance they would get.

Hunters One, Two, and Four had encountered sporadic aliens as they moved in toward where the control room should be as they checked the head-up display overlay made from the captured ship. Chief came around a corner and came back from the corner landing on his butt, almost knocking over the other two.

Wild Bill grabbed the handle on the armor carrier and pulled him back and lifted him up on his feet, face-to-face. Wild Bill said, "You're smoking, Chief."

"Well, thanks, big guy. You're okay," Chief said, odd that Wild Bill would say that.

"No, Chief, your helmet, it got scorched and still smoking. Any problems?"

"*Neg-ah-tive*, five by five, good to go."

Wild Bill turned and joined Ryan at the corner. They both went kneeling into the hall and just started shooting as rapid as they could. Chief poked around the top, sighted, and picked off a couple.

"Coming up behind you, Hunter Seven and Five," Angel announced to the others as they came up to their position.

"Good, we are near the center of the ship, the control part, probably going to be defended," Major Ryan said as he got up with

Wild Bill at his side and strode past the mess of bodies lying across the passageway.

The men stalked toward the command center.

Finally getting Lincoln on his back—he still was out cold, with a dent in his armor helmet from where the chunk of rock had hit him—Sparky Davis, Hunter Nine, got up to the new cover they had landed behind. Pulling the rifle to his shoulder, he started sighting in at the alien forms that were advancing. There was still a thick pallor across the intervening yards between him and the aliens. His optics were able to ID targets though. He took aim and hit the first one through the debris cloud floating over the battlefield.

As he started sniping the aliens, they realized it and began charging the position, which was bad news, but worse news was tight on its tail. Several bots had been summoned by the attacking aliens to now bolster their attack.

"Shit. Three, now would be a good time to wake up," Sparky said as he tried to hit a bot, but they were blowing the debris cloud toward his position, interfering with his aiming.

"Well, is this saving me, Nine? Because if it is, you need to work on it," Lincoln said groggily.

"Well, I didn't want to take them all out by myself. You would never forgive me."

"You know I probably would have, this time, mind you just this once."

The aliens broke out from the cloud of debris and began laying down heavy fire on Three and Five's position.

Nine took another hit, this time to his helmet, cracking the faceplate and killing the electronics but not injuring him. He ducked down and pulled off the helmet. He had no vision with it on. He would need to see the aliens as they overran them, and they made their stand.

"Well, at least we're going to take a bunch out. Ready, Nine?"

"As always, only way to go. Let's light them up!"

With that, the men popped up over the cover and began picking targets. From the far side of the clearing, fire started ripping into the line of approaching aliens, taking them completely by surprise.

"What the—" Lincoln said.

"Hunter Team One, you're welcome. Hunter Team Two has arrived. This is a black armor affair, is it not?"

"Team Two leader, I could kiss you," Robin said as they finished polishing off the attacking aliens.

Team Two, consisting of twelve men, helped the two soldiers up. And their two medics treated Lincoln and Davis.

"Overlook to Hunters, I found Watcher, and we are heading back. Lodge, you have coordinates of the splash?" Captain "Taco" Krauterville said over the comms.

The group looked up and saw two Blackhawks come over the horizon together. Watcher was a little scarred, but Lincoln thought she looked beautiful.

"Lodge to Overlook, copy on the location. Mover is on the way for retrieval. Hunter Team Two, your timing is impeccable. Thank you."

"Two-Two, take Two, Five, Six, Seven, Eight and go assist Hunter One and his party clear out the target," Captain Lou Anderson, commander of Team Two, ordered, keeping the rest to provide security out here for any stray aliens or bots.

Inside the alien ship, the five members of Team One had arrived at the alcove that led to the command center.

"Notice how quiet it is in there. Either no one is left, or they are waiting for us," Major Ryan said as he inched along the wall.

Chief and the major were on one side, and Wild Bill and the two weapons sergeants, Herndon and Patterson, were on the other side.

Ryan went to check around the corner, and a blue alien head bumped in the doorway. Ryan was quicker than the alien. He grabbed its head and pulled it into the hallway, throwing it into Wild Bill's arms. Realizing time was short now, to get the advantage and knowing the quick disappearance of the alien from the doorway would confuse them enough to attack first and get the surprise. Wild Bill slammed the alien into the wall, causing the wall to get a coat of blue goo. The alien went limp, most likely dead. He dropped it and went through the door, scanning and firing at any of the little blue guys.

Bang was in next, slipping opposite side from Bill. Angel came sliding in next, followed by Chief and the major, all taking targets out with practiced speed. A few shots came back at the Hunters, but none was even close to being effective. Soon, the command center was covered in blue goo and a pack of alien bodies. The Hunters moved through with efficiency and speed, clearing the rest of the ship, finding one or two stragglers along the way, none of which would surrender.

"Team Two to Hunter Team One, we are at the entrance to target 1. Do you need our support? Over."

The team was now in the engine area and looked at one another. "Team Two? Come again," Major Ryan asked.

"Yes, Hunter One, this is Hunter Team Two. Hunter Two-Two, over," Warrant Officer Jay Campo said, with a slight hint of amusement in his tone.

"Two-Two, welcome to the club. Secure the entrance and we will be up in a few," Ryan said.

Lieutenant Crane Manning was awake now, and Doc was tending to a gash on his jaw he somehow got from hitting the jamb of the helicopter doorframe. His copilot Flare Forrester was tending to the helicopter, getting her back up and running. He was sore and bruised, but he hadn't got any real injuries.

Doc was working on Crane. Grumpy, he refused help. Even with his ribs as banged up as they were, he was tending to Sleepy, preparing his body for transport back to Lodge.

Speedy stood guard. A row of dead bots and aliens stood on the edge of the clearing. Speedy and Falcon had held off the attack of the last of the aliens. Falcon had landed and put down a few yards from Hawk, the crew helping to get Hawk up and running.

Grumpy knew the pain that Sleepy had from the abduction they shared because they shared the feelings with each other. He also knew Sergeant First Class Rudy Polansky could not truly cope with being a victim. White had tried to tell him that if he accepted it, it was easier to live with and that there was no way to control the situation they had been put into. It was hard for a Special Forces operator to accept that. They lived by the fact that they controlled the situation or were able to adapt and take advantage of it.

Rudy and White had become good friends over the last few years. He allowed one tear to fall as he zipped his friend into the body bag. He would let the rest come out later alone.

White couldn't help lifting the body, but he had finished working on Crane, who came over and helped him put the body in the back of the Little Bird. They strapped the body in. The rotors started as the two crews finished getting Hawk back in order. Luckily, it wasn't anything major. Just an exhaust was shut down. Almost all the systems were still online.

Doc jumped back into Falcon and strapped in. Speedy got back into Hawk and strapped in after he helped Grumpy up in and strapped him in first.

Doc used his medical AI to access Grumpy's armor to run a check on his vitals and what, if any, he needed in treatment. Both medics had access to the team's full medical AI to perform any actions needed. Going through the vitals, he saw the stress level high with the grief and the broken ribs, so he ordered a low dose of ibuprofen shot and a tightening of the armor medical equipment around the rib area, which should relieve some pain. He first let White know what he was doing.

He nodded but realized he had to vocalize, "Yeah, go ahead, Doolie."

Both Little Birds lifted off and went to the rally point by the downed alien ship. Landing at the clearing, both Little Birds shut down until Major Ryan came out of the captured alien downed ship.

Hunter Ten came out of the wood line, scorch marks all over his armor and his rifle slung and an alien weapon in each armored hand. "It's okay, everyone, I got them, no problem. Yeah, forget that I was pinned down, taking fire from opposite side. Don't worry!" he stated sarcastically over the comms.

"Ten, are you whining again?" Hunter Nine said, as one of Team Two's medic was working on his arm, doing what he could, till they got back to base.

"Okay. Had to show me up, didn't you, Nine? Even in this armor, you got a sling. If anyone was going to, it would be you."

The two soldiers met and bumped armored fists. The joking was what brothers do, but the fist bump was for coming off another mission mostly in one piece.

"The target is clear, Watcher. Overlook, you can come in for pickup. It's secure," Major Ryan said as he and the men at the ship exited and made their way back to the impromptu rally spot.

Ryan took off his helmet, and so did Captain Anderson. They walked to each other and grasped each other's forearm, not the hands, the old Roman way to shake and greet each other. The two officers had been roommates at West Point, where they became fast friends, then best friends.

Anderson did a double take and leaned back on Ryan's armor. On each shoulder was a matte finish bronze oak leaf, enameled on the armor where epaulets would be. Anderson had flat black captain's bars on his armor. "Holy shit, Rye, Major. Damn, I guess you are my company commander. Team Two, reporting, sir," he said and saluted.

Ryan smiled and returned the salute. "I see you still show up fashionably late. I'll let it go this time." Ryan punched Anderson in the shoulder. "Damn good to see you. Where the hell did they keep a whole team hidden?"

"Long story, believe me. Suffice to say we were assigned a whole other unit as a team. We have been together for about a year and a half." Anderson paused for a moment. "SOCOM."

"Black dagger work, eh. Good enough. Well, I couldn't have a better man leading a team than you, my friend." He smiled and finished, "Besides, you running them, it's going to make me look good."

They laughed and walked over to check on Lincoln who was sporting a black eye already from the head shot.

"Robin, you know better than to use your head to stop the aliens. I really thought you had learned to duck by now," Anderson said as he slapped Lincoln on the shoulder. Lincoln winced. Anderson gave him a sorry nod.

"I'm still working on it, Cap. By the way, timing was okay. I won't complain."

"Huh? Just okay? Damn, you're a tough critic, brother," Anderson said.

As the group was standing there, they heard a rush of jets as a Marine Corps Osprey did a vertical landing in the field, dropping its ramp once on the ground.

Major Johnson in army combat uniform, with Sergeant First Class Armando Acudo, also in army combat uniform, came out. Behind them were Lieutenant Troy in Space Force army combat uniform and Dr. Fargo in a Space Force camo lab coat. Fargo was rubbing his hands together like a kid on Christmas morning.

The group just stared at the exiting men from the Osprey. Mostly, it was Fargo in the camo lab coat; no one knew what to make of it.

Anderson tapped Ryan on the arm as they stared at the doctor. "Is that Christopher…" Anderson didn't get it all out before Ryan anticipated the question.

"No, it must somehow be his twin. But no, he doesn't even know who that is," Ryan said, shaking his head.

"Crazy" was all that Anderson could think to say, but it did sum it all up.

"Major, Captain," Johnson said as he approached. "Our new vehicle, thanks to the Marine Corps Recon. Now it's part of the Thirteenth Special Wing," he said, gesturing to the shutting-down Osprey. "She is call sign Taxi. We are going to clean up here and take it in Taxi. I understand you lost a man. I'm sorry for that, truly. We also can't find Sergeant Major Whitfield. Do any of you know anything or see him at all?"

"I had an incident earlier, but he left our area and hadn't had any further contact," Major Ryan said.

"You will have to fill me in later. How about you, Lincoln?" he said, looking suspiciously down at him.

Lincoln just raised his hands, gesturing "not me" as he shook his head no.

"Okay," Johnson said, taking what Lincoln was offering as fact. "Well, head back, take care of your teams, and welcome, Captain,"

Johnson said and headed to catch up with Lieutenant Troy and the doctor, who were almost at the ship.

Sergeant First Class Acudo stood there for a second. "It's weird. It's like the sergeant major disappeared into thin air. Charlie had no idea and could not even find out how he would have got out of the base. No record on the tram or any of the base exits. He was in the command center just before this whole thing broke out, walked out, have it on video. But then, poof, he was gone, no more video." Acudo shrugged like it was just crazy. Which they all had to agree it was.

"Damn, that is spooky, but he was an asshole," Robin said.

"Well, he did a trick earlier, which makes this even more eerie, let me tell you," Ryan said.

"True, it does make it more than just an AWOL, doesn't it?" Lincoln put in.

"Well, when we get back, let me know the whole deal. It's my job to locate him or figure out what the hell is up. And oh yes, Robin, he was an asshole," Acudo said, did a short hand wave, and headed behind Johnson.

"So does this mean the base is haunted, fellas?"

They all laughed at Anderson's joke, but it was a temporary relief, considering these strange events. With actual battles with aliens, what was next, they would have to be on guard.

All the helicopters spun up their rotors, and Teams One and Two of the Hunters loaded aboard their rides, back to Lodge and getting ready for the next wave of excitement.

Ryan sat next to Lincoln. "Hey, leave the helmet off, Robin. Put your head back. I'll get the reports this time. You earned it."

"Thanks. I don't know if I'll be able to relax though," Robin said as he got his helmet ready.

Ryan winked at Doc and gave him a finger pistol. Robin looked at Doc as his suit injected him with a little knockout, just enough to have him sleep all the way back to base.

The major put his helmet on and began the paperwork, giving Junius and Tanaka part of Lincoln's. The reports would all be done as soon as they reached Lodge.

Acudo and Johnson stood outside the ship as Troy and Fargo headed in.

"Sir, Major Ryan said that something weird happened earlier with Whitfield. They seemed as surprised about him being gone as we were."

"Sergeant, I have to admit Whitfield got under my skin, like everyone else he met. It just is not what I would expect from a sergeant major in the Army, let alone in Special Forces. Something was going on. We haven't figured it out yet. I am telling you this makes me nervous. We are on new ground here. A new age of things that were myth are now real." Johnson took off his hat and wiped his brow. His mind was racing.

"Sir, as long as we know something is off, then we most likely won't be taken off guard," Acudo said, mostly trying to convince himself.

"Yeah," Johnson said, nodding his head in agreement. "All right, let's head inside and watch the toddlers, huh."

Acudo laughed, and the two men walked into the ship.

*****

Commander saw the reports come in. Commanders Two and Three were killed. Then the fact that each of their fleets lost one ship each and Commander Four lost one of his was the perfect result. He immediately promoted Leader One into Commander Two and sent him to prepare his new fleet. He turned to Leader Two and surveyed him.

Leader Two lowered his head. He hoped it wasn't too late to be a part of the grand plan of the commanders.

"Leader Two, you are now Commander Three. Go get your fleet and prepare them. We are going to station 1."

Leader Two—no, Commander Three—straightened up and smiled. "I am eternally grateful for your forgiveness and inclusion, Commander. I will not let you down."

"No, I don't believe you will, which pleases me, having my two sons at my side as we take our just positions, for greater profit and glory." He waved his hand, shooing Commander Three to get going.

Commander Three left with a new purpose and power in his step. Now the plan was coming together. He would now take the twelve fleets and head to station 1, and with the strength, he would take the station and become Superior One. Controlling the whole sector of slaving and research. Every one of his commanders now were loyal, completely or they would have died by his hand.

Considering the little-known thought monitors he had placed in his men, it cost him profits and free slaves, but it was worth it. Technology from Gregoria was illegal for Aldions to use on one another, but "illegal" and "being caught" were two different things. Since he was about to crown himself by force Superior One of Sector Ugo, then what was illegal anyways? Not what he judged good.

The commander stood up on his platform and smoothed out his cape and adjusted his gun belt. He walked down to the walkway to his command ship. His death guards were with him. He signaled for his navigator to have his death fleet move out of the dark of the moon and join his gathering fleets behind the moon, which hid his fleets from the planet below. There would be plenty of time later to come back and teach humans their place once the sector was his.

The Greelock watchman saw the gathering fleet and put the defenses on alert.

The station commander came onto the bridge. He came over and looked over the watchman's shoulder and viewed the Aldions and the gathering of their ships. He studied it for a moment and decided the threat was not to them, but it looked as if the commander over there finally got enough pieces to make a run at a new position. He chuckled a throaty sound like a gravelly growl. Aldions were such a contentious race. It was a matter that they were a thriving society at all. Slavers, bottom feeders, doing research on races for sheer profit, never trying to advance themselves.

He growled and waved to the watchman. He could turn off the defense alert. They were fine. He walked over to his communications watch stand and asked if they had a schedule of when the next ship was due. He was informed that the ship was en route and doing well. They were one jump away and would arrive in a week.

It was picking time. The supply transport would come and pick the humans and other life for the delivery to the Arca Greelock colony. He had to make a deal for about a dozen humans to be left on station. His crew needed the treat of fresh meat.

The humans thought that the Greelocks were a distant relative, which couldn't be further from the truth. Greelocks were roughly eight feet tall and were covered in "fur," which really was a natural armor to protect them. They came in different colors, from brown, tan, white, black, and even reddish coverings. Humans had very few looks at them and, insulting, called them "bigfoot," "yeti," "sasquatch," and other assorted names. The mistake humans had made and as they often did, they judged the Greelocks to be ape descendants or relations. Also, they assumed they were less intelligent than they were.

The command officer of the station always made a joke of that. "So how many Greelocks have they captured, and how many humans have we missed?" He would pause. "The answer is the same—none." Then the Greelocks would laugh.

"Well, this supply run should be very good. With the Aldions out of the way, we will have less competition of human harvesting," the younger Greelock second officer said as he approached from the command offices.

"Yes, this year's festival should be one of the best ever. The feast will be full of meat this time," the commander said, running his tongue over his sharp teeth as he thought of the savory cooked human steaks he would be having.

CHAPTER 15

A LARGER PICTURE

Lincoln woke up when the helicopter bumped down onto the lift pad. He wiped a bit of drool from the side of his mouth. His head hurt, like someone was tightening a strap around it.

Doc took his helmet off so he could talk to Robin.

Robin sat up straight and wiped his eyes. "Well, I guess you hit me with a knockout. I should be pissed, but my head hurts too much. And don't think about hitting me again. I will take some ibuprofen when I hit the med room."

Doc held up his hands in surrender. "Okay, okay, no more hits right now. You needed it though. That brain of yours had to have a rest. It took a big jolt." Doc grabbed Robin's helmet and pointed to the dent in the crown of the top.

"Damn, that is a nasty dent." Robin rubbed his head where the dent in the helmet would have been. He felt it was tender, and there was a bump starting to raise.

The others all took their helmets off and started to gather their gear to exit the helicopter before it went down with the lift. Some of the team wanted to go out and get the fresh ocean air before going downstairs, especially after having been in their armor for hours.

Lincoln, Doc, and Ryan walked over to the back hangar door to go out by the floodwall. Team Two's helicopter set down and shut off, its team getting out and heading down with the rest of Team One, all except for Captain Anderson, Warrant Officer Campo, and Master Sergeant Armstrong, who strolled over with the men of Team One heading out the back door.

"So is it always like this with the little blue guys?" Levar Armstrong asked as they all stepped into the night air, stretched, and took deep breaths of the salty ocean air.

"So far, but I am still waiting for the curveball to hit. Somehow, I can't believe it's going to be how it's been—fighting them. You know, I am waiting for the pushback. Plus, we need to study up on old reports. See what kind of alien crap to expect," Major Ryan said, then stared out at the reflection of the moon on the moving ocean.

Lincoln put his gear down and sat on the wall facing the hangar, his back to the water. Sergeant Anderson came out and looked at the men and then Robin. She sighed with relief, seeing him in one piece. Robin patted the wall next to him as he smiled at her. She walked over and sat next to him. He put his hand in hers in the space between them and squeezed her hand. It was all they needed to communicate.

Major Ryan caught the hands in his peripheral vision, and it explained Robin's actions earlier, but holding hands was definitely not him. This must be different with her.

"Good point. You got some Blue Book material, Rye?" Anderson asked his old roommate.

"Better than that, Captain. We have what was left of the Project Blue Book staff, now Space Force and part of our HQ," Lincoln added.

"Okay, so we can get help reading all the files, things like which were the most conceivable and which seemed a little far-fetched, right?" Campo asked.

"If you had asked me last month what was far-fetched and what was conceivable, my answers would be totally different," Ryan said.

"Well, when they briefed us last week that as soon as we finished the current mission my team was being redesignated, I had no idea what we were in for. Well, not until yesterday when the general did a vid conference at SOCOM to fill us in." Anderson rubbed his chin as he remembered. "It took almost all night to let it sink in, and yet I don't think till we cleared the wood line and saw the little blue things running around that I truly believed."

Campo nodded in agreement about that. He too could not think of it as totally real, but seeing actual real aliens brought it home. "It's as if they said, 'Hey, Santa is real.' You would be like, 'Yeah, okay, sure.' Then Santa comes up and pats you on the back. What can you say? 'Oh, shit, you are real.'"

"Hell, for all we know, Santa is an alien. I mean the rules are out the window now," Armstrong said as they all nodded silently in agreement everything was upside down now.

"Well, thank god, we got enough tin foil for the whole unit," Lincoln said as the group nervously laughed. This was his fourth contact with the aliens, but he knew it would happen. They lost a man, and several of them were injured. Yet it was a victory for the alien hunters, and not for the aliens.

The group heard a rustling noise from the left side of the path along the flood retention wall. It was an odd sound, just off center from being naturally occurring. The Hunters turned their heads and bodies toward the sound and became quiet and still as they started to raise their weapons.

A ripple appeared in the air from the center of the path as if the air just became liquid, and it stretched from the ground to a point, seven foot in the air. A large man, looking like an armored pro wrestler, stepped out of the ripple. He looked like a man, but his skin was red, a shifting dark-to-lighter red skin. His eyes were almost a glowing green, and he had no hair on his face or head.

The weapons raised as he stepped toward them. He raised both his hands, showing no weapons, and he slowly moved their way.

The major took a step toward the man. Squaring himself with him, he kept his rifle at the ready but pointed at the foot of the creature. Anderson mimicked his movement and stayed on his left side a step back. Doc stepped back and farther to the left but stood five feet away, weapon at the ready. Lincoln had taken to wear two guns on his hips after his second meeting with the aliens. He moved slowly off the wall from a sitting position to a kneeling firing position, his rifle across his knee but pointed slightly away from the approaching being. Andrews slid the pistol from the holster on Lincoln's side that was to her when he unfastened the catch and slid into his kneeling position. She kept it down out of view of the creature by holding it low behind Lincoln's back. Campo took two steps back and just a step toward Lincoln's position, his weapon at the ready also. The men had given themselves an excellent firing setup if it came to it.

The being was five feet away from the ripple, still stepping carefully and very slowly, when a second form came out of the ripple.

This form was about five foot six, armored, and reminded the major of an armadillo in its features. Unlike the taller being, he had a rifle in its grasp, but it was pointed down and away. It was a weapon that the men hadn't seen before. The creature moved away from the ripple and stepped off to the right of the path and stopped, taking up a guard position.

So far, neither of the creatures made any overt moves nor any sounds.

The tall creature stopped about six feet away from the major and stood with his feet apart and his arms still raised. He stared forward at the major.

A third being started to emerge from the ripple. This looked more like a large human-bison mix. It reminded the major of the old myth of the Minotaur. It was holding a large weapon, very similar to a minigun on an A-10 aircraft, but only slightly smaller. The Minotaur had it pointed up to his right in both bulging muscled arms. He too was armored in very similarly marked armor. It stepped over to the right side of the path a few feet forward.

The ripple apparently wasn't finished with birthing beings as a rock-looking creature stepped out next, very similar in form to the red being; but his skin was more like a rock pattern, looking very hard yet flexible. It too wore the same armor. He carried two holsters on either side. Both its guns were still holstered. It had in its hands a rifle, but more suited to close-quarter combat. It had it in its left hand, and it hung at its side, muzzle to the ground. It walked up to behind the red creature and stood just behind it to its right.

The red being still stood totally still and unmoving, hands still in the air.

The final being came out of the ripple. It was another rock being, very similar to the first but a little stockier and an inch taller. He had a rifle across his chest in his arms. He stood in front of the ripple. In a guard-like position.

The rock beings had no hair on them either, and as you would expect, their skin or rock, whichever, was a yellowish gray coloring.

The Hunters had stayed extremely still and steady during this whole event. The major looked over the group in front of him and calculated that, with the unknown weapons power and the abilities of the beings, they were at a severe disadvantage. He also knew he could subvocalize at any moment and set the base on alert and have all the men downstairs armed and up here in a moment.

Somehow, he had the feeling that the red being in front of him knew the same information. The way it looked him and the others over was familiar to him. The way the beings moved and formed up was very familiar indeed.

After a moment of his calculating and sizing up the situation, he dropped his weapon to a less-ready position, with one hand holding the rifle and it falling very slowly to point straight down. His now-free left hand came up palm out like he was about to wave, but he kept it up and still.

The other Hunters kept their stillness and weapon discipline. As the veteran operators they were, they did not lose their cool or react with hysterics, no matter what the situation.

The red being moved for the first time since he had taken up his current stance. He slowly nodded his head at Major Ryan. It was clear that the two facing each other head-on were both leaders of the separate groups. The two held themselves very much the same. Both had the same bearing and thoughtfulness of the situation.

Major Ryan nodded back to the red being, then looked at each of its hands, and nodded after the being gave a little bit of a mouth movement that could have been a hint of a smile. He also looked at Ryan's hand and nodded.

The two leaders both slowly, with deliberate movements, put their arms down. Ryan's went to his belt buckle where he looped his thumb into his waistband to keep it from falling on his holstered ᵤₙ. The red being did almost the same, but he gripped them in each other in front on his belt holding his double holsters.

They stood there again in silence, sizing up the situation like commanders do and not jumping into saying anything to possibly cause an incident. Neither wanting to speak first, if at all.

The Hunters had no way to know if the aliens—which they had to be since none of the equipment nor the species was vaguely familiar—could communicate like them. Or if they could, if they spoke any language they would know. No, they would have to wait to see the aliens tip their hand and let it be known what they could do in the way of communicating.

Sergeant Andrews had to give it to Major Ryan. It was a great move to hold out and let the aliens give away their secrets. Whatever they could or could not do, some of it would be given away when or if they attempted to communicate. It had to be obvious that they wanted or needed to communicate. Or why had they gone through this elaborate showing of themselves? No, they needed or wanted something to come out like this to this particular group in this particular setting. The advantage with this small factor was to the Hunters.

Major Ryan had come to the same conclusion and was not going to give up the advantage and seemed anxious to know what the aliens were about. Oh, inside, he was bubbling with questions and statements, but about his counterpart, of which he thought of as, he didn't know whether it was an ally or foe or perhaps a little of both. He wasn't going to let on. He was going to wait it out, however long it took.

The red being looked over the Hunters again, and a stray movement again at its mouth gave the distinct impression it was holding back a smile. The question was whether it was a smile that it was about to kill them and eat them or about to pat them on the head and say, "Good little humans," or just say hello.

Amusement or respect couldn't be judged, not till you knew about whatever race it was to have a guideline for its actions and emotions. Ryan wouldn't jump to any conclusions on that front. He couldn't afford to.

"Humans—I think that is what you call yourselves—I give you greetings," the red being said, his voice very strong and on the edge of being very deep. Now he had given away that his English was very good and he was fluent. He hadn't faltered or even paused any. "Yes, I speak your tongue, as do all my men," the being said as if reading Ryan's mind.

Ryan nodded to the being but still not talking. It was a good move.

That trace came and went again on his features. "I have decided to greet you on your ground, when you are armed, in a nonthreatening way to set you at a bit of ease at our first meeting," the red being said and then paused, probably expecting a response now at this point from Ryan.

None came, except a nod again, making it clear he understood.

"I am Commander Quarplek. These are some of my men, my personal team of trusted men." He paused again, waiting for some response. But again, none was given. He grumbled, and a bit of frustration was shown, but only for a moment, a very telling sign. "Is this to be a one-way meeting? I would have thought meeting a different species than yourselves would be exciting and cause to communicate," Quarplek said, showing a bit of confusion at the human's action.

Ryan understood the frustration of the commander, but he didn't really care how the being felt. It wasn't his problem to care. He was a bit angry that the being was a bit condescending, like he should be greeted like a celebrity or a saving parent. No, the arrogance was underlying there, and it gave Ryan a little nagging sensation in the pit of his stomach.

"Human, I and my men are here for you. We come to assist you," the commander said, like he was offering a wonderful gift free of charge.

Ryan knew nothing ever came free of charge, nothing. What was that old saying? "If it seemed too good, it usually was," meaning there was always a pitfall to free things. "One, you see we have just dealt with beings trying to kill us. And two, I do not remember asking for any assistance. Now I'm sure that you are very good at what you do. But the real question is what is it that you do?" Ryan said. And his tone was hard and steady, and it made the commander pull his head back and blink at the smaller human.

"I do not understand. I would think that dealing with the Aldions was difficult and you would need our help. They certainly have technology way above your human capability."

And there it was, the hook, the poor little humans were being harassed by the bad aliens. So in came the good aliens to offer help and protection. The cost came again to Ryan's thoughts. What would be the bill for the assistance of the protecting big brother aliens?

"Huh, isn't that funny? As I see it, we have done pretty good so far, us little frail humans," Ryan said very sarcastically.

"I don't understand. I have only come here to offer assistance."

"Really? And what would it cost us?"

The commander stopped and furrowed his brow and stared back at the smaller human. He studied him with a different look on his features this time. The appearance of the kind, gentle, old-uncle continence disappearing from his features and physical attitude. The commander moved his hands from his belt and placed them on his hips, like he was going to verbally scold the small human for talking back to his better.

It did not escape the notice that it also put his hands above his double holsters.

"I am surprised by the attitude you have decided to take upon my offering to aid you, human. Would it not be better to be outfitted to fight a battle correctly, trained in the ways of our combat, so you are prepared to defeat your foe?"

"You know, Commander, you didn't answer my question. As a matter of fact, you deflected it quite skillfully," Ryan said, his hand sliding an inch back from his buckle.

The commander nodded his head. "Ah, I can see you have gotten full of mistrust by the actions of the Aldions. But I assure you, not all species are as cowardly and profit driven as they."

Ryan nodded but did not respond. Once again, the commander changed the subject. He also noticed the fingertips of his hands now caressed the exposed back part of the guns in the holsters. Ryan's hand moved just an inch more.

"Human, we are offering our experience and knowledge. Why would you be offended by this? Should you not welcome us with open arms for this?"

"Well, Quarplek," he started, not using his title of "commander," "you still did not tell me what it would cost us. What would be required of us in return for your gracious assistance?"

This time, Quarplek seemed more irritated, especially with the informality and obvious lack of respect he thought he deserved. "Human," he said, and this time his voice became sterner, "you have this notion that we would ask for your children to eat or that all your females of your species be given over. You are mistaken."

"I don't care if you just wanted all our beer. You still are avoiding the simple question." At that statement, Campo chortled.

"Beer. This is that liquid that you ferment and drink to get silly. It numbs your brain, does it not?"

"You see, Quarplek, at every turn, you deflect the issue, which in turn makes me just a bit more curious and a bit more worried of your true intent." He shook his head in disgust. "You see, Quarplek, I don't trust any, uh, species that can't answer a question as straightforward with an answer just as straightforward. Maybe other species just fall in line when you come in and say, 'We are here to save you,' but not humans, I'm afraid. For all I know, these Aldions are working for you. It's all just a setup to come in and take over."

Commander Quarplek, at that statement, stood up straighter with anger and insult, and he had his palms on his weapons, just a movement away from drawing and firing. He was pissed at the little human talking so harshly to a warrior of his caliber, veteran of so many campaigns. Humans were such an arrogant little race. "Human, you tread on very dangerous ground. I don't like the kind of talk you are making. I do not think you would want me or my team as an enemy. You would not do so well. We are not Aldions, businesspeople as you would say. We are soldiers, very excellent soldiers."

"Here, see there. That's more of an honest answer, Quarplek, the true thoughts of our benefactor as it were. Now I can see your view of the situation. It makes it clearer." Ryan noticed that Quarplek's hands were tightening on his weapons. "Quarplek, before you try to draw those weapons and shoot this insolent little human, know that every one of you will be dead the second you clear your holster."

Quarplek froze and stared at the human and ran through his brain what Ryan had just communicated to him. He realized he had made a strategic error, a very uncommon thing for him. He had underestimated the little humans. This one in front of him was very good, very good indeed. He hadn't noticed that any others had come out. He had been so confident, and the human had made him angry.

"See now, you are on the same page as me. And if you think I'm bluffing, I would think twice if I were you. I don't think you would like the outcome if you decided I was bluffing and called me on it." Ryan subvocalized. Now that he had given away the play he was making, it didn't matter. "Oh, and we puny humans do have a trick or two up our sleeves, Quarplek. I see the ship you had come out of, though the cloaking and rippling effect was quite impressive and dramatic. Carefully, you can look behind you and to my men with weapons trained on you. Don't get the wrong idea. Move very carefully please."

Quarplek was taken aback. This human had played him very well and had him at a disadvantage. This just did not happen. He had been disrespected, but he could not see a way to turn it around. He lifted his hands away from his weapons and, replaying earlier, raised them up, showing no harm. He turned and saw his ship now out in the open and visible.

Somehow, the humans had found the frequency they used and blocked it. It was only the shuttle, not his command ship, but it was even more of an embarrassing action.

Oh, he had been thoroughly outclassed in this meeting, where he had been overconfident and sure of the situation. His opponent had taken full advantage of him and made him look like an inexperienced fool. He certainly was a fool at this point.

Ryan had been steady. As Lincoln and Andrews had subvocalized and alerted all the right parties, the rest of the Hunters had stealthily taken up positions, overlooking this impromptu meeting.

And there were no less than two weapons aimed at each alien head. The Thirteenth Scientific Research and Development had been notified and, with the aid of a lot of alien technology they were in possession of, had an idea of what the ripple was and what it meant and, even better, how to counter it.

Lieutenant Colonel Rivera stepped out of the shadows and walked up to the meeting.

Quarplek turned back around and faced the major and colonel as they stood shoulder to shoulder in front of him. "You must be the base commander."

"Yes, I am, Commander Quarplek. And I will tell you that the whole incident out here was relayed to me. I heard every bit of it. Understand something, Commander, this is my base. I don't take to anyone, better yet, any species, coming here and thinking that you can demand or walk in here and just make yourself at home. I don't think your little optical trick will work again, and you never did answer my man's question. But then again, I don't think it would matter. The price probably would be too high."

"Very good, human commander. I understand. You have made your point this day. You, as a species, are not ready to join the galaxy yet." He had meant it as an insult, but the humans turned it around on him.

"If you mean we will just fold and serve you as apparently you are used to, then no, we are not the race you thought we were. Be warned, we have an annoying habit of coming together as a species to combat anyone, any species, from stepping on us."

"Warning taken."

"We do thank you for giving us our current enemy's name and a profile, albeit a small profile. Nonetheless, it's something. So in return, we shall not harass you as you exit off my facility."

Quarplek almost made a huge error and acted upon his rage, but his second officer put his hand on his shoulder and held him back. The infuriating humans just stood there, staring. Quarplek gritted his teeth, nodded his head, moved his hand up, and waved it. His men turned and went through the ship's door, and then all were gone but Quarplek and his second officer.

"I think you will find that you have made an error."

"I don't think so" was all Rivera responded.

With that, the two aliens turned and stomped into their ship. It lifted off the ground and hovered, then turned in a half arc, and sped out over the water, then up, and out of sight.

All the humans just stared at the path the aliens just took, not sure how to react to the interaction they just went through.

"Well, isn't that just a load of crap?" Campo said out loud. It broke the trance they all appeared in, and they all chuckled.

"All units, stand down," Rivera said over comms and turned to all the people around him. "Okay, so earlier wasn't enough for you? Have to invite the aliens home," he said as everyone reluctantly smiled. And he clasped Ryan on the shoulder as they all headed back into the hangar and into the base.

"Good job, kid. You did well," he said to Ryan.

"This time though I don't think I made a friend, and I am pretty sure we will meet again," Ryan said, unsure if he should be afraid or jubilant, but he was neither. He just was.

Rivera stopped before he entered and motioned for the ones that were still with him to come with him. "Okay, one of the roving Space Force military police has found something over by an old storage building. He was unsure exactly what he found, but it was enough that he went to notify me straight out." He led the way toward the building which was about four hundred yards away and on the outskirts of the abandoned section of the above-ground base, the part used for pilot training and all the World War II facilities. "Since I assume this will affect the mission, I'd rather have you all with me and be informed now. Save me from going over it all again."

"Yes, sir. Any idea what it is?" Ryan asked.

"No, the MP seemed pretty shook up though," Rivera said as he turned a corner to head down a base street to the building.

As the group approached, the military police seemed relieved. He was a young kid but seemed competent enough. He saluted the colonel as he walked up. "Sir, I'm sorry to go straight to you, but I thought it was prudent to do so, considering the evidence here," he said, then pointed down to a pile of rags.

"It's okay, son. I'm sure you had a good reason," Rivera said as he, Ryan, Campo, and Doc walked over to the pile and knelt down to get a closer look.

"Holy shit," Campo said as he realized what he was looking at.

"Yeah, holy shit," Rivera said as he took in the sight. He was very grateful the young military police decided to contact him straight out. He owed the kid one.

Everyone looked on and realized the pile they thought were just rags turned out to be a set of army combat uniform, and it was covered in a gooey paste. No one was sure what it was, but they all knew from the way it stunk that it wasn't anything good.

"Andrews, get on comms and notify the Thirteenth Scientific Research and Development. Let them know they are needed up here but to keep it low-key and keep vague but let them know what they will be finding here."

"Yes, sir, on it," Andrews said as she walked a couple of feet away to do the notification.

Ryan moved his position a couple of times to try to get a good look at the mess on the grass just next to the building, about a yard off the road. Unless someone walked up on whatever transpired here, it would have been hidden from any view.

"What does it look like, Steve?" Rivera asked Ryan as the group had stood back and let Ryan move freely around the spot.

"Well, I think we solved one mystery," Ryan said, but he did not seem overjoyed.

"Yeah. What would that be, Steve?" Rivera said, sure he wasn't going to be happy.

"The mystery of what happened to Sergeant Major Whitfield. These are his clothes. Now I'm not sure this is him, this goo, but a piece over here has a tattoo just identical to the one he had on his forearm."

Now looking down at the mess, they could see among the goo pieces what appeared to be the slices of upper skin, like a broken husk.

"Yuck," Andrews said as he recognized the pile for what it could be.

"Exactly," Campo agreed.

Rivera walked over to the military police and put his hand on his shoulder. "Son, you ever get the notion to follow your gut, you do it. I don't think I would have been happy if you didn't."

"Thank you, sir," the military police said, blushing. Not every soldier would have the guts to follow their conviction on doing something outside the lines.

"So are we guessing that somehow Whitfield was melted down and this is all that is left of him?" Lincoln asked the group as he looked down at the pile, not sure if he was relieved or upset or even happy. He did hate Whitfield after all. Still looking down at the mess, it was hard to picture the man anymore.

"Actually, I'm not guessing that I have a theory, but it's out there," Ryan said as he had found a stick and was now poking the goo.

"Wait, stranger than aliens, trying to kill us, other aliens, especially ones that look like a tomato or a pet rock, threatening us, or invisible ships? You mean further out than that?" Captain Anderson asked, clearly skeptical that he could think anything was too far-out there now.

"Well, when you put it like that," Ryan said, chuckling at his old roommate.

"Not that I have experience with jellied people," Doc said as he stood, arms crossed over his chest, studying the mess that the major was poking. "But to me, it doesn't look like enough to be a whole person there. Of course, considering if any burnt off into a gas or seeped into the ground or even collected and removed, I still don't think that there is enough there to account for all of Whitfield."

They all gave a bunch of thoughtful noises at his statement.

"Like I said, I don't have experience with melted people," Doc said as he continued to stare down and analyze the pile.

"Well, accepting your qualifications or lack thereof, I feel that you are right. That's what been bothering me poking this stuff. Look, we see skin like it's been peeled off, yet there are no bones. And considering the goo, there's not enough. Finally, why is the uniform not even destroyed or damaged?" Ryan concluded.

"Excellent point. You would have to conclude that anything that would gel someone's body would do something to the fabric in some way. I mean it's not synthetic. It's an organic, not the same complexity but surely not enough to avoid any damage," Rivera added in.

"Okay, so if this isn't all of Whitfield, what are we proposing happened? What is this the result of?" Warrant Officer Campo asked.

"I don't know where that leads us. I mean, there must be something that would fit this type of thing, wouldn't it?" Ryan asked as he looked up at the group.

The military police was fidgety and looked like he wanted to say something but wasn't truly confident that he should interject into the conversation with the experience and rank sitting in front of him.

Rivera noticed this, and as a very intelligent and experienced leader and a longtime veteran of the Special Forces, he knew you never discounted anyone's thoughts, especially a young man that had already proven that he had a respectable thought process. "Son," he said to the military police, "what's your name?"

"Me, sir, I'm Corporal Roberts, sir," the young man said, obviously unsure if he should be flattered or scared that the lieutenant colonel, his base commander, should be interested in his name.

"Corporal, I see you have some thought to add. And believe me, we could use any input we could get. So feel free to tell us what you're thinking, son," Rivera coaxed, hopefully putting the boy at ease a bit.

"Sir, I really am not sure. I mean, it's going to sound silly," Roberts said, looking a bit shy.

Lincoln walked up and put an arm around the corporal's shoulders. He was a head above the boy. "Look, the only way we ever figure things out, Roberts, is if we all put our heads together. A master sergeant like me lives on the input from my whole team. Right now, you are part of my team. First, you did an outstanding job executing your job. You found this mess. Second, you thought outside the box and went against your fears and went with your gut to notify the colonel, the absolute right choice. Outstanding, Corporal, you have proven yourself to this group of experienced, seasoned men. So when we say spill it, we totally mean it. Does that make sense to you, Roberts?"

The young corporal thought about it for a minute. "Yes, Master Sergeant, it does. And thank you. Well, I know this will sound crazy. But me and my squad mates play all sorts of games from video to role playing. And in these games, we have tons of mythical creatures." The young corporal paused to see if they were following what he was saying. They all were paying close attention to what he was saying. So he continued, "So in our games, they have these things, from mostly Indian mythology. They call them 'skinwalkers.' Also, in one type of role-playing game, we have 'mimics.' And still another, we have 'shapeshifters.' But they all do the same thing—they become anyone. They take the memories of the people. Some they eat. Others they just take their souls. I know it sounds crazy. But when they leave the disguise—and I mean in all the legends—they leave behind stuff like this."

The group all sat silent, digesting what they were just told by this young man.

"Shit. Makes sense. Who knows, it could have been damn aliens that were at the root of that myth or even all the others. Son, looks like you came through again," Colonel Rivera said as he patted him on the back.

"See, Roberts? Sometimes crazy is what you need," Lincoln said as he squeezed the kid's shoulder and then patted him on the back and released him.

The kid blushed and was beaming from ear to ear from the praise from his seniors—men he respected completely. They may have not noticed him since they had been all assigned here, but he had noticed them and paid close attention to their character and how they went about their business. It made him want to work harder and be the best he could be. He respected them, and if only for an instant they had a bit of respect for him, then it was all worth it.

"Okay, that makes a lot of sense and fits what we got here. We need to do some research on this. Kid, you and Warrant Officer Campo and Doc here go to the HQ and start digging up what you can for us from every angle. You're detached to me till I tell you different, Roberts. Got it?" Colonel Rivera said.

"Yes, sir," the corporal said excitedly.

"C'mon, Doc, kid, let's get to work," Campo said as he started to the hangar, the other two falling in line behind him.

As the three made it to the corner, two four-person golf carts came around it. Right behind them came two utility golf carts with cargo beds. Dr. Brolin sat up front of the first golf cart with Lieutenant Troy driving. The two looked absolutely pumped and ready to go.

When they pulled up, Colonel Rivera explained all the facts and the theories they had. And to his surprise, Dr. Brolin agreed it was the most likely scenario.

Dr. Brolin sent out four of his researchers to do a twenty-yard circle around this scene and to comb over it very carefully while he set two more men to separate and collect the "mess," as everyone had taken to calling it.

The colonel and the rest of the Hunters headed back to their facilities, leaving the doctor and Lieutenant Troy to do their work.

Today had been a long and eventful day. Everyone needed to get cleaned up and get some food. Then they had to meet and condense all the events into concise reports.

The Hunters and Sergeant Andrews made it back to their hangar and the entrance to the underground facilities.

Everyone headed down, except for Lincoln and Andrews and a lagging Major Ryan and Captain Anderson. The two officers stopped at the door.

"Hey, do you suppose we should wait for those two to go ahead of us?" Anderson asked, jerking his head back to Andrews and Lincoln about twenty feet behind them and obviously waiting for them to go down so they could talk in private.

"You know what kind of leaders would we be if we just left our people without our guidance. I mean we should make sure everyone makes it safely back inside, especially after all the happenings out here tonight." Major Ryan threw in. They were talking loud enough for the couple to hear them and their smart-ass remarks.

Lincoln put his hands on his hips and had a deep scowl. Sergeant Andrews, even in the dark, was visibly blushing and averting her eyes from the two officers.

"I wonder, do you think they noticed that we may have figured out that there might be something going on with those two?" Ryan asked Anderson.

The two officers turned and looked at the two.

"I think they might be wise to it now. Maybe," Anderson responded.

Lincoln smiled at the two officers and turned to Louise. She turned to him. She didn't know what to expect. Lincoln grabbed her in his arms and pulled her in for a kiss. At first, she was caught off guard, but once she realized what was happening, she fully returned his kiss, equaling how passionate his was. The two became lost in the kiss. Lincoln had thought about nothing else since the battle. He just wanted to embrace her and for her to embrace him and just be this close.

The two officers just stood there, mouths open, watching as the two were lost to the world, together in their private embrace. Ryan tapped Anderson on the shoulder and hitched his thumb, indicating they should head in and leave these two alone.

It took five more minutes of kissing until the two parted their lips, looking into each other's eyes but still holding a tight embrace.

"I hope you didn't mind that. I have been wanting to do that all day," Robin asked.

"I think I have wanted that all my life. I just didn't know it was you, till the other day," Louise said to him.

Robin leaned in and kissed her lips softly several times, then kissed her cheeks and neck, and then her forehead and the tip of her nose. She giggled and smiled. There was nothing else in the world, no one else in the world, just the two of them right here right now.

"I saw you got hurt out there. I was so selfish. Then I said to myself I can't lose you now. I just found you," Louise said, her eyes getting slightly watery.

He smiled a little. "You can't lose me now. I won't let you. No, you're a piece of me I never had before. I can't be without you now." He took her in his arms again and pulled her close for that deep, passionate kiss once more.

They strode over to the retaining wall and sat together, holding hands.

"Robin, do you think this is a bad idea? I mean, I will be on comms while you are doing a mission."

"Let me ask you, Lou. Can you do it? I mean, will you be okay, knowing what I'm doing?"

It didn't take her but a second to answer. "Yes, I won't be sitting, waiting to find out about you. I can trust myself to be the best one to help you while you're out there," she said confidently.

"Exactly," he said. "You are the best. I couldn't trust anyone more to watch my back or to get me out of a jam. Knowing we're teammates makes it more complete for me. You know everything I do. We will never have to hide anything from each other."

She pulled him in and kissed him. She had been worried that he would make some sort of ultimatum that she quit doing her job, but instead, he wouldn't have it any other way. Suddenly, she felt all giddy inside and realized she had never known happiness like this. She found herself crying tears of joy.

He looked in her eyes and saw his future. Without Louise, there would never be a future. He never thought these emotions would run through him, but here they were, for better or worse.

Time seemed to stand still for the two as they continued to embrace each other. Eventually, they decided to head in and get some food, realizing they hadn't eaten all day.

After dinner, Robin walked Louise to her quarters in the headquarters section. He kissed her good night, with him telling her he loved her. She blushed but leaned in close to his ear and whispered that she loved him too. Pleasantly surprised and relieved to hear she felt the same way he did, he headed back to his office before he went to bed.

Robin made it to his office after entering the Team One section. The office area was dimly lit. No one else was in the area. He supposed Major Ryan was over at Captain Anderson's office, helping him settle in and get his team their rooms and settled into the facilities. They came straight to the battlefield from their transport to their new duty. They didn't even get to see the facility before getting in the middle of a firefight.

He sat down at his desk and clicked on the desk light and started his computer, ready to complete some work, then turn in. The message symbol was blinking in the corner. He clicked on it.

A message came up on the screen: "Hello, Robin. I was hoping to have some fun with you before I had to change."

Robin read this, then looked for any info where this was coming from. He couldn't find anything. "Charlie!"

"Yes, Master Sergeant?" the AI replied, alert for trouble after hearing his voice.

"On my computer, I just received a message. Can you trace it? Find out who sent it or where it's coming from," Robin asked.

"I'm on it," the AI replied.

The message disappeared, and another popped up in its place. "You won't have any success figuring who or what I am, let alone where."

He read it. Then it disappeared faster this time, just to be replaced by another.

"When I'm someone, I see all they did and what they know, even more than they can. That man Whitfield hated you. He wanted to kill you because you scared him."

Robin typed in response, "What do you want?"

"Well, that is a long list. I am not Whitfield. I am not afraid of you, but I saw you as an opponent not to disregard. I just needed you to know I am out here, close. But then again, I'm not. So look over your shoulder, but don't trust what you see."

He returned, "Whitfield did not scare me, nor do you. I will wait till you step in the light. Then you will be afraid. I also know you have a tell now. I hope you know what a tell is because it will kill you. Love, Master Sergeant Lincoln." He signed it. It probably wasn't smart poking this thing, but hey, it contacted him. He wasn't going to sit back and let it dictate the terms to him.

"Bravo, Master Sergeant, bravo. I see I was right. You are not just another pathetic human, are you?"

"No, but you wouldn't know that till now, and that should make you nervous. It would if I were you or, should I say, if you were me. Think on that, shifter," Robin typed.

There was no reply, no more taunting, just a cursor blinking on the screen. The computer shut off and rebooted on its own. Robin sat back in his chair and steepled his fingers to his chin, thinking. Before Charlene talked, he knew what the results would be.

"Master Sergeant! I could not trace it. I couldn't even really see it. I felt something, someone, invading me. But I couldn't see it, like it was slithering all around in my circuits. What do we do?" The AI was truly upset.

"Charlie, you know what?" he asked it.

"No, Master Sergeant. What?" It was like talking to a three-year-old with an IQ of a million.

"Trust me on this, Charlie. Don't worry about this. It is a bit clearer to me now. So I want you to trust me when I say I got this, okay?" Robin asked as he looked up at the ceiling, like Charlene was up there.

The AI remained quiet for a few minutes, running all the scenarios through its processors.

"Oh, and, Charlie, when it's just you and I talking, please call me Robin."

"Master Sergeant, I mean, Robin, I am worried. But I ran everything, and I trust you." The AI was very meek in its statement. It was almost like it thought it might be doing something wrong.

"Charlie, you have nothing to worry about, and thank you for trusting me." Robin cleared the computer of the start-up screen and went to work, finishing what he had to. Then he shut off the desk light and went to his quarters and went to bed.

CHAPTER 16

A MUCH LARGER UNIVERSE

Major Ryan gathered his top men—Chief Tanaka, Master Sergeant Lincoln, and Team Two, consisting of Captain Anderson, Warrant Officer Campo, and Master Sergeant Armstrong. They made it to headquarter, and Lieutenant Colonel Rivera and Major Johnson joined them.

The group borrowed a NASA jet to ride to Washington in, dressed in their dress uniforms for a meeting with the president.

"All right, men, the president wants a full brief. We land at Andrews AFB, then get a copter to the Pentagon. We will meet with Major General Hansen. We will brief him first. He's read all the reports, so not much to fill in other than our actual viewpoints. Then we will use the Pentagon tram to go to the White House, where we will meet the president in the conference room that he has now designated as the alien war room," Rivera finished.

Everyone sat quietly, thinking of all the events from the last few days. It was a short period of time but a bumpy long ride, and it was just starting.

Anderson lifted his bottle of water to the other operators in the cabin. "Thanks for the invite to this shindig, and now I have a very valuable answer to a very important question." He sat there, waiting for the brave soul to ask what would that be.

His old roommate didn't let him down. "I'll bite. What would that be?"

"What could be worse than a SOCOM black mission." Anderson used his water bottle to air clink his bottle like a glass, brought it to his mouth, and chugged a big gulp of cool water.

Everyone laughed, even the colonel, because some of those black missions from Special Operations Command—which encompassed Navy SEALs, Rangers, Marine Corps Recon, Special Forces, and Air Force special warfare command, pretty much any military special operation—ran through there at one point or another. To be fair, it's hard to coordinate missions that don't exist with teams that also don't exist by ways and means that also don't exist. So as it goes, that means op orders don't exist either. So no one plans, executes, or studies—things that are never done.

*****

Commander Quarplek was beyond furious, but he was in his private room, kicking things. He had been made to look like a fool in front of his men. His mission had been beyond failure. Instead of getting the humans to operate under his tutelage, they were more than suspicious. They had downright showed his men up and sent them back with their tails between their legs. He had a solid plan when he had gone in there. It was a tried-and-true plan. This plan had worked every time on every species he had applied it to.

No, not the humans. They not only turned him down; they threatened to blow his head off, but they also didn't even want to hear what they had to offer.

Oh, and that little human who had been the party leader before the base leader showed up, he was so high and mighty, a bit too clever. Humans were not that clever. No, something had been off. He knew it. He would need to behead that little human to get his dignity back for the offenses one of his kind had insulted him with. It just wasn't done.

His door chime sounded. He turned on it, ready to rip whatever was out there. He growled at the door, then fought to gain his control. He looked around. It was clear. He said, "Enter."

Zebo Martok, his second officer, entered. He appraised his commander. Then he spoke, "Headquarters contacted us. They would like an update, sir." Then as Rukians do, he just stood stoically, waiting for an answer.

Quarplek uttered a low growl and stormed past the Rukian and headed for the bridge.

On the bridge, he took a deep breath and sat in the command chair. "Open a channel to headquarters." His communications officer did the connection, which was answered at headquarters by another communications officer, who put them on a standby as he went to find the officer who was assigned to take the report.

A long pause came as they waited. Finally, one of the Finolia, the commander's race, came on screen.

"Commander, there has been a change in plans. No report is needed here, but your father is on base 34. He has ordered you to meet him there and deliver your report face-to-face."

Base 34 was a station orbiting opposite Earth rotation, in the outer rings of Saturn. It was easily out of view of the Earth.

The communication was ended just like that. There was no option for Quarplek. He had to face his father, which was not going to be easy, with the failure so complete and insulting. He had no choice. He had to report to his father. Even if he had the courage to defy his father and make a run for it, the damn Rukians would just arrest him and take him there anyways. Of all the kingdom's soldiers, the Rukians were the fiercest and most loyal, especially to the crown. Sometimes it did not pay to be the son of the king.

The Greelock ship came into the landing bay of the satellite facility above their base, below on the dark side of the moon. The imperial commander of the Greelock ship *Bortchek*, Commander Geef, walked with his personal guard into the entry deck from the docks.

The station commander greeted him with a salute across the chest. "It is an honor to have your presence on this station, Commander." He bowed after his welcome.

"It is a welcome greeting, my friend. I am honored by your hospitality on this impeccable station, a credit to the empire."

A shuttle came into the docking bay as the commander was being brought aboard. It was First Investigator Heen, the commander of the moon base. The commander and first investigator embraced, having been long-term friends and associates.

After brief greetings, Heen asked his friend, "So why has the empire sent you out here?"

Geef chuckled. "Oh, not to worry, my old friend. It has nothing to do with you or your command. The empire wants me to take out the Earth side base of the Aldions. The report that you sent was music to their ears. No, you and I shall have fun like in the old days. We shall feast on the spoils of battle."

"Oh yes, what glorious times we shall have again, Geef, sharing Aldion steaks and a side of human cuts. Yes, glory days will be had. I can't wait. I will have my troops prepare."

The two old friends grasped forearms and howled to the roof. The hunt was coming, and excitement was on the cusp of a new day.

*****

The president and the chiefs of staff, along with the director of intelligence and the head of every agency, were in attendance in the alien war room. It was time for all the top leaders of the security of his country to be read in on the covert war.

Skeptics filled the room at the beginning of the meeting, but by the time the Hunters were done with their briefing, having given all the irrefutable proof, everyone was a believer, some even terrified.

What had troubled the president the most was the interaction the Hunters had at their base with what could only be described as an alien Special Forces team. They had approached and used a standard employment of special warfare—to help the indigenous population to take on the enemy of the team.

What scared the president was that there had to be a bigger army somewhere, which meant the Aldions, the little gray or blue race, were business types, not soldiers.

The president mumbled a prayer of thanks for having set up the Thirteenth Special Forces Group and he added that he hoped it would be enough to save his planet. Only time will tell.

*****

The NASA jet touched down at Space Force Base Canaveral and rolled into a NASA-marked hangar. It actually belonged to the Space Force. The Hunters grabbed their gear and headed off to their sections.

Robin lay back on his bed and heard a knock on his door. He said, "Come in." The door slid open, controlled with an automated clearance system. He had walked out into his sitting room from the bedroom to see who had come in.

His face lit up. It was Louise. She looked up at him shyly. "Was it okay that I came over? I missed you today. It's okay if you want to be alone."

He walked over to her and held her in his arms. "Lou, I spent my whole life alone. If it's one thing I don't need anymore, it is to be alone, at least while you're in this world."

Louise looked up into his face, and her heart melted. "How is it you always know what to say to make everything all right?"

"The same way that you holding on to me always makes things all right for me. We're perfect together. You can't mess with that. I want you here always. Never ever think anything else."

She pulled him tighter. "Can I stay here tonight? I don't want to leave you right now. Would that be okay?"

She seemed so vulnerable to him at this moment. He knew she was one of the smartest, toughest women he had ever met. Yet right here, right now, he felt like he never wanted to let her go and that he needed to protect her.

"Stay please, Lou. I need you to stay also." Whatever tomorrow would bring in this new reality of a world, he had tonight, and he hoped every day, until the end of time with her. What more could he ever want? He looked upward and rested his cheek on her head and said silently, "Thank you."

*****

It is clear that humans will not sit back and be exploited by other worlds. The aliens must be stopped. With no book on how to do that, the Special Forces Group must write it as they go. Stay tuned to see how they will continue to use their resources to do just that and protect Earth.

ABOUT THE AUTHOR

Stephen Stoller lives in Florida with his wife and three alien cats. Writing, quilting, and enjoying the supreme atmosphere of Florida are his main creative outlets.

CPSIA information can be obtained
at www.ICGtesting.com
Printed in the USA
LVHW040504180523
747321LV00001B/125